PICNIC KISSES

The kids ran back to play, and she and Chase stayed at the picnic table to keep an eye on them. She was shading her eyes to watch Aiden climb to the top of the playset when Chase placed his hand on her bare thigh.

Sparks exploded inside Paula, zinging up her nerves, and making her want his hand to move higher. The heat of his touch burned her bare skin. She licked her lips. She could almost feel his hands rove her body, stopping to explore.

He turned to her, and their gazes locked. He lowered his head, and this time, his kiss was passionate and possessive . . .

Books by Judi Lynn

COOKING UP TROUBLE

OPPOSITES DISTRACT

LOVE ON TAP

Published by Kensington Publishing Corporation

Love on Tap

Judi Lynn

LYRICAL SHINE
Kensington Publishing Corp.
www.kensingtonbooks.com

LYRICAL SHINE BOOKS are published by

Kensington Publishing Corp.
119 West 40th Street
New York, NY 10018

All Kensington titles, imprints, and distributed lines are available at special quantity discounts for bulk purchases for sales promotion, premiums, fund-raising, educational, or institutional use.

Special book excerpts or customized printings can also be created to fit specific needs. For details, write or phone the office of the Kensington Sales Manager: Kensington Publishing Corp., 119 West 40th Street, New York, NY 10018. Attn. Sales Department. Phone: 1-800-221-2647.

Lyrical Shine and Lyrical Shine logo Reg. U.S. Pat. & TM Off.

First Electronic Edition: November 2016
eISBN-13: 978-1-60183-787-5
eISBN-10: 1-60183-787-9

First Print Edition: November 2016
ISBN-13: 978-1-60183-788-2
ISBN-10: 1-60183-788-7

Printed in the United States of America

I'd like to dedicate this book to Lauren Abramo, who is patient when I'm not, and does her best to guide me in the right directions, and to John Scognamiglio, my encouraging editor at Kensington Books. I'd also like to thank Kimberly Richardson and Rebecca Cremonese at Kensington for their work on my novels, and everyone else involved—the cover designer, proofreaders, and sales team. As always, many thanks to my critique partners: Mary Lou Rigdon, my daughter Holly Post, and Ann Staadt.

Chapter 1

Paula Hull walked with Aiden and Bailey to the end of the resort's driveway to wait for their school bus. The kids skipped and hopped, and she had to hustle to keep up. That was the thing about being short. Her legs had to do double time when she needed speed. Of course, if she lost twenty pounds it might help, but every chef tasted as she added ingredients. A hazard of the trade.

When the bus turned the corner, she planted a kiss on each kid. "Have a good day."

"Mom!" Aiden winced. He was almost nine. She'd better enjoy smooches while she could, because next year there'd be no public displays of affection. He'd be too old, too cool. Bailey—six—bounced up and down next to her brother, anxious to get on the bus and see her friends.

"I want to show Maddie my blue fingernail polish!" She tugged on Aiden's arm. He grimaced, but tolerated it. Since their dad's death, he'd become protective of her.

When the kids disappeared inside the bus and it pulled away, leaving behind the smell of diesel exhaust, Paula started back to the lodge. Fast footsteps. Lots to do! Her assistant chef was starting today.

She paused briefly to look at the inn's limestone exterior, like she always did. *Lovely!* Because of her own look—the stud in her cheek, her eyebrow ring, and tattoos—people assumed she liked dark and dreary. Not so. She was a cozy girl, and the inn's three-story center with a wing off each end, its white trim, red double doors, and tin roof gave off a warm, homey feel she liked.

Move it! She huffed into the foyer and lounge. Wood floors. Beamed ceilings. Leather furniture grouped around a fireplace. She barely gave it a glance. Time to switch hats from mommy to chef. She took a deep breath as she headed to Ian McGregor's office.

When he hired her last June, he'd expected business to start slow, hoping it would grow steadily. He wasn't prepared for how fast the inn became popular. He was scrambling to keep up. So was Paula.

"I'm sorry," he'd told her. "You've gone from chef to jack-of-all-trades." But she'd suspected that might happen. Startups were always messy. No biggie.

With four suites in the west wing, four rooms on the second floor, another four on the third, and five log cabins near the lake, the inn could hold up to eighty people. Thankfully, it was only the end of April, and kids were still in school. Every room was booked—had been since mid-March—but by couples. That meant thirty to forty people expected breakfast, lunch, and supper in the dining room each day. Once June hit, things would get chaotic.

She hesitated to collect her thoughts before she opened the office door. When her husband Alex died in Afghanistan, she'd struggled to hang in there as a chef in a prestigious, New York restaurant. But restaurants demand lots of hours, and she never saw her kids, so she'd come to Mill Pond to work for Ian. Thank God, the man was married and madly in love with his wife or he'd be damned tempting. Her boss was a long slurp of eye candy who could hardly wait until his and Tessa's baby was born. Paula smiled, remembering. Alex had been excited when she got pregnant, but not like Ian. The man was already mapping out tennis lessons and fishing trips with his first-born son.

Fishing trips. Paula sighed. It brought back memories of her Alex. He was a fun father and always took Aiden fishing every summer. The kids missed hanging out with him.

"I can offer you the inn's east wing as an apartment," Ian had told her.

At the time, it had seemed the perfect fit, but then the inn had gotten so popular, she put in long hours here, too. She was still trying to find her way as a single mom, to find balance, but it wasn't easy.

"This isn't working," Ian told her a couple weeks ago, and her stomach sank. Was he going to fire her? Hire someone younger and single? "You're working too many hours. You need help." And he started looking for an assistant. Betty came in every day from ten to two—ready to do anything and everything—but she wasn't enough. Neither was Howard, who took Betty's place from four to eight. Ian realized that. He was good that way. He'd asked her to sit in on the job interviews for an assistant chef, and they'd decided on Tyne Newsome, who was just off a long trek through Thailand.

"Here I thought you'd focus on cooking creds," Ian had teased. "I didn't think you'd swoon over Tyne's looks."

The man was nothing short of gorgeous, but looks alone didn't trip her trigger. She went for the aloof badass every time, and unfortunately, one happened to be delivering the inn's groceries every morning. Jason.

She gave a quick knock on Ian's door and entered the small room that held a table and his laptop. Bookcases lined the walls. Tyne was already seated across from their boss.

"Hey, you ready?" Ian asked, standing to greet her.

"Can't wait." With an assistant, she might have time to breathe, to have a life.

She took the chair next to Tyne's. *Poor Ian.* He was going to have his hands full. First, he'd hired her—a Goth mama with a New York attitude. She'd grown up an army brat, always the new kid in school, a little on the wild side. Her looks told the world that she was who she was. Take it or leave it.

Thankfully, Ian had taken it. "Mill Pond is Midwest, but once they meet you and like you, you're in. They might balk at the cheek stud, but they'll move past it. Besides, you're so cute, you can pull it off."

Cute. That had been Alex's word for her, too. She'd never win a beauty contest, or even be called pretty, but *cute* she could pull off. "What about the inn's guests?"

"After they taste your cooking, they won't care." And they hadn't. Lots of chefs sported tattoos. They even overlooked the stud, but the tiny nose ring tripped them up. So she'd stared at herself in the mirror for a long time and decided she could change it up. She had it removed and went for an eyebrow ring instead, and guests barely blinked, but then Mill Pond was a bit on the eclectic side. Lots of artists and creative types. That helped.

Hiring her was bad enough, but then Ian hired Tyne. The man was so hot, Ian would have to hang a Do Not Touch sign around his neck. Over six feet tall, he had tousled dirty-blonde hair. A chinstrap beard added a scruffy look. And dark brown eyes finished the package. Oh, and there was the body—all rock-hard abs and sinews. Teenage girls would cling to his ankles to worship.

Tyne raised an eyebrow at her. "Any second thoughts?"

"About what?"

"About allowing me in your kitchen. We have really different approaches to food."

She shrugged. "That's why I like you. I don't want a carbon copy. I want someone to make this place stand out."

His grin was as devastating as Ian's. Women would come here just to ogle. They'd be lucky if they didn't dehydrate from drooling too much.

Paula glanced at her watch, immune to the two men's hotness. If they got the intros over with soon enough, she'd be in the kitchen in time to meet Jason when he made his deliveries. Her skin prickled. Her pulse pattered. Jason was no looker like these two, but he had swagger. He played it cool, uninterested. For her, a real turn-on.

Ian leaned back in his chair. "We already went over all the specifics. Anything either of you want to ask or add?"

Tyne shook his head. So did Paula.

Ian grinned, dimples showing. "Then good luck to the two of you. This is going to be a fun mix."

That was the idea—Tyne's international fusion dishes mingled with her classic traditional style. Guests would have plenty to choose from. Mill Pond had become a foodie retreat. There were so many specialty farmers and suppliers in the area, people expected more when they stayed here.

Paula pushed from her chair and Tyne followed her to the kitchen. She had everything ready to go for breakfast. Early risers could choose from cereals or homemade granolas, fresh fruits, and rolls or donuts, but most guests opted for a leisurely breakfast at eight. She poured lemon-blueberry batter on the griddle for pancakes, checked the sausage patties, links, and candied bacon strips she'd already put in the warming oven, and started filling ramekins, nestled in a steel serving pan, for eggs *en cocotte* with smoked salmon.

Ian's wife, Tessa, owned a bakery and made a different kind of muffin each day. Today's were banana with a streusel topping. A toaster sat at the ready on the serving bar in the dining room, along with different kinds of breads, bagels, and muffins.

Tyne watched for a second, then pitched in. They worked in companionable silence until it was time for setup. "A warming table?" he asked.

She nodded.

They carried everything out, put pitchers of juices close to the coffee urn and hot water dispenser, then retreated to the kitchen as guests came and went. She and Tyne flitted in and out to clear tables and refill empty pitchers. Women stopped to gawk. He didn't notice. In between work, he asked, "Same thing every morning?"

Paula shook her head. "This is the Tuesday and Thursday menu. Wednesdays, I make croissant French toast with a peach filling in place of the pancakes. Mondays and Fridays, I switch to a southwestern strata with sausage, and Saturdays are Dutch babies with a fruit filling and whipped cream. I need to start those early while the kids sleep in."

"And Sundays?"

"We serve a brunch buffet. We'll both have to work that one. Betty's helped, but she likes Sundays off."

"Betty?" Tyne turned for an answer.

"She helps anywhere and everywhere, like most of us. Works ten to two, six days a week. Her bark's a lot worse than her bite."

Tyne blinked. "I'll try to get on her good side."

"You won't have to try too hard." He was probably around thirty, like Paula, but parenthood made her feel older, more responsible. Betty was in her sixties with two grown boys. She'd be tempted to take Tyne under her wing. "You've come to a good place to meet food people."

"That's what I've heard, why I put in for the job. Ian said I could experiment, try to find my own style. Someday I want to open my own restaurant. Mill Pond should give me lots of ideas."

The clock hit ten and the last guest left the dining room. Paula started clearing it.

"No stragglers?" Tyne asked.

"This isn't a restaurant. It's an inn. We serve breakfast at eight, lunch at twelve-thirty, and supper at six. There are choices, but no menu. If a guest wants something else, there's a diner in town."

"Reminds me of the summer camps my parents shipped me to as a kid, only classier." Tyne's voice had a bite to it. That must have been a sore point.

Paula had to laugh. "Sort of the same idea, only Ian offers golf, tennis, horseback riding, and the lake."

She'd barely mentioned his name when Ian bustled into the kitchen to pitch in with cleanup. Once school was out, a high school kid came to work the dishwasher for breakfast and lunch, but during the slower months, Ian offered a hand. When Betty strolled in, she joined them.

"Tyne, Betty," Paula said in way of introductions. "Betty, Tyne."

Betty cocked an eyebrow. Her hair was as salty as her attitude. "He's too cute to cook. You just chose him to dress up the place."

Paula sighed. So did Tyne. "I've cooked in over a dozen different countries," he told her.

Betty shrugged. "So? No girl anywhere would turn you away— except maybe her." She motioned to Paula. "All she does is work."

Tyne rolled his eyes, but let it slide. He went back to helping Ian.

Paula had heard it before. Often. Even though Jason tempted her, it had been a while since she entertained the thought of herself with a man. She'd pictured herself as a workhorse for so long, she couldn't think of herself as sexy anymore. Alex had loved her curves and cockiness. She had a sharp tongue and a temper, but she'd put everything under wraps when he died. Literally. People would be surprised she had a figure under her chef's coat and drawstring pants.

Betty gave a wry smile. "It's not going to happen, is it? Okay, do what you always do. Start cooking."

Paula's comfort zone. She showed Betty the menu for lunch. The older woman glanced at it with a quick nod. "I'll get the buffet table and dining room set up, then start the sandwich fillings. You've already roasted the beef?"

"Yup, ready to go." She and Tyne were slicing eggplants and Vidalia onions for today's veggie sandwich when the kitchen's back door opened. Paula stopped working. Her gaze followed Jason as he wheeled a stack of boxes inside, full of produce, meats, and supplies. Her pulse quickened, and the kitchen melted away as a backdrop. She turned to Jason with a smile. "Good morning."

He gave a curt nod, ignored Betty—as usual—barely acknowledged Ian, then narrowed his eyes at Tyne.

Paula hurried to make introductions. "Jason, our new assistant chef, Tyne Newsome. Tyne, our deliveryman, Jason Baxter. I don't have time to go to each of our suppliers every day. Neither do Chase or Ralph, in town, so Jason does it for us. We rely on him. He checks each item, fills our food lists, and delivers them."

"Nice set-up." Tyne glanced at the variety of suppliers' names on the boxes. "Chase and Ralph own restaurants, too?"

Ian nodded. "Ralph runs the diner. Chase owns the bar."

"Where you from?" Jason looked Tyne up and down. "You don't look like a cook. No studs or tattoos like Paula here."

Paula blinked, taken aback. He'd never mentioned anything about the stud in her cheek, never stared at her little eyebrow ring or tattoos. She thought Mill Pond had gotten used to her pitch-black hair, pulled up in a clip so it spiked at the back of her head, and her fondness for wearing black.

Tyne glanced at her expression, frowned, and then gave Jason a dirty look. "Tats from every country, bro." He yanked his T-shirt up to his chest. Blue ink swirled on his sides. He yanked at his shirt's neckline; more ink stretched across his shoulders. "Happy?" he asked.

Jason glared at his six-pack abs. "Cooking must keep you fit."

Tyne jerked his shirt back in place. "No, workouts do."

Jason reached for his clipboard and shoved it at Paula, making sure their fingers touched. "Here. Check that you've got everything, then give me your signature."

Men and their damned pissing contests. Zipping through the list faster than usual, not inspecting and counting each item, she signed that everything had been delivered.

Jason turned on his heel. He tipped his empty dolly and stalked out the door.

Ian grinned. "We put your Jason in a bad mood."

"He's not *my* Jason." She started putting the supplies away.

Ian patted Tyne on the back. "The two of us might as well disappear when Jason steps through that door. I'm surprised Paula doesn't have a tattoo of him hidden somewhere."

Tyne dismissed Jason with "He's an ass," then went to look through the boxes and whistled, impressed.

Betty whisked into the kitchen and nodded agreement. "That's what I keep telling our girl. Jason thinks he's God's gift to women, but I have more respect for our creator than that. She should throw herself at Chase. Now *that* boy's worth the bother."

That boy had women waiting in line for him. Paula didn't have a prayer.

Paula hurried to defend Jason. "I should have told Jason we were getting an assistant chef. He doesn't like surprises."

Ian finished rinsing the pots and pans. "And you know that how?"

"If somehow a supplier's out of something I ordered, it irritates him. He doesn't like to bring inferior products or run behind schedule, either." She admired that about him.

Tyne glanced out the window as Jason's box truck pulled away. "Lucky man if he expects perfection."

"And you don't?" Paula couldn't keep the snap out of her voice.

"Sure I do, but I'm not an ass about it."

Ian took one look at her face and threw up a hand to call peace. "Down, girl. It's only Tyne's first day. Don't kill him yet."

Paula sent Tyne a withering look. What did he know about Jason? Not a damned thing. But she needed an assistant, so she fought to calm down.

Ian nodded at the kitchen. "All clean. What needs doing next?"

He was trying to change the subject, Paula knew. Not a bad idea. "I thought Tyne and I could put our heads together to plan out menus and schedules."

"Sounds good. I'll get out of here and let you get to it." Ian glanced at Tyne. "A word of warning—Paula's little, but she's a firecracker. Don't get on her bad side."

"I'm not little! I'm short!" She sounded sharper than she intended, but five-one was plenty if you put your mind to it. Her height didn't bother her. She'd love to be thinner, though. Not that Jason was trim and fit. He was a little overweight, too. She adored a man with love handles, a little softness like a teddy bear—cuddly.

Tyne shrugged. "Sorry. Didn't mean to aggravate you. My brother swears I can irritate anybody. Words pop out. I say what I say, and people either listen or don't."

The tension released from Paula's shoulders. She liked people who spoke their minds, as long as they didn't push it. "Okay, let's grab a beer and get started." She went to the refrigerator and pulled out two bottles of dark ale and handed one to Tyne, then sat at the wooden worktable. It was early, but restaurants kept strange hours and she liked a beer between sets. Tyne straddled a chair across from her. Ian shook his head and made his escape.

Chapter 2

"So what have you got in mind?" Paula asked Tyne. "How do you want to divide up the schedule?"

"Ian promised me two nights off in a row each week. Other than that, I don't care." He stretched his long legs diagonally under the table.

She nodded. "I thought I could work the breakfast and lunch shift Tuesday through Sunday. We both have to work Sunday brunch. There's no way around it, but we don't serve until eleven, so it's breakfast and lunch combined."

Tyne frowned. "How does that make the dinner schedule?"

"I'd work Sunday and Monday nights. You'd work Tuesday through Saturday. Sundays and Mondays aren't the best nights to have off, though. If you'd like something else, let me know. I just wanted some time with my kids on Fridays and Saturdays."

Tyne shrugged. "Doesn't matter to me. I didn't come here to play. Sundays and Mondays will give me plenty of time to meet people, make connections."

"About the evening meal, Ian wants me to make one traditional meal each night to go with one of yours—whatever direction you take. So I thought I'd prep my choices for your nights before I go off shift."

"I'll do the same."

Either Tyne was really agreeable, or he didn't care about anything except building his career. Paula reached for a clipboard with menus scribbled until Saturday. After that, she and Tyne would work separately. "Want to pound out supper menus for your first two weeks alone? We have time before lunch prep."

"How exotic can I get?"

Paula pursed her lips. "You're in Indiana. No one's going to eat puffer fish. You can push the envelope, but you can't go crazy."

He grinned. "Fair enough. What if I start slow and see how Thai, Filipino, or other dishes go over?"

Heads together, they planned out evening meals until the middle of May. Paula was surprised how many countries Tyne had lived in, how wide his food knowledge was. He could draw from Greek, Spanish, Moroccan, and Italian, as well as Asian, German, and Polish.

"How long did you travel?" she asked.

"Overseas? Eight years."

"No Mexican or South American?" she teased.

Tyne gave his lopsided grin. "That, too. I'll add in some of those dishes later."

"Have you been to Brazil?" She'd always wanted to go there. Maybe, someday.

"Spent a year there. Worked at a ranch/restaurant."

Lucky shit. She'd be jealous, but she'd spent those years with Alex, and she'd never regret that. "I'm surprised you left. I've heard the beaches and women are gorgeous."

"Oh, they are, but I always intended on coming back home."

She cocked her head to the side, studying him. "Do you *always* stick to your agendas?"

"Always."

He was *way* too serious for her. Too driven. She thought back to her early and mid-twenties. She'd met Alex when she was twenty, married him a few months later, and had Aiden at twenty-one. Thank God, she'd gone to culinary school right out of high school, when her dad was stationed on the East Coast . . . before they moved to Fort Worth and she met Texas barbecue and the love of her life.

She shook her head, and Tyne leaned forward on his elbows, his dark eyes sparkling with amusement. "I take it you're not an agenda person?"

"Not even close, but I'm organized." She pointed to the schedule. "I might not make long-term goals, but I plan out every day. Did we forget anything? Should we add something else?" A few more tweaks finished the schedule and they started prepping for the lunch buffet. "Two soups, two types of finger sandwiches, and little, fancy desserts that Tessa—Ian's wife—makes," Paula told him. "We can make our lunches more like afternoon teas."

"What's up for today?" He frowned at the roast beef cooling on the counter.

"Roast beef sandwiches with Roquefort and caramelized onions, and grilled vegetables with fontina and pesto," Paula told him. "We use specialty breads from Maxwell's—another local you should visit. He makes great focaccia."

"When it's summer, and there are kids?" Tyne asked.

"I have two of my own. I've got that covered. Learned K.I.S.S. the hard way."

"Kiss?"

"Keep it simple, stupid. We add PB&Js and bologna sandwiches to the serving trays and Tessa adds cookies to the dessert tiers."

"Kids are hard sells, right?" Tyne started chopping broccoli for the broccoli and cheese soup while she sweated onions to add to the pancetta for her special tomato soup. Hers took longer, so Tyne got busy helping Betty with the finger sandwiches.

When they finished, Betty stretched to pat his shoulder and smirked at Paula. "He's a good boy. We should keep him, even if that tush of his is an unholy distraction."

Tyne blushed, and Paula laughed at him. She couldn't believe how much they'd gotten done so quickly. Lunch sped by and with the three of them working together, clean up went just as fast. She glanced at the clock and shook her head. "I have a couple hours before the kids get home from school. What if I drive you into town and introduce you to Ralph and Chase? You'll like them."

"Really?" He looked excited. "You've already gone out of your way for me."

Betty pointed to the time. "You'd better leave now. You're cutting it close, but the kids can live without you a minute if you're a little late." She aimed that at Paula.

Betty thought Paula worried about Aiden and Bailey too much and commented on it frequently.

"How old are they?" Tyne asked.

"Eight and six. They can function without me. There are people here who'll keep an eye on them, but I like spending time with them."

"They're lucky." His voice gruff, Tyne started for the door. "Mind if I drive? I'm a horrible passenger."

Why didn't that surprise her? He was a doer, not an observer.

"That's probably better. I think Bailey spilled her milkshake in the minivan. I wiped it up, but the seat might still be sticky."

He stared. "Once you have kids, it's minivans, isn't it?"

"There are worse things in life," she told him. "Like no sleep, no privacy . . ."

"No money," Betty added.

He held up a hand to stop them. "I like kids, as long as they're not mine. Is Jason a kid person?"

Paula hadn't really thought about it. "I don't know."

He looked serious. "That's something to consider, though, right? Parents who treat kids like pets should be shot."

Again, she heard the angst and anger. Tyne had a few issues. "Most people aren't crazy about kids until they have their own." But Jason had never shown any interest in hers, never asked about them. Tyne pulled on a hoodie and Betty sucked in her breath.

"Yowza!" When Paula scowled at her, Betty shrugged. "The boy looks damned good in that."

"You're too old for him."

"I'm not dead. My eyes still work." Betty gave her an impudent look and went to finish her work in the dining room.

When Paula and Tyne walked outside, she gaped at his bright orange Jeep. The top was off. There was only a roll bar, no windows.

"Oh Lord." She made the sign of the cross. She wasn't Catholic, but that was just a technicality, right?

His lip curled up at one corner. "I'm a good driver."

"Yeah, and I'm too young for a heart attack, so be careful." She gave him directions to Mill Pond. They could glimpse the lake behind the resort before they passed the Albertsons' place with dairy cows grazing in a pasture. The Kruses' farm sprawled to the left with its fields waiting for corn and soybeans. After that, she pointed out the Danzas' poultry farm with ducks, geese, and chickens. "We get our eggs from them." Near town, she pointed to an old, brick church. "Tessa's Grams goes there." Then, she took him to Ralph's diner.

He paused a minute to look up and down Main Street. "Tourists must love this."

The street was lined with quaint, brick buildings, sporting striped awnings, flower boxes, and old-fashioned street lamps. The aroma of baking bread drifted on a breeze.

"It adds to the charm. We get all of our bread from Maxwell's," she said, pointing. Sadie's Ice Creams and Custards sat next door to his shop. Once inside the diner, she introduced Tyne to Ralph and his new wife, Jules. Jules had worked there as a waitress for years, but it wasn't until Ralph's wife died that he'd finally really noticed her. From everything Paula heard, Jules was the better fit.

Tyne studied the specials on the signboard. "Good, solid, home-cooking. I bet you have faithful customers."

He and Ralph talked business-speak for a while, discussing start-up costs, overhead, stuff she didn't care about, before Paula moved Tyne along. "I want you to meet Chase. He runs Mill Pond's bar."

Chase was the hottest bachelor in town, besides Tyne. Too hot for her. He could pick and choose from every attractive female in Mill Pond.

The bar wasn't open yet, but it was Tuesday, and everyone knew that Chase would be starting to smoke meats for the one day he served lunch—Wednesdays. Paula decided she'd have to watch their time. Chase was as passionate about barbecue as Tyne was about international cuisine. They might never shut up once they started talking.

When the Jeep pulled close to the back of the building, Chase was just finishing spritzing his pork shoulders and ribs with his secret marinade and was closing the lid on the grill. He looked up as they walked toward him and hit them with his famous smile.

Paula bit her bottom lip. Yup, the man could turn heads. He was too handsome, too . . . everything. Mill Pond water must amp up good looks somehow. Come to think of it, though, Ian and Tyne hadn't grown up here. As tall as Tyne and Ian, Chase had streaked, blonde hair and a perpetual tan. His eyes were the color of the Caribbean—clear blue-green.

"What brings you here?" Chase asked her.

"I want to introduce you to my assistant chef, Tyne Newsome."

Chase motioned for them to follow him inside. "Want something to drink? A beer? Pop?"

Paula shook her head. "We have to get back to prep for supper soon, but I thought Tyne might like meeting a few of the locals."

"We're a pretty friendly lot." Chase offered a hand, then grinned at Paula. "What did you do to Jason today? When he delivered my stuff, he almost bit my head off."

"Me? I didn't do anything. He met Tyne."

Chase gave a knowing nod. "That explains it. Jason doesn't like competition."

"Then he doesn't have to worry about me." Tyne crossed his arms over his chest. "I follow my brother's rule. *Don't get your honey where you make your money.*"

Chase threw back his head and laughed. "Great rule. Too late for me."

So true. Paula liked Chase, but so did half the women who walked into his bar. "Chase is our local player. The steps that lead to his upstairs apartment are worn bare."

"Nope, not fair." Chase grabbed a glass and poured himself his favorite draft. "I'm no player. Just easy."

Tyne settled on a stool. "What's the difference?"

"A player doesn't like women. He uses them. They're notches on his bedpost. I love women, and they love me. I'm accommodating."

Paula snorted. "You make it sound like your civic duty."

"I listen," Chase said. "I care. If I can make them a little happier, why not?" He looked at Tyne. "What about you? Which camp do you fall in?"

"Neither. I don't have time. I have things to do."

Chase's blue-green eyes sparkled. "Ah, but it's when you least expect it that Cupid strikes."

"I'll bust his damn arrow in half."

Chase shook his head. "Good luck with that, friend, and welcome to Mill Pond. Are you living at the inn? In one of the cabins?"

"They're filled up." Tyne nodded to a shop farther up the street. "I'm renting the apartment over Daphne's stained glass shop."

At the name *Daphne*, Chase sighed. "She's a lovely person." His voice had a wistful sound to it, and Paula narrowed her eyes, studying him.

Tyne quirked an eyebrow. "Sounds like you like her."

"She's out of my league. Besides, she's seeing a professor from the university."

"A *married* professor," Tyne said.

Chase scowled and took a sip of his beer. He obviously didn't like it if someone made a disparaging remark about Daphne. "He and his wife have been separated for months now. That's why he took an apartment in Mill Pond. They're in the middle of a divorce."

Paula glanced at the clock. It sounded like Chase had it bad. "We'd better get going. The kids will be home soon."

Chase looked at her with interest. "How *are* your two young ones?"

"Fine. Almost ready for the end of the school year. Aiden's looking for someone to take him fishing."

"Really?" Chase put down his beer. "I love to fish. I like kids. Give me a call."

Lots of guys said that. Few of them meant it. "Are you serious?"

"Cross my heart." He made the motion. "We'll have ourselves a fine old time."

Paula put her hand to her throat. A lump lodged there. She managed, "Thanks. I mean that. Aiden misses his dad sometimes."

Chase winked. "Like I said, I like kids. Just don't tell Jason, or he'll start dumping my stuff in the parking lot for me to get."

Tyne laughed. Paula didn't. And that made Chase laugh harder.

Chapter 3

Supper shift was interesting. Prep had been easy with Tyne working alongside Paula. Tonight's two entrées were angel hair pasta with shrimp *fra diavolo* or chicken *Pietro* with rice pilaf. The kitchen smelled of meat searing, garlic, and balsamic vinegar. Paula inhaled. *Ambrosia.* Tyne made a spicy peanut butter slaw as a side, along with a Caesar salad, sliced heirloom tomatoes, and green beans almandine.

Howard, a guy who'd retired from the army after twenty years, came for his four-to-eight shift. He started the coffee urn and worked on the buffet table. And Lane, a kid Grams sent to them, came to bus tables, clean floors, and fill in wherever he was needed. Paula liked Lane. He was a sweet teenager, never mouthy.

At six, guests followed the aromas to the dining room. When they noticed Tyne dash in and out of the kitchen, people started calling him to their tables. Wives gaped up at him as they complimented him on the food. Paula had to smile. *Bib time.* Women needed something to catch the drool. Guests often complimented her if they saw her in the hallways, but nothing like this.

Tyne grinned and schmoozed, and Paula realized he could be as charming as Ian or Chase. When he wanted to dazzle, he was good at it. But he turned it on and off at will, whereas it was an integral part of Ian and went bone-deep in Chase.

Cody, the seventeen-year-old dishwasher who worked in the evenings, got a kick out of watching Tyne. Five-eight and skinny, he batted his eyelashes and said, "Oh, chef, you butter bread better than anyone I've ever met."

Tyne grinned and tossed a dishtowel at his head. Cody burst out laughing. The dining room cleared by seven-thirty, and between them, everything was spotless in half an hour.

Howard took off, as usual, the minute work was done. Tyne offered Cody a ride into town, and Lane hopped on his bicycle and rode the few blocks down the road to his parents' farm. The work night over, Paula had a little skip in her step as she went to her apartment to relieve her babysitter. She could spend the rest of the night with her kids.

Maya was sitting at the long, narrow table that separated the living room from the kitchen, doing her homework while she kept an eye on Aiden and Bailey. They were watching TV. Bailey glanced up at Paula and waved, then went back to the show. Aiden didn't even glance her way. Maya must have kept them busy until now.

The girl didn't believe in letting them spend too much time in front of the flat screen mounted on the wall.

Paula frowned at her, the neatest nerd she'd ever met. She secretly believed Maya had come out of her mother's womb a hundred years old. If Maya did anything frivolous, Paula didn't know about it. Every night she babysat, she came to the kitchen to collect a plate of food for her and each kid. Paula loaded Maya's plate higher than anyone else's, but the girl was still downright skinny. With drab hair and spotty skin, she didn't stand out, but she was a straight-A student, always studying. Someday, she'd make her mark on the world. At least, Paula wished that for her.

Maya glanced up at her uncertainly. "Are you finished already? My mom won't be here to pick me up until nine."

Paula walked to the refrigerator to grab a beer—her after work ritual. "No biggie, will you have your homework done by then?"

Maya shook her head. "I have six more algebra problems to do."

Paula grimaced. "I hated math when I was in school."

"No! It's one of my favorite subjects! That and biology."

"You're not normal." Paula smiled to let her know she was teasing. Maya smiled, too. She knew Paula liked her. "You know, our new assistant chef lives in town. He offered Cody a ride home tonight. Want me to ask him if he'd drop you off, too?"

Maya stared. "Not tonight. My mom's coming for me, but do you think he would? If he'd drop me by the diner, I could walk the rest of the way."

Paula knew where she lived, in a rundown apartment complex just outside of town. Tessa's grandmother had recommended her as a babysitter. Grams had found Cody for Ian, too. All the kids she sent tended to be poor. Sometimes they also had problems at school. Grams was drawn to the troubled kids.

Paula thought about Tyne's Jeep. Would it hold two kids? "I'll ask him. No guarantees."

Maya sat up straighter. "I could pitch in on his gas. It would still be cheaper than paying my stepdad. He only lets me keep ten dollars a week and takes the rest to pay for gas and the wear and tear on Mom's car."

Paula's hands balled into fists. She'd never met Maya's stepdad, but she'd met her mother and was unimpressed. It couldn't cost the woman much to deliver and pick up her daughter. She was making a healthy profit off Maya's babysitting, but Paula pressed her lips together to keep from blurting her thoughts. They wouldn't make Maya's life any better. Instead, she took a deep breath. "I'll ask Tyne and see what he says."

Maya pushed a limp strand of hair behind her ears. She glanced at the clock. "I'd better try to finish a few more problems before Mom gets here."

"You're through most of them, right? You can finish them when you get home. Want some dessert?" There'd been two thin slices of Tessa's red raspberry tart left at the end of the night. Tyne had given half of one to Cody, and she'd brought the other half for Maya. Lane and Howard split theirs.

Maya licked her lips. Raspberry heaven on a plate. Paula could tell how much the girl wanted it, but she shook her head. "When I get home, I have to help Mom with my little brothers and sister. I might not get back to my homework until it's late."

Paula tried to remember how many kids were in Maya's family. She vaguely remembered a girl a few years younger than Maya. "You have a sister, right?"

Maya nodded. "She's ten, by Mom's second husband. Our brothers are from our new dad."

"Newer than the second?"

"Mom's third."

Paula gave up. She'd do what she could for Maya, but the girl's life was complicated.

At a little before nine, Maya gathered her books and went to the inn's front door. Paula watched as a car pulled into the circular drive, and Maya ran to get in it. The car zoomed away, and Paula turned to Aiden and Bailey. "Is your show over?"

Aiden switched off the TV. "Yup, is it storytime?"

Paula gave him a look. "No, it's shower and pajama time, *then* we'll read a story."

Aiden zipped into the kids' bathroom and Bailey disappeared into the master suite. In twenty minutes, they were back, and Paula inhaled their fresh, clean scent. She loved the aroma of just-scrubbed kids. They settled on the sofa, and she started reading a chapter in *Harry Potter and the Chamber of Secrets*. If they were lucky, they'd finish the book before the school year ended. Aiden had already hit her up to read the third book in the series.

They'd just finished and Paula was tucking them into bed when the phone rang. Paula glanced at the caller I.D. and smiled. "Take turns. You can talk to Grandma and Grandpa for fifteen minutes, then it's lights out."

While the kids talked, she half-listened as she picked damp towels off the floor and straightened the house. When they said their goodnights she got on the phone for a fast goodbye to her folks. "What have you two been up to?" she asked them.

Her dad chuckled. "The old lady dragged me with her to bingo today. Lucky girl, she won us enough to go out for dinner."

"Does that mean you're a bust at bingo?"

"I think I won one round, but my mind drifted and someone called it first."

Paula chuckled. Her dad had been in the military, and they'd moved every few years. "Your quick reflexes didn't help you focus?"

"I felt secure enough to let my guard down." He laughed. "Now go put those two kids to bed. We kinda like 'em."

"Thanks for calling."

"Keep in touch," he said—his standard parting—and hung up.

When Paula went to tuck Aiden in, he had a thoughtful look on his face. "You look awfully serious."

Aiden nodded. "We had career day at school. Kids' parents came in to talk about their jobs."

Paula had done that earlier in the year. She'd taken in a tray of fruits dipped in chocolate for the kids to try and answered question after question about cooking. *No, she'd never starred on the Food Network. No, she didn't know Bobby Flay. Yes, she'd gone to culinary school.* She'd been surprised at how many things the kids asked until she realized that their teacher had coached them before she got there. She had to give the class credit. They'd followed their teacher's instructions really well.

She looked at Aiden. "Did someone talk about a job that interests you?"

He shook his head. "I've been thinking about being a soldier like Grandpa and Dad."

No! Her heart lurched. It was almost painful. Her dad was a career army guy. Howard, her kitchen help, had been an army mechanic until he bummed up his shoulder. Alex had signed up for a second tour of duty, but had never returned. She didn't want that for Aiden. She couldn't stand the worry.

Bailey voiced Paula's feelings—her gutsy little girl. "What are you? Stupid? Dad got killed in the army. I won't let you go."

Aiden rolled his eyes at his little sister. "You're a girl. You don't understand."

Paula studied him. *Because she's a girl?* Was he serious? She shrugged. "Girls can enlist. Maybe Bailey will sign up, too."

Aiden's jaw dropped. "No!"

Bailey glared. "Why not?"

"You could get hurt."

Paula smirked. "Our point exactly."

Aiden leaned back on his pillow and smiled. "That was a pretty cool move, Mom." The boy was too smart for his own good.

Paula shook a finger at him. "I have to try to stay a step ahead of you." Not that she could. The day would come when she could only voice an opinion, nothing more. She bent to kiss them goodnight, turned down the light, and said, "Get some sleep."

When she settled on the sofa, though, with her thoughts to herself, she felt bruised, as if she'd been punched. Raising kids was no easy job. She'd worried enough about Alex when he was overseas. She didn't want to go through that again.

Chapter 4

Tyne was already in the kitchen when Paula got there. His cheeks looked fresh and rosy, his dark blonde hair more tousled than usual. Damn, he was hot! She smiled at him. "You should put the glass screen back on your Jeep. Looks like you caught lots of wind on your drive here."

He was breaking eggs into a huge, metal bowl, a whisk near at hand. "I rode my bike to work today."

"For the exercise? Our spring mornings are still plenty cool. You must be dedicated." Paula started working on potato pancakes to serve with smoked sturgeon—a special treat to celebrate Tyne's start here. She usually only made it on Sundays.

He chuckled. "Not a pedal bike. A motorcycle."

He'd look good in a black leather jacket, straddling a mean machine. Alex had had a motorcycle. It was part of what had attracted her to him. "Chase owns a bike, too. He goes on Sunday rides with Harley once in a while. You should ask to tag along sometime."

Chase probably looked every bit as sexy as Tyne did, but she was sure he knew it.

"Harley?" Tyne added heavy cream to eggs in another bowl, along with a dash of cinnamon, to pour over the croissants for French toast.

"He owns the vineyard and winery on the edge of town, a beautiful spot to spend time. He's your age, works with his dad. You'd like him. He met his wife, Kathy, when he was out for one of his Sunday rides, found her stranded in a cemetery."

Tyne looked up. "Someone dumped her there?"

"No, her car broke down and she pulled in to be off the road."

Tyne frowned. "Brave girl, a lot of people get creeped out around tombstones."

Brave girl, indeed. She'd left a loser boyfriend. Paula started cooking the potato pancakes on one side of the hot griddle while Tyne cooked the eggs on the other. "Do graveyards spook you?" They'd never bothered her until she'd watched Alex's coffin lowered into the ground.

He shook his head. "I spent a lot of time in them, taking pictures on my travels. They can tell you a lot about a country and its beliefs."

She blinked. "Are you religious?" He hadn't struck her that way, but just because a man oozes sex appeal and rides a motorcycle doesn't mean he never opens a Bible.

He put the soaked croissants on the griddle. "I like to *study* religions. That's about it."

She shook her head. *Yup, too serious for her.* "Once a person gets past your stubble, you're a pretty intellectual guy, aren't you?"

"My brother says I can be intense."

She could buy that—too intense for her, but he made for one hell of a good assistant chef. When they finished cooking, they carried the food out and arranged it on the buffet lines. People came and went, women twisting in their chairs to catch sight of Tyne, lingering a little longer than usual, but by ten, she and Tyne began cleanup. They were putting the last heavy pans away when Betty stepped through the back door to start work and Jason came with the day's supplies. *Stop, world.* She gave him her full attention.

He held gazes with her a little too long, and her heart sped up. His light-brown hair had been tousled by the wind, causing long strands to fall over his sky-blue eyes. He raked the hair back. His sensuous lips curled slightly, mocking her.

He gave a small smile, ignoring Betty and Tyne. "Wanna check your supplies? I think I got them all."

"You always get everything we need." Jason knew his stuff. He might even be pickier than she was. But she went over to check things off his list and sign it at the bottom.

He usually backed away when she approached, but didn't today, which put them in close proximity. *Hot damn.* She could feel the heat radiating from his body. She breathed in the sharp scent of his aftershave. His gaze lingered on her as she worked. Once she finished, he said, "I heard the new guy's doing most of the evening shifts, is that right?"

The new guy. He wouldn't even distinguish Tyne with a name. Paula nodded.

Jason tucked the clipboard under his arm. "That means you'll have some nights open. I'm going to be at Chase's bar on Friday with my friends. If you drop in, I'll make time to dance with you. Maybe we can teach each other some new moves."

A sizzle burned through her veins. Jason had never paid attention to her, even though somehow he gave off the vibe that he was very aware of her presence. Was that his magic? That he held eye contact a second longer than usual and then pretended not to notice her? She raised her eyebrows, intrigued, but shook her head. "I have to work this Friday. Tyne's regular hours don't start until the weekend."

"No problem, doll. Just thought I'd ask." Jason shrugged. "I thought you and I might fit together pretty well on the dance floor."

Oh Lord, have mercy! He'd called her *doll*, was actually flirting with her. She could feel her cheeks burn. She imagined his arms around her. Her head came to his chest—a good place for it to rest during a slow dance. It had been a long time since a man held her. Too long. "Maybe next Friday?"

"I'll be there. I play pool every Friday with my pals." Alex had loved playing pool and spending time with his buddies. Jason stroked his goatee as if considering the possibilities, gave her a wink then tilted his dolly onto its back wheels and headed for the door.

Paula put her hand on her throat, almost breathless. Jason had promised her a dance.

When the door closed, Tyne scowled at her. "Really? The guy didn't put any effort into that, and you're going to fall all over yourself?"

"Hey, I have the hots for him, okay? It's the first time he's offered me a crumb."

"What is he . . . fifteen? He'll make your day by hanging out with you? He probably won't even buy you a drink." Tyne watched the box truck pull away. "He's a douche. He wanted to let me know he had you in the palm of his hand. Sort of pathetic, if you ask me."

"I'm not."

"You're worth more than that. Guys would line up to dance with you."

Paula motioned to her black chef's coat and drawstring pants. Everything she owned bagged on her. "I don't think so."

"Not like that," Tyne said. "But if you put on something that showed you have tits and a shape, they would."

"I need to lose weight."

"Bullshit. Every woman in America thinks she's too fat. You're cute, and if you don't know it, you should."

That word again. Cute. But it could be worse. She'd take it.

Tyne pointed a finger in her direction. "Demand a little more. My brother had to work hard to win his girlfriend."

Paula sighed. She got the same grief from Betty. She turned her back on him, started unloading the supplies from the top box and putting them away. When Betty opened her lips to say something, Paula shook her head *no*. Her temper was bubbling to the surface. "Your brother's a famous West Coast chef, right? I'm surprised women didn't chase him down."

"Oh, they did. No guy's interested in girls who are too easy." He gave Paula a look. Betty nodded.

Paula had heard enough. "Watch it, Hot Shot. I've been there, done that, remember? I'm just finally ready to dip my toes in the dating scene again. I'm not asking him to marry me. Give me a break."

Tyne looked contrite and lifted one of the heavier boxes onto the wooden worktable to help her put things away. "Sorry, I forgot. You lost your husband. I'm being a dick."

"No, men aren't so good at expressing themselves. You're trying to warn me off. I spend more time with guys than girls so I get it, but enough's enough." She pushed ingredients to the side for the soups she'd planned for lunch. "How do you and your brother get along? No competition even though you're in the same field?"

"Nope, we watch each other's backs. Our dad's an investment broker and Mom's a dancer. She does choreography now. They divorced when we were young, and neither of them wanted to spend time with us, so we got hustled back and forth. We learned to stick together."

"Do you have a lot in common?"

Tyne unloaded the pork loins for supper and put them in the industrial fridge. He loaded the sirloins on the shelf below them. "Only cooking. Holden was a straight-A student, went to a top culinary school and was the star pupil. He's Dad's favorite. Me, I got a diploma, went to a smaller culinary school, and then started traveling."

"But you two stayed close?"

He crossed two fingers together to demonstrate. "We're tight."

Paula nodded. "Aiden and Bailey are close. I like that."

"What got you interested in cooking?" he asked.

"I was an army brat, found food I loved every place they sent Dad. Got hooked on different cuisines."

"Sort of like me." Tyne emptied the last box.

The food put away, they got busy prepping, and Betty went to the dining room to work on setup.

"I like this idea of having a fancy tea service for lunch every day," Tyne said. "It makes lunch special."

"Ian aims to please." She was slicing cucumbers for the traditional cucumber sandwiches today. "The guests get a kick out of these occasionally."

They got busy, making sandwiches and two more soups for the buffet. When the guests came and went, there wasn't much to clean up. The heavy tureens on the buffet were empty. The finger sandwiches were gone. Only two thumbprint cookies sat on a dessert tier.

"Do you think we made enough food?" Tyne asked.

Paula nodded. "This time we did three sandwich choices instead of two. The cucumbers are more for fun than anything else. The last guy who got here—the one who came a little late—cleaned us out. He had seconds and thirds of everything."

Ian came to help and overheard her. "That's a good thing. That means he liked it." He tilted a tureen wrong when he rinsed it and splashed water in his face. Paula watched Tyne brace himself, ready for some cussing. He didn't know Ian. He laughed and dabbed himself off. "Well, now I'm as clean as the dishes."

Tyne shook his head. "You guys go to a lot of extra work to make the buffet fancy—tureens, three-tiered trays for desserts, fancy china to hold the finger sandwiches."

"Customers like it." Ian gave everything a last rinse and turned to Tyne. "Desserts remind me. My wife runs a bakery and makes all our stuff. Tessa said she'd give you a tour of the barn and farm stand, if you'd like to see them. Spinach and leaf lettuces are starting to come up."

"That would be great! Should I go now?" At Ian's nod, Tyne waved a quick goodbye and hurried to his bike.

When Ian headed back to his office, Paula went to her apartment. She did something she hadn't done for a long time. She went to her room, opened the top dresser drawer, and took out Alex's picture.

Tears pressed at the back of her eyelids, and she was grateful when the phone rang to distract her. She pushed the picture away and hurried to answer it.

"Yes?"

"Hey, Paula, this is Chase." *Even his voice was attractive.* "I was calling about Aiden. I could take him fishing on Sunday, if he's free. The bar's closed, and it's supposed to be sunny. Thought I'd take the boat for a spin."

He'd remembered. She pressed a hand to her forehead, she was so relieved. Chase was as thoughtful as Ian. "That would be perfect. Aiden would love it."

"You and Bailey are welcome to come along. You can sit on the shoreline and have a picnic. Bring Tyne, too. A lot of my friends are going to be there."

"And you want to fish with a little boy?" Alex had ditched the kids when friends showed up. "Wouldn't you rather visit?"

His voice held a smile. "I'll do that later in the day when the beer flows. What do you say? Meet up around two? I've got some leftover pulled pork."

"I'll bring German potato salad." No mayo, safer for picnics.

"One of my favorites. See you then."

When he hung up, Paula stared at the phone. *How nice was Chase!* She didn't know him that well. Until now, she'd worked too many hours to spend time with anyone but the kids. She'd go all out to make something special for Sunday's picnic. Tyne would love it, too. He could meet lots of people at once. She'd guess Harley and Kathy would be there, for sure. Maybe even some of the local suppliers.

She frowned, her thoughts turning to Jason. She wondered what kind of friends he hung out with. She couldn't stop the flutter of butterflies in her stomach when she pictured him. If Jason spent most Friday nights at Chase's bar, maybe Chase knew him. Maybe he could tell her a little about him. Sunday was sounding better and better.

Chapter 5

The kids had just walked in the door, home from school, when Tyne roared into the circular drive with Tessa on the back of his bike. When she removed her helmet, her wild, copper hair flew in all directions. A smile stretched across her face. She went to unstrap large, plastic containers strapped behind her. Tyne held the door for her as she entered the inn.

Ian hurried from his office and scowled at her. "Should you be riding on that thing in your condition?"

Tessa patted her stomach affectionately. "The baby loved it. I could feel him giggle."

Ian took the containers—filled with desserts for tonight's dinner—relieving her of her burden. "Well? I suppose you want to buy a Harley now."

She laughed, grabbing for a bag she'd balanced on top of the boxes. "Only if I get to drive. You have to sit behind me."

"I could do that, the better to hang on tight." He put the boxes on the counter to wrap his arm around her. Ian was always reaching for his wife. Paula loved watching them together.

Tyne patted Tessa's shoulder as he passed her. The smile he gave her was warm and affectionate. Ian's wife had won another convert. While the three of them headed to the kitchen, Paula herded the kids toward their apartment. She'd already butterflied the pork loins and stuffed them with chopped dried cherries, apricots, and walnuts before tying them into rolls. That way she wouldn't have to rush to finish prep.

"Hey, wait!" Tessa turned to toss Aiden a bag and he peeked inside.

"Cookies!"

"Don't eat them until your mom says it's okay." Tessa followed the men to the kitchen.

Paula took the cookie bag from Aiden and motioned the kids toward their rooms to change their clothes. "So, how was your day?"

They both still liked school, so she got lively reports as they changed and followed her to the kitchen for a snack. They gazed at Tessa's bag. "Three cookies each. With milk." They hadn't gotten around to homework yet when Maya's mother dropped her off, and the girl came to join them.

"Did you ask Tyne about giving me a ride?" Maya asked. She must really want to be able to keep more of her money.

"Not yet, I'll ask him while we prep dinner." She'd thought about it a couple of times during the day, but then a new subject would come up, and she'd forget. She'd ask first thing when she saw him again, though. Which would be soon.

"I'd better get going. I'm making stuffed pork loins and sirloin kebabs tonight," she told them. "Decide which you want for supper."

"What's a kebab?" Maya asked.

Aiden answered. "It's cubes of steak with cut-up vegetables grilled on a skewer. Mom usually makes a sauce to go with it."

Paula's step turned a little lighter on her way to the kitchen. Her kids knew their stuff. They listened when she talked food. She'd packed their lunches for a long time before Aiden told her that the other kids teased them about the food she sent them. "No one knows what half of it is. We'd rather just buy lunch like our friends."

At first, it had bothered her that they'd be eating chicken nuggets instead of chicken salad, but then she remembered how much kids want to fit in, and she'd caved. Both kids still ate healthy breakfasts and suppers, so they'd survive.

Tyne was prepping the vegetables for the kebabs when she pushed through the double doors to the kitchen. After washing her hands and donning an apron, she went to the worktable and started slicing potatoes on the mandolin.

"Potatoes au gratin?" Tyne asked.

"I thought they'd go with the pork." Paula glanced at him. "I wondered if you'd be willing to give my babysitter a ride home since you offered to take Cody into town every night. She's offered to pitch in on gas."

Tyne scowled. "I can't tonight. Not enough room on the bike. I guess I could if I let her off the same place I drop Cody."

"Maya said if you dropped her at the diner, she could walk the rest of the way."

Tyne pushed chunks of pepper to the side of the table. "That works. She'd be the first out of the Jeep. I don't like to be alone with a girl I don't know."

Paula stopped working to study him. "Why? It sounds like there's more to it than that."

Tyne grimaced and started to thread the seasoned cubes of steak on the skewers with the mushrooms, onions, and peppers. "There was a waitress who worked at a restaurant with me in Toronto. She said her car didn't work and asked if I could give her a lift home. Once we got in my car, she kept hitting on me. When I didn't stay at her place for beers, she told the owner—who turned out to be her boyfriend—that I wouldn't keep my hands off her, kept groping her every chance I got. It was her word against mine. I got fired, but after I thought about it, I got off easy. She could have said something more serious, and who knows how it would have turned out?"

Paula stared. "Maya would never do that."

"But her mom might. Or a sister or friend. I don't want to take any chances."

Paula couldn't argue with his reasoning. "I get it. I'll tell her."

Tyne nodded and went back to prepping.

"Oh, I almost forgot something else." Paula told him about Chase's phone call and the picnic on Sunday.

"I'm in. Sounds great." He finished the kebabs and started work on the dressing for the warm spinach salad. "It's nice of Chase to include me."

"That's just his nature. He makes everyone feel welcome."

"But you're not interested in him?"

Not this again. "Chase? Women stalk him at the bar. Too much competition. And then there's Daphne."

"He does have a thing for her. God help anyone who bad-mouths her."

"If Daphne ever runs away with her professor, women will elbow each other out of the way to get to Chase. I wouldn't stand a chance."

"You underrate yourself."

"Maybe, but I'm not holding my breath. Tessa says he's a great shoulder to cry on, the best listener she knows, so he'd make a great friend."

"Sounds like the makings of a great partner to me." Tyne glanced at the clock. "Cripes, we'd better move a little faster!"

They quit talking and concentrated on their cooking. By the time the first guests walked into the dining room, the buffet was loaded with food. The supper shift went quickly, and by eight Paula was on her way back to her apartment.

Life is good!

She told Maya what Tyne had said, and the girl was fine with that. Better than fine—ecstatic. When her mom came to pick her up at nine she'd finished all of her homework, and the kids were ready for showers and storytime.

At the end of the day, Paula stretched out on the sofa with a sigh. She'd suffered a twinge of guilt when she realized she wouldn't need Maya on the evenings Tyne took the evening shift. But once it was summer, she'd use her during the days and drive her home when her shift ended. Maya seemed fine with that, too.

"I'll have a lot more papers to write and tests to take in May. I'll make enough money to buy lunches, and I'll make more once I'm out of school."

"You'll still work Saturdays and Sundays," Paula had assured her.

Maya nodded. "But my stepdad will still charge me for the days Tyne doesn't work."

Paula let that slide. It was none of her business.

Chapter 6

Thursday was a breeze. She and Tyne worked so well together, the day flew by. At the end of the shift, after cleanup, Paula actually had energy when she headed back to her apartment to see the kids. Maya had been moody when she came to babysit. Paula had meant to ask her if she'd start riding with Tyne tomorrow, but decided to wait.

When she walked into the apartment, the kids were watching TV and glanced up at her nervously. They seemed restless. Paula forced a smile. "How did it go tonight?" she asked.

Bailey came to hug her leg. "Maya let us watch as much TV as we wanted to."

Paula glanced at Maya. The girl believed kids should play games, keep their minds active, before they vegged in front of the TV. She was stricter than Paula. For her to stick the kids in front of the flat screen was unheard of. Worse, the girl was sitting at the kitchen table, homework in front of her, tapping her pencil on the wood top relentlessly, her expression miles away.

Paula nodded. "Why don't you two take off and play on your computers for a while? Maya must be tired today."

Aiden heard the invitation to play computer games and shot off for their room, Bailey close behind him. Maya usually timed that, too. Paula took a deep breath and went to sit across from Maya. The girl didn't notice her, lost in her own thoughts.

"Hey," Paula said. "How's it going?"

Maya looked at her and blinked. "My stepdad said *no*."

"To the ride?" Paula hadn't expected that. She used to hate having to drop off and pick up the kids in New York. She could glance at her watch and see time trickle away while she sat in traffic. She figured Maya's mom could live without chauffeuring, too.

"He said he doesn't want me around a strange man."

Was Maya's stepdad that protective? "Did you tell him you'd be riding with Cody, too?"

"I told him, but Mom agreed with him. She always does."

"Would it help if they met Tyne?"

"He doesn't give a fig about my safety," Maya snapped. "Neither does Mom. She brought strange men home all the time between husbands. They want to keep my money. They're the ones who told me I had to get a babysitting job, and they always pester me to work more hours."

Paula bit her bottom lip. She didn't know what to say. She wished she'd never asked Maya about it, never made the girl unhappy. Finally, she said, "I'm sorry it didn't work out."

Maya gave a curt nod. "It's better this way. Now I know just how much of a selfish bitch Mom is."

Paula gaped. "I don't want to be the one who caused trouble between your mom and you. She *is* your mother." Hadn't she gone through a phase when she didn't get along with her parents? Wasn't that normal? Best not to think about it. She probably gave both her parents headaches and gray hairs.

Maya shut her book with more force than necessary. "Please. Don't give me the lecture. Mom spouts it all the time—I have no idea all the things she gave up for me. If she hadn't gotten pregnant so young, she might own a business, travel, or who knows what? I'm not buying it."

Paula scrambled to change the mood. She hadn't meant to bring Maya pain. She glanced at the girl's closed book. "It sounds like you could use a decadent dessert. There's ice cream in the big kitchen. What if we go there and I make hot fudge, and we have sundaes?"

Child experts would cringe. She was offering food to alleviate a bad mood. Wasn't that a no-no? Wasn't that like self-medication with calories?

Bailey stuck her head out of the kids' bedroom. "Ice cream? Us too?"

Paula should have known. She'd never met a kid who didn't have radar ears. They could hear a whisper you didn't want them to from a mile away. She shrugged. "Why not?"

Aiden hurried to take Maya's hand. "Ice cream always makes me feel better. Come on."

They tugged her to the restaurant kitchen and invaded the freezer.

In no time, Maya and the kids were slicing bananas over scoops of chocolate ice cream and Paula had hot fudge ready to drizzle over it. As they sat around the wooden worktable, Paula realized that ice cream might not be a cure-all for every ill, but it sure made things better for a little while.

When Maya's mother came at nine, Maya hurried out to her car, and Paula watched as she told Aiden and Bailey, "Maya and her mom are going to have a rough time. I don't want that for us. We're going to get mad at each other once in a while, but I hope we always like each other"

"Her mom's selfish," Aiden said. "You aren't."

Probably the best endorsement she'd had in a while. She'd take it. She felt sorry for Maya, but didn't know how to help her. She'd worried that Maya's misery might affect the kids' night, but they took it in their stride, and she realized that it didn't surprise them. They'd already realized Maya's relationship with her parents wasn't the best. It often surprised her how astute they were.

After showers, she read to them longer than usual, enjoying their company. When she tucked them in and went to bed herself, she considered herself a lucky woman. Part of her had been fretting because she couldn't go to Chase's bar tomorrow night to see Jason, but what was wrong with her? After Alex's death, she'd promised herself she'd never be one of those women who put a man ahead of her kids. Her kids always had to come first.

Did Jason like kids? She had no idea. But if he didn't, she was done with him. A little clutch tightened in her stomach. *Please let him like kids*, she found herself praying. Alex had loved Bailey and Aiden, even though he didn't get to spend much time with them. No, correct that—even though he *chose* not to spend much time with them. He let them hang out with him and his buddies, just like Jason invited her to hang out with him. Paula didn't need a hands-on dad for her kids, just a steady one, someone they could count on.

As she drifted to sleep, Chase's face popped into her mind. He genuinely seemed excited about kids. But was that because he was a big kid himself? Was that an attribute? She wasn't sure.

Chapter 7

Friday was the last full day Paula and Tyne would work together. After that, they'd work separate shifts. Which was wonderful. Paula would have time off. *And horrible.* She'd miss him. It was fun having Tyne work alongside her. They'd only team up on Sunday brunches from now on.

Friday meant a sausage strata for breakfast. She'd fed the kids in the big kitchen, while she cooked and slid the food in the oven before she walked them to the bus. Tyne was already busy making potato pancakes when she returned.

He looked up and nodded. "The kids must be off to school. Do they freak out on Fridays? I could hardly wait till the last bell rang."

He hadn't changed into his chef garb yet. The T-shirt he had on was snug across his broad shoulders. His worn jeans hung lower than usual. She was glad the overhead sprinkler didn't go off. The man made the kitchen steamy.

"Aiden and Bailey still like school," she told him. "I've heard that'll change soon."

"It hit me in second grade." Tyne finished the potatoes and put them in the warming oven. He came to help Paula make a fresh fruit salad. This early in the season, there wasn't much variety to choose from, so she settled on citruses from the sunshine states.

"Almost forgot," Tyne said. "I went to Chase's bar last night when I left here, and he wants to buy a fishing rod for Aiden if he doesn't have one. Is he set?"

"He has one." Paula shook her head. She couldn't believe that Chase had volunteered to buy him one if he needed it. "That was really nice of Chase."

Tyne raised an eyebrow. "I keep telling you, the guy's a winner. And he loves kids."

"Okay, I get that. That doesn't mean he's interested in their mother."

Tyne grinned. "You've got me there. Chase only has eyes for Daphne, but she's a lost cause. She's hooked on the prof."

"I rest my case. People never fall for the person who falls for them."

"Somebody must." He started carrying things to the steam table. "People get married all the time."

"Odd, how do you think that happens?"

He leaned his hip against the door to the dining room to hold it open for her. "You should know. You signed on for life, didn't you? One person in the relationship must decide to go for it."

Alex had gone for it, all right. He'd worked with her dad when they moved to Texas and went on a hunting trip with him. When he met her, he'd managed to hang out with Dad even more. "To see you," he'd told her. "And win you over."

She smiled, remembering. It had worked.

Their conversation had to stop when guests started drifting in to eat. Tyne hurried to change, then kept busy with her, refilling dishes and chatting at different tables. At the end of serving, when the last guest left, Betty came to help strip the buffet table and clean the dining room. She was dressed for business as usual, in twill trousers and a plaid shirt.

"You got a new perm, didn't you?" Paula asked. Betty's short salt-and-pepper hair looked curlier than usual.

Betty nodded. "Bumped into Chase at the marina today. He was buying life jackets for your kids. Didn't think he had anything to fit Aiden and Bailey."

Paula blinked. She hadn't thought about life jackets. "Bailey's staying with me on shore. Chase is taking Aiden fishing."

"He's got the hare-brained idea that he'd like to take all of you boating sometime. Wants to teach the kids how to tube. You'd have to spot for him."

"Isn't Bailey too young for that?" Panic slid through her.

Betty laughed. "She's six. Jed and I have lived on the lake all our married lives. Started our boys tubing young. Take our grandkids out now. Chase isn't going to go full speed and drag her through the water. He'll take it slow."

Paula fought for a little calm. Chase had spent his entire life on the lake. His parents had docked their boat at the marina, just like he did now, only a short drive from the bar. He knew what he was doing. "Aiden used to fish with his dad—off a pier."

"Yup, Chase told me. The man's all pumped up. Said no kids should miss summer lake fun."

Tyne hitched his hip against the door again, holding it open for her. "I don't know who's more excited about the fishing trip—Aiden or Chase."

Paula carried the last metal serving pan into the kitchen, Tyne right behind her with a tray full of dirty silverware. She wasn't sure how she felt about Chase spending so much time with her kids. Would he make her look stodgy? Boring? But Aiden could sure use a man in his life. She decided to welcome and appreciate anything Chase did with Aiden and Bailey.

Ian came to run the dishwasher and caught the end of their conversation. "Are you talking about Chase? He wants to put together a cookout at his place for the beginning of May and have a burger contest. He expects you and Paula to be part of it."

Paula stared. She'd lived in Mill Pond since she first took the job here—almost a year ago. She'd met people, but only as acquaintances. She worked too many hours. A mixer would be fun. But a contest?

Tyne locked gazes with her. "I'm going to take you down, woman. My Asian burgers bring people to their knees."

Betty came in to get washcloths to wipe down the dining room. She smirked at Tyne. "Probably not the only reason women fall to their knees in front of you."

A fiery red blush climbed all the way to Tyne's forehead. Paula gaped, and Ian threw back his head and laughed. "Betty, I think you're worse than Tessa's Grams."

Betty snickered on her way out of the kitchen. "Your generation wasn't the first to get a little frisky."

For once, Tyne was speechless. He ran a hand through his already tousled hair. "Damn, I thought I'd heard everything in restaurant kitchens, but that woman's got a mouth on her."

Paula was laughing with him when the back door clunked open

and Jason wheeled in. He looked at her and scowled. "I must have missed the punch line."

"Be glad for that," Ian said, and went back to his rinsing.

Tyne got busy loading dirty plates in the racks to pass under the dishwasher. Not part of his job description, but he didn't mind pitching in. Paula appreciated that about him. He wasn't too high-and-mighty as a chef to help with whatever needed done.

Jason turned his attention back to Paula. "Your salmon filets look especially good this time. I think you're going to be really happy with them."

Paula went to look inside the box from the seafood market. "They're perfect."

Jason nodded. "And Tessa had plenty of fresh spinach for you."

Paula loved to sauté spinach with garlic and seasonings as a bed for the salmon.

Tyne couldn't stand it. He came to peek in the boxes, too. He handed Jason the list of supplies he'd need for supper on Saturday night.

Jason frowned. "Flatiron steaks and bok choy?"

"Can you get them?" Tyne asked. "Paula thought you could."

Jason's eyes narrowed, insulted Tyne would ask. "Oh, I can get them, but this is a classy place. Are you going to make it into Chinese takeout?"

Tyne's brown eyes blazed. "No one's ever complained about the Korean beef I make."

Jason shrugged to let him know he was unimpressed. He handed Paula the clipboard to check and sign, but got distracted when a woman with spiked, bleached hair poked her head inside the kitchen door.

"Hey, Ian, the baskets of Brie and crackers we put in each new guest's room are almost gone. Have we got more somewhere?"

Ian dried his hands on his apron and started toward the door. "I have them in my pickup. Got them this morning. I'll get 'em for you."

When he disappeared outside, the woman looked around the room. Her gaze landed on Tyne, and she smiled. "I'm Jodi from housekeeping."

Paula guessed her to be in her late twenties—pretty enough, with an impressive bust, but rough looking. Tyne gave a curt nod, but Jason's eyes lit up.

"Haven't I seen you at Chase's bar?" he asked.

Damn! Paula tried to keep her face expressionless.

Jodi threw him a coy look. "I hang out there with my friends sometimes on Friday nights."

Paula's heart stopped beating, waiting for Jason's answer.

"Really? I play pool with my buddies there on Fridays." He motioned toward Paula. "I've been trying to talk sweet thing here into stopping in sometime. Promised to save her a dance."

"Will you save one for me?" Jodi could do flirty really well. Paula hated her.

"That depends. Do you dance dirty?"

"Honey, I can make you wet yourself."

"Enough!" Tyne gestured around the room. "Let's keep it professional. We're working."

Jodi laughed. "Sorry, babe, didn't realize you were so uptight. Are you gay?"

"No, not that it's any of your business. But this is my kitchen . . ." He paused and nodded toward Paula. "Our kitchen. Paula doesn't need to hear any of this."

She'd heard worse. She'd been in kitchens a long time, but it was nice of Tyne to care. Ian hurried back inside and glanced at each of them.

"I put the baskets on the check-in counter. There are more in my office."

Jodi nodded, winked at Tyne, and went to finish her cleaning. Distracted, Paula looked through the rest of the supplies, signed for them, and handed the clipboard back to Jason.

He held her gaze. "I'm at Chase's every Friday night. I'd rather see you there than Jodi."

Tyne glared at his retreating back. Ian blinked, confused, and Paula let out a long, unhappy sigh. Just what she needed. Jodi as competition.

Betty bustled through the dining room door. "Get over it, girl. You're wasting your time. Don't you have something to cook?"

Paula grimaced at her. "You can hear everything from the dining room, can't you?"

"Not quite as well as when I stall in here, but good enough. I have to keep tabs on you three kids."

Kids. But they probably seemed like it to Betty. Hell, at sixty-three, her kids were probably older than any of them. Paula shook her head and went to grab the day's menus. Lunch was rich mussel soup and fifteen-bean soup with ham hocks. She and Tyne had cooked the beans yesterday. All they needed to do was heat them and add finishing touches.

Betty came to help Tyne assemble the sandwiches—BLTs made with prosciutto and fried green tomatoes, while Paula sliced tomatoes, red onions, and artichoke hearts for the Parisian tuna salad. Together, they loaded the buffet in no time. Paula had learned to make extra bean soup when it was on offer. People often went back for seconds.

When lunch service was over, and they'd cleaned up everything, Tyne looked at the dinner menu—roast prime rib with baked potatoes and Provençal salmon on a bed of spinach with rice. Easy, but with panache. Tyne glanced up at her.

"This isn't a killer. If you want to take off at seven tonight, you'll be at Chase's before the action starts." He threw the offer out casually, and she knew it cost him. He didn't like Jason, but he was trying to let her meet him there.

She was tempted, but Maya had already told her that she was babysitting for her mom when she left Bailey and Aiden tonight. No babysitter, no leaving. She shook her head. "Thanks, but I can wait one more week."

"Jodi might have her evil talons in him by then."

Paula lifted her chin. "If he'd rather be with Jodi, that's his choice."

Tyne gave her a thumbs-up. "Smart girl."

Was she? She didn't feel smart, just frustrated. Besides, she didn't want to look too eager with Jason. If he was interested in her, he could wait one week. But later that night, after watching *Harry Potter* for the umpteenth time with her kids, she wasn't sure if she could.

Chapter 8

Working breakfast and lunch on Saturday seemed almost overwhelming. She'd done it for a year, but had already gotten spoiled, having Tyne in the kitchen with her. And now, she got Saturday night off. She'd be free!

She was prepping Cornish hens for her traditional part of the meal when Tyne sauntered into the kitchen. He looked rested and pleased with himself. She gave him a sour look.

He grinned. "I spent the day hiking nature trails at the national park. The outdoors revives me, clears my head. And I saw Daphne there."

"She lives right on the border of the park." Paula had driven past her house once when she took the kids on a guided tour offered by one of the naturalists.

"Yeah, I was trekking down an overgrown path, and I saw her in her backyard. I wasn't sure she'd like to be bothered, but when she saw me, she waved."

"Daphne? She's usually pretty reclusive. You'll have to tell Chase. Maybe he should start hiking on weekends."

"He should." Tyne propped his butt against the counter to watch her stuff the Cornish hens with wild rice and truss them for roasting. "She invited me in to show me her place and offered me coffee."

Was Daphne hitting on Tyne?

He crossed his arms and added, "She'd just finished making a batch of table runners for Grams's church. She showed me her sewing room. I've never seen anything like it. Four different kinds of machines and stacks of fabrics and tons of thread."

Now Paula was confused. "But she sells stained glass."

Tyne nodded. "She only sews for fun. She said she finds it relaxing. She was on a sewer's high this morning."

"And the professor? Is she still seeing him?"

"Oh yeah, told me all about him. She'd build a pedestal for him if she knew how to."

Paula winced. "I guess Chase doesn't have a shot."

"No one does. She's obsessed."

"I don't have a good feeling about the prof."

"Stand in line." When Paula reached for melted butter to drizzle over the hens, Tyne said, "Do you care if I make a glaze for them instead?"

"What kind of glaze?"

"Soy and ginger. The flavor will meld with my Korean beef."

"Sounds good to me." She pushed the tray of hens toward him and started putting away the herbs she was going to season them with.

He went to the refrigerator to dig for soy sauce, ginger, and his type of flavorings. "I can take it from here. This is your first free Saturday in a long time. What are you going to do?"

"I promised to take the kids into town for pizza, then we're going bowling."

He laughed. "Not my idea of a fun Saturday night."

"I signed them up at the kids' sports center on Thursday nights, too. They'll learn gymnastics, martial arts, whatever's in season."

He shook his head. "My brother says parents are only glorified taxi drivers once their kids hit a certain age."

"Your brother knows what he's talking about. How old are his kids?"

"Doesn't have any, but his wife's sisters do. He says their lives revolve around their kids' activities."

"I've always worked too many hours for that."

"Well, you don't have to work tonight. Get out of here." He nodded to the door.

It felt odd leaving the kitchen so early. She looked back, worried.

Tyne grinned at her. "I've run restaurants before. I can handle this. The inn's restaurant won't go down in flames."

"It's not that." She hesitated.

He waved her away. "Go! Have fun!"

Laughing, she went to get the kids and send Maya home.

"Are we really getting pizza tonight?" Aiden asked. "You don't have to cook?"

"You're going to get sick of seeing me," she told him. "I have five nights off."

Bailey frowned and glanced out the window as Maya's mom pulled up for her. "What about Maya?"

"She'll still come during the day on Saturday and Sunday."

Aiden shook his head. "Her parents are going out when she gets home. She has to watch her sister and brothers tonight."

Why hadn't Paula seen that coming? She stayed mum. It didn't help kids if you trashed their parents. Instead, she said, "She'll still babysit from brunch to supper on Sundays, too. And I work Monday nights."

Bailey smiled and reached for her hand. "Good, we'll still get to see her."

The kids liked Maya. Paula nodded. "Once summer vacation gets here, you'll see a lot of her."

Paula changed into black jeans and a loose, black sweater. Aiden frowned when he saw her. "What?" She glanced down at herself.

"Don't you ever wear anything happy?"

"Happy?" What the hell did that mean? "You mean like ribbons and bows?"

He shook his head. "Never mind."

They grabbed jackets on their way to the minivan, and they chattered the entire drive into town, but Aiden's comment stayed with her. She always wore black. It made life simple. She didn't have to think about what matched and what didn't. It had never bothered them before. Why now?

The pizza parlor was crowded, but they'd gotten there early enough to get a table. After they ate, they went to the bowling alley. Paula had reserved a lane for them. She hadn't bowled for so long, she started with two gutter balls.

"Damn! I used to be decent at this."

Aiden shook his head. "Not anymore."

She glared at him. "Give me a minute. It'll come back."

And it did. Soon, she found her groove. She wouldn't make strike queen, but her game was respectable. Bailey put her ball on the wooden floor and then shoved it down the lane.

"Go, girl!" Her daughter wasn't going to get any strikes, but she knocked down enough pins to keep her happy.

They played two games before calling it quits. Paula had promised they'd rent a movie on the way home. When they were turning in their rented shoes, Jason walked in with three other guys. Paula's breath caught. Her pulse stopped. He was dressed in worn jeans and a T-shirt with his league's logo on it. She'd never seen him out of his work uniform before—blue pants and a striped, button-down shirt. He looked good in his civvies. He hadn't shaved and had a five-o'clock stubble. She loved stubble. When he saw her, he came to say hi.

"Are you leaving already?"

Had the room heated up? Paula motioned to the kids. "We came early before the leagues start. Just wanted to have fun."

Jason glanced at Aiden and Bailey, then looked away. "Does this mean the new guy's running the kitchen most nights?"

Bailey tugged on her arm, and Paula pulled her close. "I'll only work Sunday and Monday evenings."

"Great!" He frowned at Bailey, who was smiling up at him, then looked back at his friends. They were getting ready at their lane. He looked apologetic. "I've gotta go. We're in a league, but I'm here every Saturday night if you want to hang with us." He hurried to the guys who kept glancing his way.

"Who was that?" Aiden asked on their way to the minivan.

"The guy who delivers supplies to the restaurant every day."

"I don't like him."

A knot tangled in Paula's stomach. Aiden liked almost everyone. "You don't even know him."

"He didn't look at us. He doesn't like kids."

Paula tried to explain. "He's just never around them, doesn't know how to interact with you."

Bailey shook her head. "I smiled at him. He didn't smile back. He doesn't like us."

She decided not to argue about it. What good would it do? Jason either won them over or not. If not, it was no big deal. She'd get a babysitter when she went out with him, and he and the kids would never spend time together. She'd date him, and nothing more. "Let's go rent a movie."

They dropped the subject of Jason, but on the drive home, Paula pictured him in his jeans and wine-colored T-shirt. The deep burgundy showed off his brown hair and blue eyes. She was a fan. Why didn't he just ask her out on a date? They could go someplace cheap—for pizza and beer. But she knew, for sure, that he expected her to make the first move—to drop in the bar to watch him play pool or go to the bowling alley to cheer his team. Then maybe he'd ask her out.

Maybe.

Chapter 9

Sunday morning was always busy. Guests expected something extra for brunch. There was always a ham to slice, chocolate Belgian waffles, a station for rolled French-style omelets, and crepes with lemony cheese filling, along with a slew of sides—lox and bagels, fruit salad, stuffed artichokes, grilled eggplant parmesan, and more. Tessa provided cinnamon rolls, and Maxwell sent brioche from his bakery. Specialty jams and clotted cream sat grouped together beside bottles of champagne for mimosas. Tyne and Paula worked in silent concentration, hurrying through the preparations.

At serving time, Howard took his place behind the meats, Tyne tackled waffles, and Paula zipped through omelets. Lane worked quietly and efficiently at bussing tables, as serious as usual, and Cody worked the dishwasher. Tyne was looking forward to Chase's picnic as much as she was. She could feel the energy pour off him. She felt sorry for Maya this morning. Aiden was close to bouncing off the walls. Luckily, this was the one morning Maya rented a movie to watch with them—their pick.

When the last guest left the dining room, she and Tyne burst into super speed to finish up. "Are you in good shape for tonight?" he asked her.

She nodded. "Gnocchi with ragù sauce, both already in the fridge, and almond-crusted baked cod with roasted potatoes. Simple. I won't have to get back until four."

He grinned when he gave the stainless steel counter a last swipe. "Good, then let's have fun. See you at the lake." He nodded to Cody. "Let's go."

Lane hung up his dishtowel and followed Paula out of the kitchen.

"Have a nice day," she told him.

Instead of his usual nod, he looked down at the floor, not meeting her eyes, and said, "We're going to the 4-H fair this afternoon. I'm hoping my woodworking wins a ribbon."

It was the first personal information he'd ever shared. Paula asked, "What did you make?"

"A desk with two drawers on each side and cubby holes across the back. My grandpa's a master carpenter. He's been teaching me. I don't want to be a dairy farmer like my dad. I want to open a woodworking shop in town."

"That sounds pretty ambitious, but I'm guessing you can do it."

"Grandpa and Dad said they'll help me. My older brother likes farm work. He plans on staying on to help Dad."

Paula smiled. "You must have a nice family."

He blushed at the compliment, but then, it didn't take much to make him blush. "They're the best." He looked flustered. "I'd better go. I promised Dad I'd help finish the chores when I got home." And he dashed for the door.

Paula watched him get on his bike and ride away. He was so shy, working in the restaurant was good for him, interacting with so many different kinds of people. She wondered why he'd opened up today, but then realized it was because he was so excited about competing at the 4-H fair that he couldn't contain it. She crossed her fingers for him as she hurried to get the kids.

The minute she opened the apartment door, Aiden jumped to his feet. "We're ready to go."

Paula glanced at Maya. "And it was all right with your mom for me to drop you off today?"

Maya nodded.

"Good. Let me change, and we'll hit the road." She'd worn black trousers and a black blouse to serve brunch. She traded those for jeans and a black sweater. It would be cool at the lake today. There was usually a breeze.

They went out through the back kitchen door so that Paula could grab her German potato salad and the brownies she'd made. By the time she dropped Maya at her house and parked in the marina's lot, Tyne was already there, standing at the grill with Chase and Harley. Harley—

tall and dark-haired—and his wife, Kathy—lithe and blonde—made an attractive couple.

Paula spotted Ian and Tessa talking to Tessa's best friend, Darinda, and her husband, David, at the picnic tables by the shore. Darinda's boys were already finishing hot dogs. When Paula and the kids joined them, Chase handed his tongs to Harley and came to greet them. He held out a hand to Aiden and Bailey.

"Hi, I'm Chase."

Bailey stared up at him, then stepped behind Paula, suddenly shy.

Chase motioned to the grill. "You hungry? We started hot dogs early because Gianni and Luigi swore they'd die of starvation if we didn't feed them. There's chips, too."

Bailey, who usually vied for adult attention, didn't budge. Paula tried to step away from her, but she clung to her leg.

Darinda's boys came to hurry Aiden and Bailey along. They had dark hair like their Mom and Dad and the same dark eyes. One had Darinda's mocha coloring, and the other his dad's olive complexion.

"Come on!" Gianni tugged on Bailey's hand. "We're getting another hot dog. After we eat, there's a playground over there." He pointed to a small park near the marina. "It's fenced in, so Dad said we could play there."

Aiden glanced over at swings, monkey bars, and basketball hoops. "Can we, Mom?" At her nod, he handed Chase the plastic container of brownies, then went to stand in line for food with Luigi.

Tyne came to check on Bailey. "What's up, princess?"

Paula cringed at his new nickname for her daughter. Bailey ducked farther behind her, completely out of sight.

"Oh for Pete's sake!" Tyne reached around Paula and scooped Bailey up, tossing her in the air. "Even a princess has to eat." The higher he hurled her, the higher Bailey's giggles rose in pitch. Then Tyne caught her and hugged her close. "Move it, kid. Have fun. Meet some new friends."

That's all it took. Bailey hurried to join the others for a hot dog.

Chase watched her jostle in place with Gianni, then motioned for Paula to follow him to the food table. "So, your daughter's shy?"

"Not usually. I think she took one look at you and was smitten."

He grinned. "I have that effect on females."

"If they're six." Shaking his head, Harley filled the kids' plates.

When Paula found a spot on the table for the German potato salad, Chase grabbed a plastic spoon, lifted her bowl's lid, and nabbed a taste. "I love this stuff! Yours is the best I've had."

It was ridiculous how happy his compliment made her. She needed to pinch herself. *Earth to Paula.* She was a chef. Her food was *supposed* to taste good.

They went to mingle with their friends, and Paula found herself laughing and talking. She felt comfortable here. Chase made sure of that. The man was so smooth, it looked effortless. Maybe it was for him.

After they ate, Chase put his fingers to his lips and gave a loud whistle for Aiden.

"Hey, kid! You ready to fish?"

Aiden and Darinda's boys came running. Bailey followed, looking left out.

Ian grinned and grabbed her hand. "You're my star pupil. Tessa's better at fishing than I am, but she gets carsick right now. I don't want to find out how she does on a boat."

Bailey glanced at Paula, surprised. "I'm going too?"

Chase pulled on her ponytail. "Everyone knows a girl brings us luck. You have to come."

Paula could have kissed him. Well, maybe not a kiss. But definitely a hug.

Darinda looked at Tessa. "At least the morning sickness is gone, right?"

"At last. For which I'm grateful. But I don't need to push my luck. No boats for me." Tessa smiled as she watched Ian carry Bailey aboard. David followed with his two boys, and Chase held out a hand to help Aiden make the jump from the pier to the boat. "This was Chase's idea. He didn't want to leave any kid behind."

Nice. Paula breathed easier when the men fastened each kid into a life jacket. Chase had made sure to have ones that fit them.

Harley helped with the launch and waved them off, then he, Kathy, and Tyne came to join the three women. Harley shook his head. "It's a good thing Chase has a decent-sized boat. That's a crowd."

Darinda shaded her eyes to watch the boat speed off to Chase's favorite fishing spot. "His biggest worry is that they won't catch anything. He wants each kid to at least snag something, even if it's too little to keep."

"There are no guarantees. Even the best fisherman comes home empty-handed sometimes." Harley turned to Tyne. "Chase told me you own my namesake."

"My bike? That I do. Did your dad name you after one?"

"Yup, we rode ours here today. Wanna see it?"

Tyne stood. "I'll show you mine if you show me yours."

Harley laughed, and they went to check out each other's bikes.

Kathy shook her head. "Those two are going to have a lot in common."

Darinda glanced out at the lake. Chase's boat was anchored far enough away that it looked tiny, bobbing on the waves. "David wants a motorcycle. It's the only thing I've ever vetoed. If you have an accident on one of those, you leave parts of yourself on the cement."

Kathy shrugged. "They're not so bad on the back roads. Harley doesn't ride on the highway."

Paula had been attracted to Alex because of his daredevil side. "Alex went full throttle on highways with me on the back of the bike. He liked speed. Did rock climbing and flew gliders."

Tessa blinked. "And that didn't drive you crazy, worrying about him?"

"I was young and stupid. His wild side was what made me love him."

"And now?" Kathy asked.

"I have two kids. Being a mom changed everything. Now I worry when they cross a street."

Tessa rested her hand on her belly. "I'll be that way, too."

"Who isn't?" Darinda shook her head. "Besides, could you see a pudgy, little Italian guy straddling a big bike?"

"David's short, not little." Paula gave her standard answer, and everyone laughed.

Kathy poked Paula's arm. "That's what you always say."

They'd settled into small talk and gossip by the time Chase pulled to the pier an hour later. Paula glanced at her watch. "Damn, I have to pick up Maya to babysit and get back to the inn. I'm on duty tonight."

"Ian will bring the food containers back tomorrow," Tessa told her. "Don't worry about those. The potato salad was delicious."

Aiden and Bailey came running toward her, grinning from ear to ear. Chase followed, his grin every bit as wide, holding up a stringer of fish. Paula blinked at him. With a breeze ruffling his blond hair and old jeans clinging to his long legs, he looked more attractive than she'd ever seen him. *Hot damn.* Her insides went woozy. She knew he was a looker, but that had never interested her before. *What the hell is wrong with me?* How could Daphne choose a stodgy professor over him?

He nodded to Bailey and Aiden. "Your kids have the touch. They caught us supper for tonight. Too bad they can't stay to eat it."

Bailey wrinkled her nose. "Ick, I don't like fish."

"You've never had it on a grill," Chase told her. "I make the best fish in town."

Aiden laughed. "You say everything you do is the best."

"And I never tell a lie." Chase winked, and Aiden snickered.

Harley and Tyne wandered back from whatever they'd been up to, and Paula stood to get ready to leave when a pontoon boat slowed down and someone waved and called.

"Hey, nice day to be out on the lake, isn't it?"

Paula tried for a smile and failed. Jason was waving from the boat and Jodi and a group of her girlfriends were partying behind him.

"I didn't know you had Sundays off. We'll have to connect some time."

Paula could feel everyone's stares on her. She gave a quick nod, feeling self-conscious.

Tyne crossed his arms over his chest. If looks could kill, Jason would drop dead and sink into the water. Chase looked from Paula to Jason and frowned. He gave a quick wave, and Jason and his friends moved on.

Chase gave Paula a serious look. "Steer clear of him. He's nothing but trouble."

"What kind of trouble?"

He glanced at the kids and hesitated. "He's not the type to settle down."

Alex hadn't been either . . . until he'd met her. Besides, she wasn't ready for that yet. She smiled. "Thanks for a perfect day. The kids and I really enjoyed ourselves."

Chase grimaced, but let it drop. "Aiden brings me luck. We have to go fishing again sometime."

"See, Mom? I'm good at it!" Aiden told her.

"Glad to know you have a new skill, but I have to get back to work. Thanks again," she told Chase.

On the drive home, though, a glow of warmth lit inside her. Jason had been with Jodi, and he'd still stopped to wave at her. Definitely a good sign.

Chapter 10

Paula saw the kids off to school on Monday and realized she didn't have to work until the evening shift. When was the last time she'd had that much time alone? *To do anything she wanted?*

How would Tyne do on his first breakfast and lunch alone?

She was tempted to pop in and check on him, but that was silly. Tyne worked as fast as she did, maybe faster. He'd have everything under control. Then a thought struck her. *She wouldn't see Jason today.* He'd deliver supplies to Tyne.

How would that go? Would Jason miss seeing her? She'd meant to ask Chase about him yesterday, but had never gotten the chance. Maybe a good thing. Chase didn't seem very open to her seeing Jason. She got the vibe that Chase didn't even like him.

She'd go crazy if she sat in the apartment all day. She needed to keep busy. First, she cleaned—swept, mopped, dusted, and scrubbed until everything sparkled by eleven. *Good God, the apartment has never been so clean.* What the heck would she do until the kids came home at three-thirty?

She'd clean her closet! On moving day, she'd done a grab-and-hang routine, too much in a hurry to organize anything. It wasn't until she hung her black, long-sleeved tees by her black blouses and sweaters and arranged her black slacks by her black jeans and stretch pants that she went to the mirror and looked at herself. Still Goth. *Okay, maybe it was time to switch things up.*

Instead of yanking her black hair into a spiky twist at the back of her head, she went for a softer look—a high, loose knot that looked more feminine. She chose beiges and brown for her eye makeup, and peach blush and lipstick. She stared at herself in the mirror. *Holy shit!* She wasn't beautiful, but didn't look too bad. She frowned at the delicate eyebrow ring and the silver cheek stud, but those stayed.

She'd gotten a nose ring during her first year of high school. When she'd gotten on the school newspaper and the senior in charge put her in charge of the "social" column, she'd been ecstatic.

"You're a great writer. You'll meet people," the girl told her.

A few months later when she'd made friends and began feeling settled and accomplished, her dad told her he'd been stationed overseas for a year, *after* he'd promised to stay in one place until she graduated. That's when she'd pierced her left nostril.

In Europe, she didn't even try to fit in. She hung out with the cool kids—the ones who didn't have four-year plans. They went to school to have fun and pass time. When she had her first mad crush on a guy, her dad put in for the East Coast, and she got the stud in her cheek. Every time she looked at it, she remembered how she thought she'd never survive losing Dirk—until Brent swaggered down the new school's halls in her direction.

Nope, the ring and stud had sentimental value.

Satisfied with her softer look, she went to her trusted minivan and drove into town to shop. She had to chuckle at herself. It might shock her kids to see her wearing a rainbow of colors. Had they ever seen her in something bright or pastel? Black was so easy. She didn't have to think. She just reached into her closet and put something on.

She parked across the street from the courthouse, in front of the boutiques in town square, and went to browse through racks of clothes. To find jeans that fit, she'd have to go to the mall in Columbus or drive to Indy. But the small specialty shops had a lot of unique tops to choose from. They weren't cheap, but she didn't have to sell a child to buy them. She reached for a loose, flowing top, and stopped herself. She had a figure, damn it. Maybe not a model's long, thin form, but she had a waistline. She chose something more formfitting.

Five shops later, she was bagging her third top. It had splashes of rose and gold on cobalt, and she loved it. When she paid and started to leave, a woman entered the shop, stared at her, and headed in her direction. *Uh-oh*, she looked serious. Paula searched her memory, but didn't remember her face. As far as she knew, they'd never met.

The woman stopped in front of her. "You're the chef at the resort, aren't you?"

Ye gods! Had someone she fed gotten food poisoning? The woman looked ready to blast her.

Paula nodded.

"Look, this is none of my business, but my husband is a friend of Jason's. Rick says Jason's doing his mating dance with you, trying to lure you in."

Paula blinked. "Jason's the delivery man at the inn."

"My BFF fell for his routine. She regretted it. I'm warning you off. He's a jerk."

The woman sounded sincere, not spiteful. But Jason looked to be a little older than she was and still single. Some woman was bound to have tried for him and failed.

She gave the woman a nod. "Thanks for the warning. I appreciate it."

"Damn it, you're already hooked." The woman shook her head. "Just don't go to bed with him. The minute you do, he'll ditch you and talk trash about you."

What did you say to that? Paula nodded again. "I'll keep that in mind." She had no intention of going to bed with Jason anyway. She just wanted to go out once in a while and to try dating again. Flustered, she pulled her bags closer, like protection, and hurried out of the shop.

On the drive home, incoherent thoughts popped in and out of her mind. Alex had gone through a string of girls by the time they'd met. There had to be a couple of them who didn't think well of him. Jason obviously did the woman's friend wrong, but if he tried anything with her, she'd cut him off. She didn't need any drama in her life. She made it to the lodge just in time for the bus to drop off the kids. They walked with her to their apartment. Their chatter helped calm her, and she dropped back into her routine.

Aiden stared at her. "You look different."

"I changed my hair and makeup."

Bailey looked at the bags. "Did you buy us presents?"

"No, I bought myself some new tops."

"Show us!" Bailey might have the dark coloring of a Goth princess, but she was all girl.

Paula tried on the tops for them, and both kids actually got excited. It made her think. PTA mothers always looked more stylish than she did. Maybe Aiden and Bailey noticed. She vowed, from now on, she'd put a little more effort into her appearance when they went out together.

Their fashion show ended when Maya came to babysit and Paula had to rush to the kitchen to get things going for supper. Dressed in her black uniform again, she reached for an apron. Tyne stopped what he was doing to stare at her. "You look nice. What happened?"

She rolled her eyes. "You're not going to win any charm awards. I went shopping today, so I monkeyed with my hair and makeup." How bad had she looked with just mascara and a touch of blush? Had her hair looked hideous and she didn't realize it?

He grinned. "You're always cute, but you clean up good."

She let out a frustrated sigh. Men were freaking lucky. If they washed their faces and brushed their teeth, they were presentable. Especially Tyne. "So, what's your dish for tonight?"

His grin deepened. "Back to business, huh? Okay, I made barbacoa beef for tacos. Remember?" He pointed to the menu schedule.

They'd planned all of their meals to harmonize. Barbacoa would match well with her lobster mac and cheese. She'd added plenty of side dishes and guessed that the guests would leave happier than usual. "Where are you off to tonight?"

He untied the apron he wore around his waist and hung it on a hook. "Harley offered me a tour of his winery. He's even throwing hamburgers on the grill."

"Lucky you! When I first got here I was too busy to socialize, but I can now, and I'm excited about it." Paula waved him out the door. "Go. Have fun."

A few minutes later, she heard his motorcycle roar to life. Cody's dad would have to pick him up tonight, but two nights out of the week wasn't bad. She blocked outside thoughts from her mind and got down to business. When Lane walked in to bus tables, she had everything ready to carry to the steam table.

"Well, how did it go?" she asked him.

The boy blushed and beamed. "I won first place."

"Congrats! Woohoo!"

When everyone cheered him, he turned beet red, but he sure looked happy.

The guests came in, a few at a time, devoured everything, and left. No leftovers—a good sign. One man looked like he'd have licked the steel pans if he could have gotten away with it. When the kitchen staff kicked into gear and everything was squeaky clean, Paula realized she hadn't thought about Jason once tonight. *Thank Cupid!* She'd been too busy to chew on what the woman in town had told her.

Maya's mom came for her soon after Paula got back to the apartment, and Paula kicked into Mommy mode. Once she finally tucked the kids into bed, she asked, "What do you want to do tomorrow? I don't have to work."

They looked at each other, at a loss.

She laughed. "Maybe we'll eat at the diner and go mini-golfing."

Bailey's eyes went wide. "You're taking us out to eat twice in one week?"

"Don't get used to it. This is a splurge. We finally get to spend more time together."

It would take a while for them to fall into a routine. They couldn't go out every night, but she was determined to celebrate her new schedule. Tomorrow was the start of a new era for them. If she knew her kids, they'd order bacon cheeseburgers at Ralph's and go crazy with ice cream sundaes. That worked for her!

Chapter 11

On Tuesday, she worked the breakfast and lunch shift. It was the first day in a while that Jason delivered supplies and she was alone. He'd come a little early, and Betty hadn't arrived for work yet. He grinned when he saw her, slicing a mountain of carrots and daikon radishes on the mandolin for today's Banh Mi lunch sandwiches.

"Getting fancy," he said.

The Vietnamese sandwiches were a bit of a chore, but they were unique enough to be worth it. "Everything else is simple," she told him. "Minestrone and cream of mushroom soups, and sloppy joe sliders."

"You call that simple? You're a miracle worker." He shook his head, then glanced around the kitchen. "Where's Mr. Attitude and Mrs. Prickly?"

"You'd like Tyne and Betty if you got to know them better." Paula started work on the pickling liquids to make the slaw.

Jason gestured to the top box on his dolly. "You're getting fancy for supper, too. Twenty ducks don't come cheap."

"Ah, but I use every ounce of them. Tonight, I'm making duck breasts with mushrooms and cranberry sauce, but I save the legs for confits and roast the rest of the carcass to pick over for gumbo meat."

He raised his eyebrows. "I'm impressed. Pretty slick. You know your way around a kitchen, but what are you doing with your free evenings these days? Surely you get rid of your kids once in a while."

She didn't like the term *get rid of your kids*, but let it slide. It meant he was trying to find time to spend with her. She turned off the heat under her pickling solution to let it cool. "I'm giving myself Friday nights. Thought I'd try Chase's since you made it sound fun."

His blue eyes sparkled. "Will you be there this Friday?"

"I was planning on it."

"Good, then we should bump into each other." He glanced at the kitchen clock and grimaced. "Want to check your supplies? I'd better get going. Ralph has a bigger order than usual this time."

That interested her. "Is he expanding his menu?"

"No, but business has been brisk. He ran out of lots of staples."

Business had been brisk at the inn, too. People must be tired of winter and ready to get out of the house.

Like before, he didn't move out of the way while she checked through the boxes. When she bent to peek in the bottom carton, her hip bumped his thigh. "Sorry," she mumbled.

"Don't be. I liked it."

She shook her head and reached for the clipboard, signing it quickly. She could feel the heat in her cheeks, but luckily he couldn't see the heat that spread through her body.

He locked gazes with her. "I like it better when I get to catch you alone. Maybe I'll have to get here early more often."

She twined her fingers together. She didn't know what to do with her hands. She felt like a schoolgirl, and that was just plain stupid. She'd been married, for heaven's sake! Forcing a smile, she found her voice. "Thanks. Everything here looks great. Hope to see you on Friday night."

"Oh, you will. I'll be looking for you." He smirked and turned to leave.

"I'm taking the kids to Ralph's diner tonight, and then we're playing mini-golf," she told him.

"Mini-golf?" He shuddered. "Sounds like torture to me."

"The kids love it."

He hesitated. "I'm not much of a kids-type guy."

"Chase likes my kids." She sounded a little defensive, but couldn't help it.

Jason shrugged. "He would, wouldn't he?" And with that he zipped out the door.

Paula stared after him. What the hell did that mean? She started putting the food away. Lord, she needed to step up her game. How juvenile could she sound? What in the hell was wrong with her? Had someone tied her tongue when she wasn't looking? She couldn't think of one clever thing to say to Jason, and she hadn't drilled him about kids. Did he hate them? Or did he just avoid them? She hadn't been a kids' person before she had her own.

Thankfully, Betty burst through the kitchen doors, ready to get down to business. She pointed an accusing finger at Paula. "If I have to listen to Chase tell me how wonderful your kids are one more time, I might shoot myself."

Why didn't Jason feel that way? But she wasn't being fair. Jason was interested in her, not her kids. Chase was interested in her kids, not her. Too bad she couldn't find someone who wanted both. "My kids *are* wonderful." The words sounded forced.

"Don't you start, too." Betty headed to the dining room.

Tyne said the same thing when he came in to work at three-thirty. "Chase won't shut up about Aiden and Bailey. He can't wait to plan something else with them."

Paula motioned toward the other side of the kitchen. Her kids were standing at the stainless steel worktable, chowing down on ice cream. "Don't make them sound too good. Their heads will swell until they burst."

"Will not," Aiden said.

Bailey gave Tyne her sweetest smile. Paula's daughter had a crush on him.

Tyne was clueless. "Hey, princess, how was school today?"

"Princess?" Paula rolled her eyes.

Bailey's smile grew brighter. She started telling him about her day. Tyne listened, asking questions now and then, while he started prepping his Korean ribs. Occasionally, he'd interrupt Bailey to ask Aiden a question. Paula had to give him credit. He didn't gush over kids, but he didn't mind them either. When Aiden and Bailey finished their after school treats, Paula motioned them out of the kitchen. "Move it. Change clothes and start your homework. I'll be there soon."

When they scurried off to the apartment, she looked at Tyne. "They like you. Thanks for putting up with them."

"They're cool kids. No problem."

She took the huge steel tray of duck breasts out of the refrigerator and put them on the counter. Tyne whistled. "Those are gorgeous."

"That's David Danza's doing—he raised them. I seasoned them.

They're ready to go. I have fingerling potatoes ready to roast, too."
She opened the refrigerator door wider to show him the duck legs
confit.

"I'm in love," he told her.

"Some men are so easy."

Laughing, he slid the ribs in the oven. "If you cooked like this for
Chase and let him play with your kids, you could have him."

"I doubt it. I'm no Daphne."

He grimaced. "She's the only person in Mill Pond who can walk
on water."

"See? I'm sunk."

"Is that a play on words?"

"Maybe." Her wit might be returning. It only disappeared when
she was around Jason.

Tyne started work on his fennel, orange, and parmesan salad. "I'm
in good shape. Go have fun with your kids. And thanks for all the
duck."

"No problem." The diners were in for a treat tonight. She zipped off
to grab Aiden and Bailey and drive them into town. She'd promised
them Ralph's diner and mini-golf. And they'd have a great time together. Jason didn't know what he was missing.

Chapter 12

On Wednesday, Paula and the kids headed to the kitchen at suppertime. They'd always gotten free dinners, but tonight Tyne tried to entice Aiden and Bailey into trying his food instead of Paula's.

"If you like rice, you'll like paella," he told them.

Aiden wrinkled his nose. "You put shells on the rice."

"Clams and mussels."

Bailey glanced at the meatloaf and twice-baked potatoes Paula had made. So did Aiden. They chose that instead.

"You don't know what you're missing." Tyne looked at the menu for Thursday night and grinned. "Do you guys like leg of lamb?"

"Yuck." Aiden made a face.

"Lambs are soft and wooly." Bailey's hands went to her hips. "They're only babies."

Tyne wiggled his eyebrows at them. "I'm making brats and potatoes."

"We like those!" Bailey clearly wanted to please him. She frowned at Paula. "You're cooking a baby sheep?"

Paula let out a long breath. What did you say to that? "Doesn't matter. We won't be here tomorrow." She opted for diversionary tactics. "I'm grabbing chicken nuggets on the way to your martial arts."

"Hooray! Nuggets!" Aiden almost did a happy dance.

Tyne grimaced. "I can't believe they'd choose fast food over brats."

"Really?" Aiden and Bailey would gladly sign her up to flip burgers somewhere if she'd let them. "What did you want when you were a kid?"

He tousled Bailey's hair. "Ah, I lived for French fries." He tossed a glance Paula's way. "Do you watch while they're in their classes?"

"The instructors encourage parents to drop them off and leave. I thought I'd go to Chase's bar to hang out."

"You're going to see Chase?" Aiden asked.

"At work. He'll be busy. I'll grab something to eat there."

"Tell him I said *hi*." Tyne's smile was too sweet.

"Will do." But she frowned when he tried to look innocent. Tyne was many things, but innocent wasn't one of them. "Don't look so pleased with yourself."

"Me?" Tyne grinned.

She let it drop and led the kids off to eat their meals in the apartment. She was beginning to feel as though they'd have a routine soon, and she liked that. Wednesday passed with homework, a game of Clue, and finishing their Harry Potter book. Her parents called and talked to the kids for a while, and by the time Paula was ready for bed she was happy with her world.

Thursday proved to be almost as good a day. Again, Jason came earlier than usual and flirted more than she expected before Betty popped in for work. The day flew past, and when the kids got home from school she rushed them through their homework before driving them into town for karate class. They each ordered ten chicken nuggets and fries to nibble on the way.

"What did you have for lunch at school today?" she asked.

"Pepperoni pizza." Bailey looked happy. Paula inwardly grimaced. Two questionable meals in one day. School lunches were bad enough. She'd make them eat at home more often and use Thursday nights as their splurge meals.

After she dropped them off at their classes, she drove to Chase's. A double burger and a mound of fries danced in her mind, but when she reached the bar, she walked in and sat down along with half the people from town. Chase looked frazzled.

"You okay?" she asked when he came for her order. Dressed in his usual jeans, white T-shirt, and apron tied at the waist, he was easy on the eyes, but his expression said he was doomed.

"Your food might take a while. My waitress called in sick, and so did my line cook. They probably shared the same germs last night."

Paula glanced around the room. Every table was full. "Do you need some help?"

Chase ran a hand through his blonde hair, mussing it. Damn, if it didn't make him look even better. "I couldn't ask you to cook on your night off. It wouldn't be right."

"You didn't ask. I'm volunteering. I'm no line cook, but I can flip burgers." Her mind went to the conversation she'd had with Tyne the day before. Fast food or gourmet? Yup, her kids would be proud of her.

"If you mean it . . ." Chase hesitated. "It's gonna be hectic."

"You took my kids fishing. No one else volunteers for that." She stood and followed him to the kitchen. "I've never done this before. Keep that in mind."

He sorted through his tickets. "I need fifty burgers. With cheese." He motioned to the premade patties, ready to toss on the griddle.

"Done." She pulled an apron over her head and started cooking. She toasted buns, threw fries in the hot oil, and kicked into gear. The orders kept coming. Chase helped all he could between waiting tables. He served up the cole slaw and pickle spears, refilled drinks. An hour and a half later, the rush finally died down.

Chase looked at his watch. He raised his hands and bowed to her. "You're nothing but awesome. Thank you."

"No problem." Her feet hurt. She had splatter burns on her hands. "Glad I could help."

He checked his watch again. "You'd better eat something before you have to pick up your kids. Free. On the house. Beer, too."

She couldn't make herself eat a burger. She'd fried too many of them. Instead, she made herself an order of nachos. Okay, not all that healthy, but it was Thursday. Their cheat night. She was sitting at the bar, eating, drinking, and talking to Chase. Enjoying herself. The man was easy to yak with, could cover a lot of different topics— everything from the weather to sports to food and kids. He knew everyone in town, all the goings on. He didn't dip into gossip, kept it positive, and she liked that. Then Daphne strolled in. And just like that, Chase became tongue-tied.

His reaction said it all. Daphne drifted, ethereal, with a willowy grace, to an empty table. Her wavy light-brown hair and hazel eyes made you think of the outdoors—a young, verdant forest. And Chase was mesmerized.

"She's beautiful," Paula whispered.

Chase nodded. "The professor's wife makes fun of her. Can you imagine? Calls her the professor's lapdog."

Paula grimaced. "Horrible."

"His wife comes in sometimes. A brittle woman. No softness. She made me an offer, but I just couldn't. It would have been like a business transaction. Nothing more."

"So there's a reason the professor left her?"

Chase shook his head. "He's no better in his own way. Totally wrapped up in himself."

"So Daphne's going to get hurt?"

Chase sighed. The sigh said everything.

Tyne had it all wrong. No woman could compete with Daphne. Chase had put her on a pedestal and spent his free time polishing it. She hoped when Daphne's world crashed around her shoulders, he'd be there for her. They both deserved happiness.

Chapter 13

By the time she put the kids to bed, Paula was exhausted. Flipping burgers took more energy than she'd realized. When she crawled into her own bed—queen-sized and lonely—her thoughts turned to Chase. He *was* the good guy everyone said he was. She felt comfortable around him. No wonder he was the shoulder most women chose to cry on.

He deserved to be happy. Maybe she could talk to Tyne and have him put in a good word for him to Daphne. Tyne and Daphne seemed to get along well. From things Tyne said, Paula suspected that Daphne thought of him as more than just a renter. She liked him as a friend.

She was forming a game plan to bring Chase and Daphne together when sleep claimed her. She was too tired to dream. When her alarm went off, she rolled to hit the snooze button, but then thought better of it. Today was Friday. When Jason stopped to deliver supplies, she wanted to look her best. She wanted him to look forward to seeing her at Chase's tonight.

She dragged herself out of bed. After a quick shower, she went to the kids' room and stood between their twin beds. "Rise and shine, munchkins!"

Bailey, as always, sat up and smiled at her. Aiden grumbled and tugged his pillow over his head. The boy woke every morning like a grumpy bear disturbed during hibernation.

She smacked the blankets where his fanny protruded. "Move it, kid!"

He tossed off his comforter and glared at her as he headed to the bathroom. Five minutes under streaming water might improve his personality.

She went to her room to get dressed. A workday. Easy choices.

She reached into her closet for her black, elastic-waist, chef pants, grabbed for a black T-shirt, and pulled a black chef's coat over it. She blow-dried her hair. Instead of snagging it in a clip at the back of her head, she let it hang loose. For now. She'd pull into a knot before she went into the kitchen, not her usual clip. She put on a quick job of makeup.

When she walked into the living area to lead the kids to the restaurant kitchen, Aiden looked at her suspiciously. "You look nice. What are you doing today?"

Aiden and Tyne could take lessons from each other. Both could be blunt and direct. "I'm going out tonight, didn't want my hair to dry crimped."

He narrowed his eyes, studying her. "You put on makeup."

"Get used to it, brat. I'm making an effort here."

He smiled. "I like it."

And she melted. How could such an outspoken kid make her feel so good?

Bailey tilted her head, studying her. "If you want to borrow my blue nail polish, you can."

"Aww, that's sweet. Thank you, babe, but I'm not allowed to wear it when I cook. It's a health thing." She led them to the kitchen, poured orange juice, and made them scrambled eggs and bagels. While they ate, she soaked the challah to make French toast, then started the bacon, sausage patties, and scrambled eggs to put in the warming oven. By the time she walked them to the bus, she had a good start on the guests' breakfasts.

Once breakfast was finished, she started prepping for lunch and gearing up to see Jason. This time she'd be witty and funny when he came. She'd flirt. She was out of practice, but it was like riding a bike, right? The skills came back. Eventually.

The minute hand on the clock ticked away. Betty showed up at ten. She did a double take when she saw Paula. "Lookin' good. Do we have a celebrity coming for lunch?"

"Very funny." How bad did she look most days? "I'm going out tonight. It put me in a good mood."

"Well, it's about time. You've had your nose to the grindstone for so long, you're lucky you have a nose left."

"And a cute nose, it is," Ian said, popping in to check on them.

"Jason called. He's running late. Had a flat tire. It can happen to the best of us."

Paula had to smile. She'd heard the story of how Tessa had rescued Ian on the side of the road when his rental car had a flat.

"Jason said not to worry. He'd be here soon and hopes it doesn't mess up your lunch prep."

She shook her head. "I'm okay. All I need is the ham for ham and cheese toasties. Fast and easy." She always ordered most of her lunch supplies the day ahead.

Ian left with a nod, and she got back to work on the meatballs for the Italian wedding soup. By the time Jason rolled his dolly into the kitchen, both soups were done, and so were the crab salad crostinis.

"I'm so sorry," Jason said. He glanced at the clock. "Here's your stuff. I have to get to Ralph and Chase's."

She didn't detain him. She signed the sheet and handed it to him.

"Will I see you tonight?" he asked with a smile.

"I'll be at the bar," she told him.

"Good! I have something to look forward to. Gotta go." He wheeled away. Disappointment colored her mood.

She didn't have time to dwell on the wasted effort of doing her hair and make-up. She and Betty sped through the prep of the ham and cheese toasties. Then Ian came to help clean the kitchen, and after that, she started the prime rib and greased and salted the potatoes to bake. She'd finished the popover batter when Tyne's motorcycle flew into the parking lot exactly at three-thirty . . . right when the kids walked in the inn's front door. No alone time. It was going to be one of those days.

Aiden and Bailey followed Tyne into the kitchen.

Paula washed her hands and smiled at them. "How was your day?"

"Friday's show-and-tell," Bailey said. "Emily brought in a corn snake her dad found in his field. She got to show it to us, and then she has to set it free. Her dad said snakes are friends for farmers. They catch mice."

Aiden shrugged. "I had a test today. Greg tried to cheat off me, and he got in trouble. I felt sorry for him. He isn't very smart."

"No worries. He'll learn to cheat smarter." Tyne pulled a huge container of Brussel sprouts out of the refrigerator and started trimming them. Fridays were easy: prime rib and baked potatoes along with roasted salmon and pilaf. Tyne was adding brussels sprouts with bacon as a side and making a huge Greek salad. Paula loved Greek salads. He looked at her and asked, "How long on the prime ribs?"

"I put them in the oven at three o'clock at four hundred twenty-five degrees."

He nodded. "I'll turn them down and take them out at five-thirty."

Bailey tugged on Paula's chef's coat. "When will Maya get here?"

"At five."

Aiden made a face. "Do we have to eat prime rib again?"

Tyne laughed at him. "Poor you. Most people would beg to have your problem."

Aiden wrinkled his nose, unimpressed. "It's expensive, right?"

"Yeah, and it's top grade. Get over yourself." Tyne punched his arm. "Enjoy classy once in a while, kid."

Bailey giggled, and Paula shook her head. "Get out of here, you two. There's a snack waiting for you on the coffee table at home. Change out of your school clothes and I'll be there soon."

"What kind of a snack?" Bailey started dancing from one foot to the other.

"It's a surprise. Go see." Paula watched them dash for the apartment.

"It's good, right?" Tyne asked behind her.

"I made them Rice Krispie treats this morning. Their favorite."

He sighed. "I remember those. Our nanny used to make them for us."

"Your nanny?"

Tyne shrugged. "I told you my parents didn't want to spend time with us. When we were little, it was either Nanny or school. Our parents made it home sometimes to eat dinner with us."

"That's sad." She couldn't help herself. The words slipped out.

He didn't seem to mind, just nodded. "It *is* sad. Our parents were a wash, but it made my brother and me closer."

"At least some good came from it."

"Get ready," he warned. "You're going to meet Holden soon. Hope he doesn't make you nervous. He can't wait to see Mill Pond and the resort."

"I'm okay with that. I've worked with a few famous chefs. You won't see the kids tonight at supper, though." She blew on her fingernails and rubbed them on her shoulder with a grand flourish—a gesture of winning. "I'm going for the Mommy gold star of the year. I bought fish sticks and tater tots for Maya to throw in the oven for the kids."

He stared. "Tell me you're kidding."

She shook her head. "You have *so* much to learn. Kids would choose burgers over steaks almost every night of the week. They'd take nuggets over Cornish hens, and they'd take fish sticks over prime rib. Maya might rather have salmon, though. She's older."

Tyne stared for a minute. "I thought parents could train a kid's taste buds, teach him what's good and what's not."

"Yeah, I heard that rumor, too. I tried it. No luck." Paula patted Tyne's cheek and smiled at him. "Make sure Maya gets something good, though. See you later."

Poor Tyne. He looked confused when she left him. She'd read all of those articles about raising kids, too. What no one told you was that no kid was the same. There was no single, secret method that saved you from headaches.

She got to the apartment right when Maya arrived. Paula glanced at the clock. "You're early."

"I'm sorry. You don't have to pay me, but Mom needed to buy beer and get back before my stepdad's friends got there."

"No problem. The kids are settled for right now." Aiden and Bailey were in their sweats, munching on Rice Krispie treats, playing on their laptops. Paula motioned to a stack of DVDs on the coffee table. "Every *Lord of the Rings* you can rent. Some of the scenes scare Bailey, but Aiden promised to hold her hand and cover her eyes. This should be a good night."

Maya glanced at a stack of books she'd put on the table. "Perfect. I have a paper due on Monday. I want to get started on it. I'll work while the kids watch the movies."

"Really? On a Friday?" She'd never hit the books on Friday nights when she was Maya's age, but Maya just gave her a look. The girl took school very seriously. It was her ticket to get out of Mill Pond and away from her family.

Paula zipped into her bedroom to change. She slipped on her black jeans and flowered blouse. She touched up her makeup and poufed her hair. Then she went to kiss her kids goodbye.

Aiden studied her. "You used to dress up to go out with Dad."

Ouch! Her heart constricted until it hurt. Aiden had been so young, she didn't think he'd noticed. She ran her fingers through his hair. "Yeah, I miss that. Thought I'd try it again."

Aiden nodded. "Have fun, Mom. Other kids' parents go out together. You should have a good time, too."

Her grouchy son thought too much, but that's what made him special. She hugged him a little too tightly. "Love ya, kid."

He looked smug. "Yeah, I know. We want to watch our movie now."

She laughed at herself as she walked to her minivan. Kids loved you, but you had to know your place in their lives. And they grew up. You couldn't build your world around them.

She flipped her hair and started to town. It was time she had more in her life than a job and mommyhood.

Chapter 14

S he stopped to grab a few things at the drugstore on her way to the bar, so she didn't walk through its doors until six. The place was full. All of the side booths were taken and every round table had an occupant. Someone perched at every stool at the bar. Paula scanned the room to find a place to sit, and Buck Kreiger, who owned the nursery a little outside of town, motioned for her to join him.

As she made her way to his table, she noticed Jason and his friends, already bent over a pool table in the side room. Jason noticed her and gave a quick wave. When she joined Buck, she smiled her thanks. "I thought I might have to stand in a corner to eat."

He laughed. "The place fills up early." Buck was a nice, nice man. At fifty-six—she'd attended his birthday party at Ian and Tessa's place—his skin was weathered from outdoor work. Deep creases fanned at the corners of his eyes. Dirt permanently stained the skin around his finger-nails. He'd started running the landscape business with his dad when he was in his early teens. Now his parents lived in a retirement community near Harley's winery.

"How's your mom?" she asked after Louise Draper, Chase's waitress, came to take her order. Paula looked at Buck's burger and onion rings and asked for the same.

Buck chuckled. "Oh, she's doing great. If wine helps a person age, Mom should live a long time."

"How long have they been in their new place? Do they like it?"

"Three years, since Mom turned seventy. They love it. I'm not al-lowed to visit them on Thursdays. That's their card party day, and they watch a movie in the community center and get free popcorn after supper."

Paula understood. "My mom's a bingo fanatic."

Buck gave a knowing nod. "Whatever makes them happy."

Paula's food came and they made small talk between bites. When Buck finished his meal, Louise brought him a slice of apple pie. Paula raised her eyebrows. "No blueberry?" Everyone in town knew that Ian's wife, Tessa, had Buck wrapped around her little finger with the blueberry pies she made for him.

"Tessa only sells those in her bakery. She rations her blueberries. Ralph and Chase can only get apple and cream pies from her."

Buck would know. The man loved his pies. Paula would offer to make one for him, but she doubted she could ever live up to Tessa. When they finished their meal, Buck reluctantly paid his bill and laid down a tip. "I'd better get home. I have to start work early tomorrow morning. The nursery's always busy on the weekends."

As she watched him go, she realized he was lonely. He'd spent his whole life with his parents rambling around in the background. He'd never moved into a place of his own. Chase dropped into Buck's empty chair. "Nice to see you here. This is a first, isn't it? You're finally free on Friday nights."

"The kids were happy to see me go. We've never had this much together time. It might be Mommy overload for them."

He laughed. "If things slow down a minute, maybe I can grab you for a dance. The band starts at nine."

"You'd better be quick. I have to leave at nine forty-five. I only hired Maya to babysit until ten. I work the breakfast and lunch shifts tomorrow."

He grinned. "Isn't the restaurant world glamorous?"

"Yeah, there's nothing that beats long hours and splattering grease."

He motioned for Louise to bring her another beer. "On me." And then he started making the rounds again, making sure customers were happy. Whenever he got a free minute, though, he dropped in to check on her.

Paula glanced at Jason a few times, but he was busy with his buddies, serious about their pool. She wondered if he thought she should walk over and join them, but that wasn't going to happen. He'd invited her to the bar. She'd come. It was his move.

She sipped beer and visited with townspeople who came and went at her table. She was connecting with people she only saw occasionally. Garth Roarke, who owned the service station where she'd had the minivan's tires changed, brought Leona, the town's favorite hairdresser, to sit with her. Leona had moved in with Garth, and they were redecorating their house. Paula listened to them discuss crown molding and cement counters until Gladys Whittaker—who worked with Leona—waved them back to her table.

Finally, the band started setting up. When the music started, Jason came to ask her to dance. The first few songs were fast, and Paula found herself remembering old moves. Alex had loved to dance, and they'd made a great couple on the floor. Jason planted his feet in one spot and jerked to the music. A little disappointing, but hey! Not everyone had rhythm and style.

A few more people crowded around them, and the band started a slow song. More couples came. Their space shrank. Jason pulled her against him, grabbed her ass, and swayed in place. The man had no style. She pulled back to talk to him, but he shook his head and closed his eyes.

"I'm in the moment."

She wasn't. She wanted to be. She'd thought about being in Jason's arms enough, she expected to have near orgasms when he held her. And maybe she would have if he wasn't such a bad dancer. She couldn't help but compare him to Alex. Not fair, she knew that, but disappointment washed over her. She glanced up when Chase swirled past them with Iris Clinger in his arms.

Paula smiled. Iris was going to turn sixty this summer. Grams had already lined everyone up for a birthday party for her. Iris was beaming up at him, thoroughly enjoying herself, and Chase laughed down at her and dipped her gracefully. People stopped to watch them, cheering as they passed. Not Jason. Eyes closed, he still swayed.

When the music stopped, he led her to her table and sat down beside her. "I'm a little thirsty. Are you?" She expected him to buy her a drink, but instead he nodded to the bar. "I've noticed Chase keeps your glass full. Do you think he'd spring for a drink for me, too?"

She stared, but he didn't get the hint. Finally, she motioned for Louise to bring them two beers. She glanced at the clock. "I only have half an hour more. I have to be back at the inn by ten."

Jason frowned, obviously put out. "But the band didn't start until nine. That hardly gives us any time to dance."

"I thought you'd come to visit before the music started." Paula didn't know how to play coy. It wasn't in her nature. Why the hell did she have to wait until nine for him to spend any time with her?

"I told you I came here to play pool with my buddies."

She shrugged. "That's your choice, but then we only get to dance for a little bit. I have to work tomorrow morning."

They'd finished their beers when Jodi walked through the front doors with her friends. She looked around the room, spotted Jason, and came to sit with them. Her friends pulled extra chairs to the table.

Paula glanced at her watch. Nine-forty. "I have to go."

The band started a new song, and Jason said, "I'm still in the mood to dance."

"I'll be your partner." Jodi gave a seductive smile.

Jason held out a hand and led her to the dance floor. Paula handed a twenty-dollar bill to Louise as she passed. "For the drinks and your tip." Then she left.

On the drive home, she tried to see the upside to the night. She'd enjoyed spending time with Buck Kreiger. It had been fun talking to Garth and Leona. Chase was the sweetest man she'd ever met. And Jason?

Well, Jason had been a bust. But first dates were always awkward. Always. It wasn't fair to judge him so soon.

Chapter 15

She had a hard time getting started on Saturday morning. When her alarm went off, she thought of her old job in New York. No breakfasts in a swanky restaurant. She didn't have to report for work until the dinner shift. Of course, she worked late hours and had to get up to drive the kids to preschool and school before she could climb back into bed. Restaurant hours were killers.

She got ready for work as quietly as possible, so that she wouldn't disturb Aiden and Bailey, and, as always, glanced inside the kids' bedroom before she left. Her insides melted as she watched them sleep. How could they look so pure, so beautiful? She locked the door when she left the apartment. Maya would get here around nine, and when the kids finally got up and moved around, they knew where to find her if they needed her.

Ian came early to help her. Dutch babies always took a bit longer to make, and he'd asked her to add homemade oatmeal to the buffet table today, too. A few guests had asked for it. Paula didn't usually take requests, but she could make the oatmeal ahead of time and just reheat it, adding raisins, apples, and brown sugar for flavor, and topping it with fresh strawberries or blueberries. Not much of a bother, since she filled the Dutch babies with a fruit filling and whipped cream anyway.

When guests crowded into the dining room at nine, Paula was surprised to see that over half of them took the oatmeal, and they seemed to really enjoy it.

Ian grimaced. "I'd say that was a hit. Can you add it to the Saturday menu?"

"If I get a little extra help."

"I'll work something out. I've already asked Grams to find a couple of people to help you with breakfast. Once June hits, our numbers will double. You can't juggle everything alone." When the last guest left, Ian carried the steel pan into the kitchen, grabbed a clean spoon, and pried what was left of the oatmeal out of the corners. Her boss was a notorious spoon-licker. "Mmm, this is good."

Paula shrugged. Who knew? To her, oatmeal was everyday food, not special enough to rate space on the buffet, but whatever pleased people was fine with her.

Betty came in time for cleanup and then began setting up the dining room for lunch. Paula had the soups finished and was starting on the sandwiches when Jason came with the supplies for supper and Sunday.

He took a deep breath and nodded. "Smells good in here. What is it?"

"Probably the Italian sausage soup with tortellini." Paula lifted the lid, and Jason nodded.

"You should have happy customers today." He didn't hand her the check-off list. He glanced away from her instead, licked his lips, then turned back to her. "Hey, about Friday night, I sort of blew it. I didn't stop to think about you getting up to work the breakfast shift. I'd been looking forward to dancing with you all week, and then you had to leave early. I shouldn't have gotten shitty about it."

The kernel of anger inside her dissolved. She'd been looking forward to Friday night, too, and it hadn't lived up to expectations. She shrugged. "No biggie."

He looked her up and down with a sly smile. "I know women better than that. I'd lay money on it that I had a black mark after my name."

She smiled. "Okay, a small one."

"Well, I deserved it. If you show up next Friday, I'll get over to talk to you sooner."

Sunshine exploded in her chest. "In that case, I'll be there."

"Good." He handed her the list. He watched her go over it and sign the last sheet.

"Are we good now?"

"We're back on track."

He held her gaze a little too long. "I hope that track leads somewhere great."

She could feel the blush creep up her throat and cheeks. "That would be nice."

With a small salute, he whipped the empty dolly around and went out the door.

Paula breathed out a sigh of contentment. Betty heard it as she whipped back into the kitchen from the dining room and scowled.

Paula shook her head. "Don't say it."

"I can wait. *I told you so* is more fun. I've had to eat crow before, but it's not going to happen this time."

Maybe a change of topic would deter Betty. "I have one more batch of sandwiches to make. You could fill the soup tureens and take them out to the buffet."

Betty made a long face. "I like you, girl. I'd spare you, if I could, but girls in love don't ever listen. You finish up here, and I'll set things up."

By the time Betty had the two soups and the plates of ham and cheese sandwiches arranged, Paula had the tuna and artichoke paninis finished. Guests filed in, ate every scrap of food, and filed out. Ian came to help clean up after lunch and shook his head in amazement. "We never have leftovers, and you make some unusual stuff. That's a pretty wonderful compliment to your cooking."

Paula let herself bask in his praise. Ian was a warm, easygoing boss. He treated his employees like they were part of a team, and that made her want to please him. Not that he was a pushover. She wouldn't respect that, but Ian was fair, and she felt safe about that.

When Betty finished cleaning the dining room and left, Paula started on the chicken saltimbocca. When Tyne zoomed in at three, he smiled at the beautiful stuffed chicken breasts.

"They're almost a complete meal with the spinach and prosciutto rolled inside. All I have to do is add some buttered spaghetti."

"That was the idea." Paula took off her apron and hung it on a peg by the door. "You look all windswept and rosy again."

"Daphne asked if I'd help her rearrange her sewing room. Lots of heavy lifting. I had to hustle to get here in time."

"Did you ask Chase to come and help? That might have been an opening for him."

Tyne gave her a look. "As a matter of fact I did, and he declined."

Paula stopped on her way to the door, surprised. "Why? He doesn't serve lunch today, only on Wednesdays."

Tyne folded his apron in half and tied it around his waist. Dressed in a tight T-shirt, the man could be an ad for eye candy. "He didn't elaborate, just said he was busy."

Tyne could have knocked her over with a limp napkin. "Too busy to help Daphne?"

"Maybe he's losing interest."

Paula thought about that on her way to the apartment. Why hadn't Chase jumped at the chance to see Daphne? Her kids had never shown up for breakfast or lunch either. They were probably stuffing their faces with peanut butter sandwiches and gorging on all-day cartoons. Maya hadn't come for a free lunch either. She was probably working on some term paper and hadn't bothered to stop to eat.

The conundrum left her once she walked inside the apartment. The kids attacked her, ready for some company. As she'd suspected, Maya gathered a load of books and got ready for her mother to pick her up.

"I'm sorry I didn't play with the kids," she told Paula. "But I have a ten-page paper due on Monday, and I can't get any homework done at home."

Paula didn't ask. She had a feeling that Maya took care of the house and kids when she wasn't at school or babysitting. "Don't worry about it. School's out in two weeks. Do what you need to do."

Paula spent the rest of the day playing Uno, building Lego kits, and baking cookies. At suppertime, Tyne talked Aiden and Bailey into trying his red shrimp and mango curry over rice, and they loved it. *Really?* They'd have never touched it if she'd made it. *Shrimp? Ew! Curry? Are you kidding?* But for Tyne, they tried it . . . and liked it. He went to a chalkboard he'd installed by the pantry, wrote his name on one side and Paula's on the other, then put a line under his half of the board.

"What the hell is that?" Paula asked.

He gave a wicked grin. "You're zero to one, Mom. You'd better step up your game."

She rolled her eyes and led the kids back to their apartment.

They watched a movie and then she put the kids to bed. She half-expected a phone call from her parents, but it didn't come. Oh, well, there was always tomorrow. And Sunday came early.

Brunch was a brutal bustle to get everything ready. Tyne had slid the hams in the oven to cook at two-hundred degrees overnight, so all they had to do was glaze them. That left the crepes and potato pancakes to prepare, along with the waffle batter. The omelet station needed setting up, besides the lox and bagels, fruit salad, and regular offerings. The dining room was ready to go by eleven, and service and cleanup was done by two. The kitchen crew wanted to get out of the resort as fast as possible. Lane jumped on his bike to peddle home.

"I'm building a corner cupboard for Nick Hillegard. He's started flipping houses in Indy and doesn't do much handyman work anymore. He wants me to make specialty pieces that will add character to older homes."

"That's perfect for you."

Lane gave his shy smile. "I've been researching rehab projects, so I know the styles and looks of old houses, what they'd use." He glanced at the clock. "Gotta go."

While they talked, Howard, who hated mornings, sped away with a wave instead of saying goodbye. Even Cody was in a rush.

"I'm meeting some guys to play hoops," he said. "My dad's picking me up."

Tyne had told her that he, Chase, and Harley were going on a long motorcycle tour since the weather was nice. "Do you need any help with prep for tonight?" he asked.

She shook her head. "I keep Sundays simple. I've already made the chicken and noodles to dish over mashed potatoes, and you made eggplant parmigiana for me to heat up. I'll add a big tossed salad, Tessa's desserts, and I'm done."

Satisfied, he grabbed his leather jacket and took off.

Paula was as bad as the others. She hustled the kids to the minivan to explore the national forest for the afternoon. When they ran into Tyne and the others on one of its back roads, Aiden and Bailey got so excited, everyone parked and gathered for a short greeting.

When Chase removed his helmet and ran a hand through his sunstreaked hair, Paula had to force herself not to stare, the man was that good-looking. He hadn't shaved, and stubble covered his chin. Tyne and Harley were nothing to sneeze at either, but there was something about Chase. Bailey ran to hug his leg, and he tugged on her ponytail. "Maybe someday your mom will let me take you on a short ride."

"Really?" Aiden looked at the three motorcycles. Chase's was old school, Tyne's was shiny and sleek, and Harley's was big and bad. From Aiden's expression, it was a tough choice which he considered the best. Alex had taken the kids on his bike after he'd sworn never to go over twenty miles an hour and to be extra careful. They never went far.

Chase gave Paula a considering look. "Maybe we can even get your mom on the back of mine sometime."

Bailey nodded. "She used to ride with Daddy. She liked it."

"She did? Then she's a pro, right?" Chase turned his smile on her. He knew how effective it was and used it shamelessly.

"Maybe someday." Paula had no intention of clinging to Chase on the back of his motorcycle. The man was irresistible enough without her plastering herself to him.

His blue-green eyes danced with naughtiness. It was as though he could read her mind. "I'll promise to go slow and careful."

She blinked. Now he was mocking her. He must be feeling pretty damned frisky on his day off. She looked pointedly at her watch. "We have to get back. I—"

"Work the supper shift," Chase said with a grin. "I think you do that on purpose so that you've always got an excuse to leave."

Her hands went to her hips. "Why would I need an excuse? I can do what I want."

"Can you? I wonder." He studied her, then lifted Bailey off the ground. "I'll carry you to your car. Your mom's on the clock tonight." Bailey giggled as he lowered her onto the seat and fastened her into her booster seat. Then he looked at Paula. "It would be fun to spend a whole Sunday with you some time, but we work such different hours it's going to be hard."

Paula blinked, confused. What was Chase up to? Had he run out of quick lays to solace himself until Daphne came around?

Tyne overheard and called, "I'll trade hours with her if you guys can figure something out."

Traitor. Tyne was supposed to be her friend. Mr. Matchmaker wasn't helping either of them. She'd be a poor substitute for Daphne, and Jason would move on to someone else if he heard she'd spent a day with Chase.

Paula shook her head. "I'm just getting used to my new schedule. Maybe later."

Chase laughed. "There are a lot of maybes in your life, Paula Hull, but we'll work something out eventually."

Like hell they would. But she gave a warm smile and pulled away. When life got messy, she could always bury herself in the kitchen. With a wooden spoon in her hand, she'd forget Chase's taunts. She left the kids with Maya and raced to the kitchen. Between prepping and cooking, though, Chase's face kept swimming before her eyes. Betty was right. He'd be a good catch. But not for her. She didn't want someone who was hung up on someone else.

Chapter 16

Supper went fast and easy that night. No hiccups. She was back in her apartment by eight. Maya left, and by nine, she was reading a story to the kids when her mom called.

"What's Dad up to?" Paula asked when it was finally her turn to talk.

Her mom hesitated. Unusual. The Jabberwocky—Dad's nickname for her—usually jabbered away, nonstop. "He went to bed early tonight. He's been a little tired lately."

"Did he catch something?" Paula couldn't remember her dad ever being sick.

"I don't think it's a cold or the flu. We've just been doing more than usual lately."

Worry settled in. "Has he been tired for a while?"

"Close to a week."

A week? He had to be sick. He always had more energy than anyone in their family. "Has he seen a doctor?"

"You know your dad." Her mother sighed. "But if he doesn't start feeling better soon, I'll drag him to one if I have to."

When they hung up, Paula shivered with uneasiness. Then she chided herself. Her dad wasn't young anymore. He turned fifty-nine last September. Lucky for him, he could retire younger than most people since he was in the military, and if he wanted to go to bed before her kids did, why not? But she didn't like the idea of her parents getting older, slowing down. She wanted to wave a wand and make them immortal. Then she laughed at herself. *If wishes were horses . . .* She, of all people, knew magic wands didn't work once you hit a certain age.

She felt old when she got the kids up on Monday to get them ready for school. "Only two more weeks, and then you're on summer vacation." She shooed them into the bathroom to get ready.

Bailey's bottom lip protruded. "I'll miss my friends."

Aiden shook his toothbrush at her. "We live on a lake now. We have fun in the summer."

"And since I don't work every night, you can have friends over once in a while," Paula added.

"We can?" Bailey hopped up and down on one foot, she was so excited. She grabbed her backpack and tugged Paula to the door. "Hurry up, Aiden!"

Her brother groaned. "The bus won't come any sooner, no matter what we do." But he followed them outside.

They didn't even need long sleeves, it was so warm. The flowerbeds burst with tulips and hyacinths. Daffodils bobbed their heads. Paula stopped to enjoy them, but Bailey yanked on her hand. "Come on." When Paula walked too slowly, she started to skip ahead. She called back, "Once school's out, Maya will babysit for us almost every day, won't she?"

"Yup, you'll be in little girl heaven." Six-year-olds looked on the bright side. Paula was grateful for that. Even Aiden was looking forward to summer break. She waved as the school bus pulled away. On the walk back, Paula stopped to admire the fieldstone inn, the rolling lawn that led to the lake, and the horses grazing in the side pasture. Two guests drove toward her in one of the inn's many golf carts. They waved as they passed and the woman called, "We'll be back for breakfast! We love your cooking."

"Thanks! See you soon." The compliment buoyed her. She didn't cook breakfasts on Mondays, but Tyne's food would make them just as happy.

She headed for her apartment and debated whether she could call her mom. She usually made a habit of staying out of other people's business, even her parents', but she couldn't shake her worry. So she braved a rebuff and made the call.

"How's Dad feeling today?"

Her dad took the phone. "Ask him yourself, kiddo."

Relief made her shoulders relax. The little knot in her stomach, that she hadn't realized was there, dissipated. "How are you doing, Dad?"

"Pretty good, just a little under the weather." He was using his *happy* voice, the one he used to deliver bad news. When she was younger and he told her the family had to move overseas or he was being sent to active duty for a few months, as long as he used his *happy* voice he figured that would make everything okay. Those days were long gone.

"Maybe you should see a doctor."

"When I don't have a fever? My friends would never quit laughing at me."

"Maybe you should come here and stay with us for a while. You could see your grandkids."

Her mother called from the background. "We just got back from visiting your brother, Dave, in Georgia. Probably why your dad's tired. We'll get to Indiana to see you in a month or two."

There was no rushing her mother. She wove through life at a leisurely pace, drinking beer and playing Bingo. She rarely went against Dad, just rolled with the flow, letting him take the lead, and it worked for them.

"If you're not better by the end of the week, will you ask your doctor about vitamins or a checkup?"

Her dad chuckled. "You worry too much."

A non-answer, something her dad was good at. She wasn't going to win this skirmish. When they hung up, she kicked the couch, frustrated. Her parents never listened to her. If she thought about it too much, she'd rev herself into a bad mood, so she turned on the TV instead. She spent the morning binging on shows she'd DVR'd that she never got to watch on work nights. As she watched, she picked up her needlework. Cross-stitching small x's to make patterns relaxed her. Her walls were covered with projects she'd finished. So were her mother's. She'd have to find someone else to give her stuff to. By lunchtime, she was so relaxed she had to kick herself into gear to dust and sweep before the kids got home. And still, deep in her gut, her parents' brush-off rankled.

Tyne frowned at her when she walked into the kitchen. "Is everything okay?"

She grabbed her apron and pulled it over her head. "Fine. Why?"

"You look like you just stepped in dog shit. Are the kids all right?"

She sighed. Tyne was too astute for his own good. "My dad called, and he's not feeling so good."

"Does he have health problems?"

She shook her head. "He's the type who never gets sick, always exercises, and stays fit."

"He's older now. Even if he takes care of himself, he might have to slow down a little."

"Yeah, tell him that." She started breading pork chops. "He's always followed his own path."

Tyne gestured toward the lamb shanks and white beans he'd made. "They're ready to go." He shook a wooden spoon at her. "You always felt loved, right?"

"In spades. Can't complain." She might want to throttle Dad once in a while, but she knew he loved her.

Tyne grinned. "Consider yourself lucky then. And remember what they say—old age isn't for sissies."

"Dad's not old. He's only fifty-nine."

"But you probably gave him gray hairs."

She laughed. Tyne was working hard to put her in a better mood, and she appreciated it. "Thanks, I'm okay now. What do you have planned for tonight?"

"Mondays are slow at the bar. Chase promised to teach me how to mix drinks and bartend if I hang out with him."

Paula blinked and shook her head. "You don't get enough restaurant work here?"

"Hey, if I ever want to open my own place, I want to know all the ropes."

"You're going to cook *and* bartend?"

He wagged a finger at her. "No, but I want to know *how* to mix drinks and do it right. Then I'll know what to look for and who to hire."

Always thinking. Tyne never lost his focus. Paula turned her back on him and started browning the pork chops. "Get out of here, and don't test too many of your own drinks."

"What are you now? My mother?"

"Hell, no. You'd make me nuts. I think of you more as a brother."

He threw back his head and laughed. "Yeah, that works." He came behind her to give her a quick hug. A brotherly hug. "I'll try to be a good boy tonight."

"You're pushing it."

"I'm out of here before you throw a pot at my head." He hurried out the door and a few minutes later, she heard his bike roar away.

Chapter 17

Paula didn't mind working the breakfast and lunch shift on Tuesday. She thought she'd be tired. She'd worked Monday night, but the guests were in especially good moods. They called her to their tables to compliment her grilled tuna Niçoise platter. They loved Tyne's lemon capellini with caviar, and they especially loved the beets with orange vinaigrette she made. But really, the main reason she hummed as she prepped and cooked on Tuesday was because she had Tuesday night off. When she left the kitchen at three-thirty, she didn't have to come back until tomorrow morning.

She was still humming when Jason came to deliver supplies. He gave her an odd look and narrowed his eyes. "Do you have news? Did you win the lottery or get engaged over the weekend?"

"Hardly." Then she decided to test the waters, to push a little further than usual. She gave him a direct look. "Not many guys want to get strapped to a woman with two kids. Do you like kids?"

He shrugged. "They're okay, I guess."

Just okay. He didn't ask her how old Aiden and Bailey were, didn't ask anything about them at all, which left her with a tinge of disappointment, but it wasn't like Jason was a chatterbox. He was the silent and mysterious type on good days. She went to check through the supplies, and he came to look over her shoulder.

"I couldn't get any acorn squash, so I brought you butternut instead. Will that work?"

She could feel Jason's body heat, inhale his musky aftershave. "Perfect. No problem."

He stepped back to his dolly and lifted the boxes onto the steel table for her. He grunted when he grabbed the last one. "The brisket's damn heavy, wasn't sure you could manage it."

She wasn't sure she could either. She'd have had to take each brisket out individually. "Thanks for lifting it. I bought a lot. I'm braising them all, but I'm freezing some to make sandwiches in a couple of weeks."

He gave a quick nod, clearly only half-listening. "You have tonight off, don't you? You should stop by the bowling alley again. It's tournament time."

"Betty tells me the place is packed from morning 'til closing during the bowl-offs. It would be too busy for the kids and me to get a lane."

He grimaced. "I see Betty there. We don't talk."

Betty couldn't stand him, but Paula could hardly say that. Instead, she said, "Her husband's a pretty good bowler, I guess. She's not bad either."

"Their team wins most years." He didn't sound happy about that. "Couldn't your kids just come to watch? I didn't get to vote on what my parents did when I was growing up. They dragged me with them wherever they went until I was old enough to stay home alone, and if I was smart, I kept my mouth shut and didn't bother Dad."

"You must have been raised old school."

"There's nothing wrong with that." He tucked the checklist under his arm, close to leaving. "Kids don't always have to be the center of attention."

"Do you have any brothers or sisters? Nieces or nephews?"

He made a sour face. "Three sisters, all spoiled rotten. They all have kids, spoiled even more. Dad thought his girls should be princesses. We don't get along."

"You and your sisters, or you and your dad?"

"All of the above."

That sort of negated his belief that kids didn't need attention. He obviously resented that his dad doted on his sisters and not him. "What's your mother like?"

He puffed up with pride. "She's the best. I drive to Indy almost every Sunday to go to lunch with her."

Paula stared at him. "Only your mother? Not your father and sisters, too?"

"Nope, Dad takes them and their families out, and Mom and I go somewhere else."

"And that's all right with her?"

"I only drive to Indy once a week. Mom can see them anytime. Besides, she doesn't approve of my sisters' morals. All of them slept around before they got married."

"You haven't?"

"It's different for men."

Was he serious? "Why?"

"Our bodies don't make babies. We don't have to be responsible for a life growing in us. Mom's always told me that it's the woman's job to say *no*."

Okay, his family was odd. No wonder he didn't understand kids and family dynamics. She bit her bottom lip. Did he mean everything he said? *Double standard* didn't even begin to describe how he and his mother viewed the world.

He looked at the wall clock. "Gotta go. Ralph and Chase will get on my case if I'm late with their stuff."

She watched his box truck zoom away and went over their conversation in her mind. Was he for real? Did he live in the same century she did? She remembered the warning about him. "Don't sleep with him, or he'll drop you."

If they were going to get along at all, they'd have to have a serious discussion about that. But Betty flew into the kitchen and her thoughts turned back to meals and menus. She needed quiet, uninterrupted time to take in everything Jason had told her.

Betty started on the dining room, and Paula returned to her soups and sandwiches. While they loaded the food onto trays and poured the soups into tureens, Betty said, "I miss seeing our hottie boy since he started working evenings. I only see him on Mondays."

"Tyne? Maybe you and Howard could switch hours." Paula smiled as she said it, and Betty snorted.

"All right, little Miss Smart Ass. My Jed's glad to see me leave during the day, so he can play on his CB radio, watch the History Channel, and go fishing, but he likes his supper on the table every night and thinks I should be in the recliner next to his in the evenings."

Paula grinned. "I guess you'll have to look at Jed instead of Tyne then. And Tyne's mighty good scenery."

"Like you'd know! You hardly notice. You're more impressed with his cooking." Betty barked a laugh. "Thing is, Jed's like our old sofa—pretty damned comfortable and well worn. That suits me just fine these days."

A small twinge tightened in Paula's chest. She'd thought she'd have that with Alex—old age and longevity. Life always threw you curves.

After the lunch guests left, Ian came to help with cleanup. He looked excited.

"What's up?" Paula asked.

"Tessa had to start wearing maternity clothes. She looks sexy as hell."

How much in love was her boss? He'd think Tessa looked good if she was smeared in mud and covered in sticks.

His hand went to his hard abs, unconsciously rubbing his stomach. "She's so happy about it. Now everyone will know."

Paula thought back to when she was pregnant with Aiden. She'd been busy with her new job at a Texas restaurant, before Alex had gotten transferred to the East Coast. Ironic, that, doing her dad's military journey in reverse. She had to work through morning sickness and the mid-day tireds. She dreaded the day she had to tell the head chef she was pregnant. She was afraid that he'd fire her. And he might have, except Alex got transferred first.

She was happy for Ian and Tessa. Her hand went to her stomach, too, rubbing the memory of her pregnancies. "Tell Tessa to be happy it took this long for her to start to show. The first baby's like that. The second time? Your muscles are already stretched out, and boom! You look big two seconds after you conceive."

Betty got a kick out of that, nodding agreement. "With our second boy, I felt like I was carrying a bowling ball in front of me for eight months."

Ian's chocolate-brown eyes glowed with excitement. "But that's wonderful! I love Tessa's baby bump."

Betty gestured to the dirty dishes piled by the big spray unit. "You'd better love rinsing those, or we're going to be here all afternoon."

He laughed and turned to start working. "I don't know how I'm going to stay here all day once the baby's born. If I run home, I can hold it."

"Trust me," Betty told him on her way to finish the dining room, "when you lose enough sleep and the baby spits up every time you burp it, you'll be happy to get away for a while."

Ian looked dubious, but Paula remembered those days. She'd

waited to find a job in New York until Aiden was a few months old, but she was still the one who sat up with him in the middle of the night when he cut teeth or was sick. She'd go to work, dragging from lack of sleep. Hell, after Tessa had the baby, Ian might come to the resort and hide in his office just to catch a quick nap.

She thought about that. Everyone was working more hours than they'd expected. Tessa had hired Kayla to help make the desserts for the resort, and Kayla was pregnant. Grams worked Thursdays to Saturdays with Tessa at the bakery, and Tessa was pregnant. When babies came into their world, schedules were going to get jumbled. She had no idea how they were going to cope. But that was a problem for a different day. For the moment, she'd better get busy.

When they finished, and Ian and Betty left, Paula started work on the briskets. They had to cook low and slow. They wouldn't be ready for tonight's meal, but she made a special rub and smeared it all over them before putting them in the refrigerator. Tomorrow morning, they'd go into the oven. Then she got busy on tonight's Dijon and cognac beef stew. By the time Tyne arrived, the stew was simmering on the back burner of the stove.

He inhaled the scent of bacon, onions, and seared beef. "Damn, that makes me hungry. A perfect one-dish meal."

She smiled. "The guests are getting lucky this week. We're serving two beef dishes in a row, tonight and tomorrow night."

He grinned. "Thanks for that. The stew will go great with my sea bass, and the brisket will pair with my spicy lemony clams with pasta."

"That was the point—something traditional and something unique." She pursed her lips, studying him. "You look like you've had another adventure. I'm getting jealous."

He reached for his apron. "I visited David Danza's farm today to see the free-range chickens, ducks, and geese. It's an awesome operation. I came back with a bunch of eggs just because they looked so good."

"Yeah, it's hard to resist all the specialty items around here. I have trouble resisting Evan Meyers's cheeses. He raises goats, and his son works with him. They make all types of different cheeses—all of them good."

"On the way back, I stopped to help Chase carry a baker's rack upstairs to his apartment. It's an antique, really cool. His parents come to stay with him a few weeks every year. They run the bar so he can take time off. He wants the place to look good for them."

"When are they coming?"

"He's not sure, but he doesn't want to have to rush to get things ready."

Her parents weren't particularly fussy, but she still did a deep clean every time they came. "Parents do that to you; get you all in a cleaning frenzy."

Tyne shook his head. "I don't have to worry about that. My parents wouldn't like my place whatever I did to it."

"Really? Daphne's such a perfectionist I thought your apartment would be pretty nice."

"Oh it is, but I could live in a penthouse filled with treasures and they still wouldn't approve. Nothing I do will ever be enough, so I quit trying." He shook his head, dismissing the topic. "Anyway, while he was cleaning, Chase found a box full of remote control cars and boats he saved from when he was little. He asked if you'd like to swing by his place when the kids get out of school some night. He thinks they'll get a kick out of them. He tried them, and they still work."

"Does he have time for that? The bar opens at five."

Tyne gave a knowing grin. "He'll make time. He's so ready to tinker with his old toys he can't wait to have the kids come for a playdate. He said if you give him a night, he'll prep everything ahead so they can try things out."

She couldn't help it—her lips pressed into a tight line.

"Does that make you mad?" Tyne scrubbed at the stubble on his chin. "I thought you'd like the idea."

"I do." Her voice came out hoarse. "Sometimes old memories hit me. Alex bought Aiden a remote control tank, and they set up toy army men and fought wars together." She swallowed hard. "Chase is so good about the kids, it gets to me, you know?"

He pulled her to him, held her tight against his chest. "You and your kids are pretty damned awesome. Some lucky man's going to scoop all three of you up and count his blessings."

Tears stung, and she blinked them away. "I hope you're right. The kids deserve a good dad."

His hug tightened. "And you deserve a good husband. Don't sell yourself short, Cheffie." Then he chuckled. "Sorry. I used the word *short.*" He patted the top of her head. "I won't go there."

She sniffled and stepped back, forcing a grin. "You're pretty wonderful. You know that, right?"

He flexed his impressive biceps. "What's not to love?"

She laughed and started for the door. "Be careful. Some woman's going to figure you out, and then you'll be in trouble."

"No way. Feminine wiles bounce off me like I'm made of Teflon." He took the sea bass out of the refrigerator to start prepping it. She wondered if he felt as awkward as she did. When she needed normal, she started cooking. She'd bet he did, too.

"Okay, then, have a good night, Teflon boy."

His chuckle followed her out of the kitchen.

Chapter 18

Paula called Chase while the kids changed out of their school clothes. "Tyne told me about your remote control cars. The kids would love those. What's a good time for you?"

"What about Thursday afternoon after school? We can play until they have to go to their sports class."

"Won't that make you late at the bar?"

"Yes, schedule person, it will, but I'll prep everything ahead, and my line cook will be ready to go. Louise can take care of the rest until I get there, and I asked Harley if he can bartend for an hour or two."

"Harley knows how to bartend?"

Chase laughed. "Not many people order anything too exotic on Thursday nights. Harley serves wine at his place. He can serve beer at mine."

She thought about that. "Who'll cover for Harley at the winery?"

His voice brimmed with amusement. "His dad used to run the entire show. He can handle a few hours on his own, and if he needs backup, Kathy will pitch in. Satisfied?"

"Okay, that works."

"Good, because I'm looking forward to racing remotes with Aiden and Bailey."

She hesitated. "It's awfully nice how much you like my kids."

"Maybe I'm getting a little fond of their mom, too. She makes a mean line cook."

Was he flirting with her? Or was that just part of who he was? Didn't he flirt with every woman?

He read her hesitation correctly. "Don't freak out, Shorty, but it's nice getting to know you better. There's a lot more to you than the Woman in Black."

"I'm not short, just vertically challenged." She could hear her voice relax. "Thanks, it's mutual. You're a lot more than a hottie who beds women."

This time, his laugh lasted longer. "Good to know. I'll try to develop my character more. See you on Thursday."

When they hung up, Paula smiled at the phone. Chase didn't need to work on his character. There wasn't one thing about him that needed to be changed. He was perfect, as is. But she couldn't tell him that. He'd read it the wrong way and try to charm her into his bed. But was that true? Did Chase have to try to bed women? If she remembered right, it was the women who worked to charm him.

Her thoughts were interrupted when Bailey came running out of her room. She wrapped her arms around Paula and smiled up at her. "Mommy, I want to grow up and be a cowgirl."

Well, there you had it. Last week, Bailey wanted to be a princess. "Why a cowgirl?"

"Our teacher read us a story about Annie Oakley. She could stand on horses and ride in a circle and still shoot the target. I want to do that."

"Well, who wouldn't, kiddo? You'd better start practicing."

Bailey raced to find her toy gun. It shot plastic darts that stuck to walls. Paula had drawn a circle with chalk on their closet door. She heard trigger pulls in their bedroom and glanced in to see Aiden and Bailey aim and fire.

She shrugged. That wouldn't last long, but it gave her time to change out of her chef clothes into sweat pants and a loose top. They were staying close to home tonight. Might as well be comfortable.

They started with a long walk outside, exploring the lakeshore and the stream that fed into it. They kept a safe distance from the ducks with their ducklings, trying not to disturb them. Paula told them the story of Ian and his brother Brody rescuing the female duck from the ice.

"She was frozen in it?" Aiden asked.

"Yup, they had to use a saw to get her out."

When they crossed the road, they searched for tree frogs that had started singing again after a long hibernation. Then they returned to the shoreline, and she pushed them on the rope swing that went over the water. By suppertime, they were famished and chose her stew over Tyne's sea bass. With a smirk, Paula marked a line on her side of the chalkboard.

After supper, Aiden rolled a long piece of butcher's paper across the floor, and they drew an Old West town, complete with a black-smith shop, a saloon, and a few cattle ranches outside its borders. Before bed, they played two games of Yahtzee. Then it was time for a Harry Potter chapter and sleep.

Paula didn't tell them about Chase's invitation on Thursday. She'd learned the hard way that kids weren't patient about waiting. She'd tell them when they came home from school that day. She smiled as she drifted into slumber, anticipating how excited they'd be.

She was making a remote control airplane dip and soar when a strange buzzing sound kept distracting her. It took her a minute to pull out of the dream to realize it was her cell phone. She glanced at the clock—two a.m.—and her stomach clenched. No one called in the wee hours of the morning. "Yes?" *Please be a wrong number. Please be a wrong number.*

Her mom's voice was a mess. She was *never* a mess. "He's dead, Paula. Gone."

Dead. The word anchored itself to her stomach and spread cold through her whole body.

"A severe heart attack. The EMS took him, but he didn't make it to the hospital."

The floor opened and swallowed her. Like Jonah in the whale. A huge, yawning cavity. Time stopped. The world stopped. Mom had to be wrong. Dad couldn't be gone.

"Honey?" Sobs shook her mom's words. "I'm sorry. I have to call Dave and Kirby to tell them."

How would her brothers react? "Are you okay? Do you need help?" How stupid was that? Of course her mom wasn't okay. How could she be?

"I'll call you when I know more. We made all our plans. The funeral home knows what he wants." A choked cry. "I have to go."

Paula stared at the phone in her hand. Then her hands started shaking. Men in uniform had knocked on her door to tell her about Alex. They'd stood there and watched her fall apart. Dad couldn't leave her, too. It wasn't fair! The trembling took her entire body. She curled on the bed and pulled her knees to her chest. Then everything went numb.

Her alarm went off in the morning, and she climbed out of bed. When she saw herself in the mirror, she doused her face with cold water. Maybe that would help. No one would be in the kitchen this early, so she threw on her chef clothes and went to start breakfast. Her usual routine. Routines were good. The room was quiet, a blanket of comfort. She listened to the sausages sizzle, spread the bacon strips on the baking racks. She placed everything in a low oven before she went to wake the kids. She didn't tell them. Wasn't ready. Why ruin their day?

She waved them off at the school bus, then returned to finish up things. Cooking was good. She busied herself in the kitchen, going through the motions. Guests came and went, excited to start their days. When Ian came to help with cleanup, he took one look at her face and asked, "Are you all right?"

Betty, who for once had worked silently, stopped to hear her answer.

She kept her voice calm, emotionless. "Dad died last night. Mom's going to call with arrangements later today. I'm going to need to take a few days off."

Ian stared. Gently, he said, "You could have called me. You didn't have to work today. We'd have figured out something."

"I know, but I need to keep busy. I need to be in the kitchen." When Alex died, she'd cooked at work and cooked at home until her emotions finally dulled, until she could glimpse a man in uniform and not fall apart, until she could glance at his favorite chair and not expect to see him there.

Ian hesitated, then nodded. "If you change your mind, if you want to leave early, just tell me. We can help you through this."

Tears threatened. She waved away his offer. "I'm fine."

He looked like he wanted to hug her, but instead, he went to rinse the dishes. Betty patted her shoulder and disappeared into the dining room. Paula started cooking. She made four pots of soup—two extra as backup for when she had to fly to the funeral. Both basil-vegetable soup and lentil and escarole soup froze well. Then she rolled the tuna and crab wraps and finished the crostini with avocado and green pea hummus.

Someone had talked to Jason before he brought the supplies. He stayed a short distance from her and handed her the checklist. "You'll probably have to leave to go to your dad's funeral."

"My mom's in Texas. The kids and I will have to fly there."

"This probably puts a damper on things, doesn't it? You'll be sad for a while and stay home and cry."

She rubbed her forehead. She needed some aspirin for the headache that was forming. "I won't be at Chase's bar this Friday, if that's what you're asking." She was surprised by how sharp she sounded. She hadn't meant to.

"No, no, I didn't mean that. I'm not good with women crying, that's all, and it sort of felt like we were getting some place, and I'm asking if that's over now."

"It's going to slow it down, for sure." What was he asking? Was this his idea of trying to comfort her, to let her know that he was interested in her?

He unloaded the boxes from the dolly and shook his head. "If you show up at Chase's, I'll buy you drinks. I'll try to show you a good time."

"Thanks, I appreciate that." A tiny bit. At least he'd made an effort. He really was bad at anything emotional.

With a nod, he hurried out the door.

Ian and Betty came to check on her frequently, but stayed out of her way. By the time Tyne came, she felt like an automaton, cooking by rote. He sniffed the air, smelled the briskets in the oven, and then held out his arms to her. She walked into them.

"Has your mom called yet?" he asked.

"No." She buried her face against his strong chest.

He rested his chin on the top of her head. "The waiting will make you crazy. Want to stay and cook with me?"

She shook her head. "The kids will be home. I don't have a babysitter."

"Ian said he'd take them to his place. He and Tessa will watch them."

Tears came again. She wiped them away with the back of her hand. "No, I haven't told them yet. I need to."

"If you change your mind, you can come back, and I'll give you a corner of the kitchen to do your thing."

He understood her. He knew cooking grounded her. "I called Chase. He's offered to help with anything you need."

She fought back more tears. "That was nice of him."

Tyne opened his mouth, most likely to say the usual—the man *is* nice—but then he closed it. He settled on, "He likes you."

"I'm not sure if he likes me or my kids."

She caught a glint in Tyne's brown eyes. "I'd say a heavy dollop of both."

"Well, that's sweet." She heard the inn's front door open and shut and wiggled loose from his hug. "The kids are home. Wish me luck."

"Good luck, and if all of you want to hang out in here, I'm game. I'll teach them some knife skills."

That brought a smile. She couldn't help it. Tyne could lift her spirits. "Thanks. You're the best."

He waved her off, and she went to see her kids.

Chapter 19

Tyne and Ian told her not to worry about the resort. They'd cover for her. Chase volunteered to help with Sunday brunch. He offered to play sous chef with Tyne for Sunday supper. Paula was touched. No one could have better friends.

She and the kids flew to Texas for the viewing and funeral on Friday and Saturday. They'd fly back on Tuesday.

The kids usually fidgeted on the flight, excited to see their grandparents. This trip, all three of them sat silently, flipping through books and magazines. Paula kept waiting to wake up and discover it had all been a mistake. Dad couldn't be dead. He wouldn't leave her. Alex hadn't meant to, but he knew the risks he was taking when he went overseas. He could have gotten an office job, sat behind a desk where the only thing that might kill you was a freak storm. But the man loved the military. And it had taken him from her.

Her older brother Dave came to fetch them from the airport. When the kids scrambled to hug him, he patted them clumsily. "Hey, there now."

Paula was surprised at his unease. "How are Matt and Lizzie?"

"Okay, I guess. Don't see 'em much since the divorce. Matt graduated and got a summer job before going off to college. Lizzie's learning to drive, always going somewhere."

"And your job?"

"They still need die setters in the state of Georgia."

Clearly, he wasn't in a talkative mood. She shifted topics. "How's Mom?"

"Drinking a little more beer than usual, but holding out."

"And you and Kirby? Are you okay?"

"Why wouldn't we be? We haven't lived at home for twenty years now."

Typical of the men in her family. They didn't talk about their emotions. Neither had her dad.

The drive to Mom's apartment took half an hour. The kids pointed and commented on landmarks they remembered. By the time they got there, Paula's nerves were close to unraveling.

When Mom opened the door for them, Paula searched her face. Red, puffy eyes. Dark circles. "You look worn to the bone."

"You don't look all that great, either." Her mom motioned them inside. Paula's other brother, Kirby, sat on the couch, sipping a beer.

"You still single?" Paula asked. "I wasn't invited to a wedding."

"Won't be, I'm too old to change my ways." At thirty-seven, Kirby would rather drive a truck in Houston than settle down. He raised the can to her in a salute. "Hey, sis!"

Her big brothers had been both her tormenters and protectors when they were growing up. She shook her head at Kirby. "You're getting a beer belly."

He smiled and rested his hand on his expanding stomach. "Nothing says happiness like a little weight."

"You sit on your ass and drive a truck all day. A little exercise wouldn't hurt you."

"I'll start when you start."

Before Paula could retort, their mom gave a wan smile. "Some things never change."

Dave sat on the couch and patted the seat on both sides of him. Aiden and Bailey went to join him.

"What's Matt going to study in college?" Aiden asked. "He told me he was going to play baseball for a living."

"Yeah, I was going to be a pro football player. The odds aren't good for those dreams."

"So what's Matt going to do now?" Bailey asked.

"Business and finance, the boy's good with numbers."

Like his dad. There wasn't anything Dave couldn't figure out and put back together. Well, except his marriage. As far as she'd heard, his divorce had been a friendly one.

They tried to keep up a stilted conversation, but finally gave up. "When's the viewing tonight?" Kirby asked.

"Six to eight." Their mother didn't really look up for it. Sudden

deaths knock the stuffing out of you, leave you limp. Paula didn't remember much about Alex's funeral. Everything had happened in a haze.

Kirby drank a few more beers and was buzzed by the time they
got ready and left. It didn't help that they ordered in a pizza that people only picked at. No one had an appetite.

The viewing seemed bizarre to Paula. Lots of people came, but
she didn't know most of them. A few were friends of her mother's.
The rest were men who'd served with her dad on the base or overseas. When they went home, they were all tired, even the kids.

Paula had made reservations at a hotel. Mom's apartment wouldn't
hold them all. They all sat as a family for a while, and her brothers
made clumsy efforts at conversation, but her mom withdrew into stoic
silence, and finally, they gave up. Paula grabbed Aiden and Bailey
and had Dave drive them to their hotel.

She'd purposely picked one with a pool. She bought a beer at the
hotel bar, then dropped onto a chaise lounge and let the kids splash
and swim, working off their excess energy. When they finally took
the elevator to their room, they fell into their beds, exhausted.

Saturday's viewing started at eleven, an hour before the funeral
service. Rows of people passed by her and smiled and shook hands,
but inside, Paula was empty. The one thing that stuck, that she'd remember, were the beautiful flower arrangements on each side of her
father's coffin. The biggest was from Chase—a glorious combina-
tion of roses, daisies, and exotic flowers. The other came from Ian,
Tyne, and Betty—orchids and carnations. She focused on those during the ceremony. She couldn't concentrate on what the minister
said. The words bounced around inside her head, not connecting. She
stood silently at the graveside service. When the trumpet player
played taps, she almost lost it, but fought for control. And then it was
finally over. She smiled and shook hands some more before people
got in their cars and left. They were finally alone.

Mom got in Kirby's car to drive back to the apartment. She'd told
people she wasn't up for a carry-in meal. She'd break down while
people passed scalloped potatoes and casseroles. People brought
food anyway, more than they could possibly eat. But Mom could
freeze it for later.

When they all gathered in the apartment for dinner, their mom
nudged food with her fork, then went to bed. Kirby went out to buy
more beer, while Dave turned on the TV and found a sports station.

"I'll call a cab tonight," Paula told him. "It's not that far." Her brother looked wiped out.

At least Aiden and Bailey had a good time. They swam and played outside on the playground equipment. Once back in their room, they all fell asleep while watching a rented movie.

Dave left on Sunday. Kirby got drunk and passed out on the couch. Mom never came out of her room. Paula took the kids to the zoo. They found a hamburger joint for supper. On Monday, Kirby drove back to Houston, and Mom came to sit on the sofa and watch TV. She never noticed when shows changed, and Paula heated up a casserole someone had made for them and brought her lunch on a TV tray. After they ate, she asked, "Are you going to be okay? I'm supposed to leave tomorrow, but I can stay longer if you need me."

Her mom put a hand to her throat. "No, you go home, hon. I just need some time to adjust. I have to do it in my own way."

Paula understood. She'd needed time, too. "You'll call if you need me?"

"You'll be the first on my list."

"Do you want me to check on you in the morning before we leave?"

"No reason to. I'd rather sleep in."

So Paula and the kids flew back to Indiana on Tuesday, and Paula couldn't help but feel like a failure. She hadn't been able to ease her mom's pain. But then, who could have made her feel better when Alex died? No one. Only time had helped her heal.

She was hollow inside. Aiden and Bailey each took one of her hands to walk her out of the Indy airport when they landed. Ian had dropped them off. Chase was there to pick them up.

"Hey, I don't have to work until five tonight," he told the kids. "I vote we drop your mom off, and then you come to my place to help me try out my remote control toys."

"What toys?" Aiden asked.

Chase glanced at Paula. "Smart mom, she didn't tell you. It's not safe to tell kids ahead of time." He explained about cleaning his apartment and finding his old cars and boats.

The kids' faces lit with excitement, but Aiden shook his head. "I think Mom needs us tonight."

"And you'll be there for her," Chase said. "But she looks like she hasn't slept in a week. Let's let her have a nap. What do you say?"

That won them over. Chase dropped her at the resort, then took off with the kids. Ian helped her carry her luggage into the apartment and gave her a quick hug. "We all missed you."

Once she was alone, with no kids to be strong for, she broke down. Tears started and wouldn't stop. She curled up on the sofa and cried herself to sleep. It was almost eight when the kids came bursting through the door. She blinked. "Where have you been? Chase had to work at five."

"Tessa's Grams came to get us, and Miguel made us supper at her house."

Tears threatened again. Damn, was she going to cry over everything? The good and the bad? She pushed herself to her feet and flipped on more lights. Her stomach rumbled, and someone knocked on the door.

Tyne poked his head inside and motioned for Aiden. "For your mom, she's probably hungry by now." He handed Aiden a plate piled high with fried calamari. "I know she likes these."

"I'll be there to fix breakfast and lunch tomorrow," she called to him.

He laughed. "Good, it'll be like the old days. We can work together."

Her smile felt lopsided. "You're all too nice to me."

"Hey, we're a team. When we're up shit creek, you're there for us."

Suddenly she was all weepy again. "Thanks."

He gave a wave and took off. "See you tomorrow."

Aiden plopped down next to her when she reached for some calamari. "I want to make a memory box for Grandpa. Chase showed us the one he made when his grandpa died. He said it helps you remember all of the good things about the person you loved. He said to remember the good and flush the bad."

"Smart man." Did Chase have a fix for everything? "Tell me what he had in his box."

The kids talked while she ate, and soon, they were sharing memories of her dad and laughing about some of the funny things he'd done. By the time they went to bed, Paula felt better. She still had a lot of healing to do, but she could tell it was going to happen. And part of that was due to her friends at the resort. And to be honest, a big part of it had to do with Chase.

Chapter 20

The next few weeks were a bit of a blur. Paula dove back into her routine, but each night, she and the kids added one more item to her dad's memory box. Finally, it was full, and Chase had been right. They'd concentrated on her dad's life more than his death. It felt good.

The resort filled to capacity, and the two young people Grams found for Ian started working forty-hour weeks. Paula saw potential in both of them. Ian had to add another full-time employee to help Tyne with dinners—a teenage boy with a chip on his shoulder.

Tyne grinned. "Reminds me of me at that age. That kid's gonna learn his stuff."

School ended, and Maya came to babysit on the days Paula worked. The girl had Aiden and Bailey outside more often than not. She didn't believe in sitting around, watching TV. She seemed nervous, though, on edge.

"Is everything okay?" Paula asked.

She shrugged. "My stepdad didn't like it that I didn't work nights. He found another family for me to babysit for. The parents both work second shift. I won't be able to babysit for you on Mondays anymore."

"Is that what's been bothering you? Were you worried about telling me?"

Maya twisted and untwisted her fingers. "You've always been good to me. I don't like letting you down."

"It's one night. I'll figure out something." Paula hesitated. "But I'm sorry you're going to spend your whole summer working."

Maya let out a long sigh. "The other kids are brats. I don't like them."

"I'm sorry." Paula couldn't think of anything else to say.

Maya shrugged. "It's better than being at home."

A sad comment. Paula felt for the girl.

On Thursdays, when Paula dropped the kids off for karate and went to the bar, Chase came to sit with her whenever he could. He asked about the box, what they'd added—clearly his way of letting her talk out her grief. He never pushed, just listened.

Jason never asked about her father. He never asked if she and the kids were coping. Instead, he forced himself to make small talk about things happening around town. It was a strain for him, she could tell, but she appreciated the effort. Jodi frequently managed to bump into him on his way to and from his truck. Paula had no doubt Jodi met him at Chase's on Fridays and maybe even cheered for him at the bowling alley, but Jason still was interested in her, she was sure.

After a month, Jason finally said, "It might do you good to get out again. I'll be at Chase's on Friday night."

She nodded. "It's time." She'd been through this before, when Alex died. She didn't want to lose another year or two to grief. She loved her dad, always would, but she needed to get on with life.

She thought about her mom a lot. Tried to call her, but Mom never picked up. Paula understood. Her mother would call her back when she was ready. Still, she thought about her every night when she drifted to sleep.

On Thursday, Chase called while she was prepping for lunch. "Aiden told me he was having trouble with a karate move they learned last week. If you can swing by here before their classes, I can work on it with him."

"When did you talk to Aiden?"

"He calls me once in a while."

"He does?" He'd never mentioned it to her.

"It's a guy thing. He's not going to ask you about pitching or karate."

"That's fair. Will you have time?"

Chase laughed. "Do we have to go through the entire drill again? I prepped everything for tonight. Louise can cover for me."

"Is Harley going to man the bar?"

"No, my new part-time bartender is. It's summer. I'd like to squeeze in a boat ride or two during the week."

"You've cut back on hours?" She didn't mean to sound so surprised.

"Harley and I both have. We found a college kid who wanted to make money this summer. We're sharing him, each giving him two nights a week."

"That's a good idea." She was impressed.

"I like to think I have the occasional, rare, brilliant thought." He hesitated. "So what do you say? Can you bring the kids when you get off work?"

"We'll be there."

She could hear his smile. "And don't forget. I've put it off because . . . well, you weren't up for it yet. And now Tyne wants to wait for his brother to show up, but I still intend to have the grill contest."

She *had* forgotten. "If Holden's coming, you don't need me."

"Oh, but I do. You make everything better. See you soon." And he hung up.

She frowned out the kitchen window, watching guests wade in the lake, sit on the pier, and wander from one thing to the next. *So freaking happy.* Turmoil stirred inside her and she tamped it down. Chase had been different lately. It almost seemed . . . She shook her head. No, she was being silly.

Betty cleared her throat behind her. When Paula jumped, she laughed. "Quit daydreaming, Goth girl. We don't have sandwiches on the lunch buffet yet."

Paula scrambled to finish the dill chicken salad, and Betty spread it on Maxwell's freshly baked bread. Paula tossed quesadillas on the griddle and let her two, new helpers quarter them and add them to the plate tiers. They finished just before the first guest entered the dining room. *Jeez, that was close!* Kids milled at the buffet now, and she watched half of them reach for PBJs. A few tried her tomato soup from scratch, but not many asked for the minted pea soup. *Go figure.* She smiled at herself. Warmer temperatures, lighter fare. But every kid grabbed for a few of Tessa's homemade cookies.

When Tyne and Cody walked in together to start their shift, she was ready for them. She and Steph—the new girl—had prepped everything for seared tuna, and Josh—the new guy—had finished the mango chutney to serve with it. Even better, she opened the refrigerator and pointed to a huge container of old-fashioned potato salad—enough to serve eighty—and then pointed to another container filled with three-bean salad.

"Did you save some of that for Chase?" Tyne asked, motioning to the potato salad.

Paula lifted a filled, plastic container from a bottom shelf.

"A good thing. It's his favorite." Tyne went for his apron. "Are Aiden and Bailey still at class?"

"Yup, they're working on karate now."

"Really?" Tyne took a stance she'd seen Aiden and Bailey do. "I have a black belt."

Why didn't that surprise her?

"So does Chase," he added.

That *did* surprise her.

"We spar once in a while."

Boys. She shook her head. "Do you keep it friendly?"

"Us? We get a little competitive once in a while."

What else was new? She watched him pull trays of meat out of the refrigerator, all nicely cubed and marinated. "You're making shish kebabs tonight, right?"

Tyne put a hand on Cody's shoulder. "My friend here is going to learn the fine art of skewers."

Tedious work. Paula started for the door. She didn't want to be volunteered, but Tyne's helper should be here soon. She glanced at the clock. Correction. Austin was late. He'd hear about that. "Have fun, you two."

Tyne's grin mocked her. "You have a fun night, too. You're going to be at Chase's, aren't you?"

She pointed a finger. "Don't go there."

He laughed as she retreated.

The kids were dressed for their classes when she got to the apartment. Maya had already left. She had to be at her next job by three, but Ian had let the kids hang out with him while he made his rounds, and if they needed something she was only a few steps away.

"Can Chase really help me with karate?" Aiden asked on the drive to town.

"He has a black belt. I think he's good at it."

"A black belt?" Aiden's eyes went wide.

"Chase is a man of many talents. Be careful what you wish for. He might know a little about it."

Bailey giggled. "He can't braid hair."

"See? You just burst my bubble. Now I know his limitations."

Bailey rolled her eyes at her mom. When they pulled into the bar's parking lot, Chase was waiting for them. He had on a pair of exercise pants, ready for action. He looked good as he blocked and kicked. But then, when didn't Chase look like temptation waiting to happen? Paula watched him with the kids. By the constant grin on his face, he was enjoying them as much as they enjoyed his attention.

Did Daphne want kids? Paula pictured the beautiful stained-glass artist. She was probably in her mid-thirties, a little older than Chase. She'd been an only child and still ate supper with her parents a couple nights a week. The professor she was dating was at least five years older than she was. She seemed happy living a quiet, serene life. That didn't happen with kids underfoot.

When it was time for Aiden and Bailey to go to their class, Chase walked them to the minivan. He leaned in the window toward Paula. "I don't have to work tonight. Want to go to Harley's for dinner with me?"

His face was inches from hers, his blue-green eyes smiling, his full lips so close she could brush them with her own. She didn't have to think about it. "Sure."

His gaze went to her lips, and her breath caught, then he pulled away. "Let me change into my jeans, and I'll be ready." He was back in five minutes. His jeans clung to his muscular thighs. He looked just as good as he had before, and he was sitting right next to her. She could stretch her hand across the seat and squeeze that thigh.

Down, girl. She wasn't ready to tumble down that rabbit hole. One touch and she'd be in trouble. After she dropped the kids off, they headed to the winery. It was on the edge of town in beautiful, rolling countryside. The white stucco house with a red-tiled roof sat on a knoll, surrounded by lush landscaping—forsythias frothing with yellow blooms, almond bushes with blushing flowers, and gleaming green boxwoods. The tasting room, Spanish-style, too, sprawled in a side yard. Grape vines stretched in neat rows behind it.

When Harley saw them walk in, he called Kathy to come and join them. Plenty of tourists stood in line for wine tastings, but Kathy led them to an outside table and brought them a platter filled with a variety of nibbles. There was no full-scale kitchen here, but the winery offered breads from Maxwell's bakery and specialty cheeses from

Evan Meyers's farm, along with fresh fruits and fancy crackers. On Friday nights, for their jazz evenings, Harley catered in antipasti platters, too.

Soon, Kathy had to go behind the bar to help her husband. "We didn't expect to be so busy tonight. No time to talk, but we'll have to have both of you over some time when the winery's closed."

Chase and Paula both understood catering to customers. They satisfied themselves with breads, cheeses, and Riesling. "I'd quote the famous poem, but I can't remember the lines," Chase said.

"A loaf of bread, a jug of wine, and thou . . ."

He cocked his head, studying her. "I didn't think you'd know that."

"I love to read. Don't tell anybody."

"So do I."

"You?" She bit her lip. "That wasn't nice."

He shrugged. She'd never realized how broad his shoulders were. "Not many people would guess. I don't look the type. I've thought about wearing big dark-rimmed glasses so that I look more scholarly."

"They'd show off your eyes. You have beautiful eyes."

His gaze settled on her. "So do you, sapphire blue."

Sapphire? She liked that. "Daphne goes for the scholarly look. She'd like you in glasses. And you know karate. You could protect her."

"And I'm good at boating. And mixing drinks. I'm a Renaissance man, of many talents, but I try to stay humble."

She laughed. "Modesty becomes you."

"Yeah, neither of us likes to toot our own horn."

She wasn't sure how much she had to toot about. "It wouldn't do us much good. Our friends would be happy to shoot us down."

He chuckled. For a man who was so good-looking, she'd wondered why he wasn't full of himself. "It would be hard to get a big head around Tyne and Harley."

He was right about that. "Those two don't put up with any crap."

"I've noticed. Ian keeps it real, too."

They drifted to small talk until it was time to return to town and pick up the kids. On the ride back, Paula asked, "So, was a night off everything you thought it would be?"

"All that and more." He turned on his seat to study her. "You know my parents are coming soon?"

"Tyne told me."

"Would you think about helping me entertain them? I always run out of ideas, and then they just spend time hanging out with me in the bar. This time, I'd like to do a little more."

She thought about her dad. She wished she'd been able to convince him to spend more with her and the kids, but he and Mom never stayed with them very long. "Fish and company stink in three days," he always told her. But she wished she'd have come up with sneaky ways to keep them longer. So she found herself nodding. "We'll think of something."

Chase smiled and settled back to enjoy the rest of the ride. When the kids climbed into the minivan, sweaty and worn out, after their class, he shook his head at them. "Looks like you two need a break on Sunday."

"This is Thursday," Aiden told him.

"That leaves three days for you to rest up. I thought maybe we could talk your mom into boating with us after she works Sunday brunch."

"Boating? Yes!" Aiden shouted.

Paula shook her head. "I have to be back at the restaurant by four."

"I know." Chase looked as naughty as her kids. "But let's get her hair all messed up and give her a sunburn first."

Bailey laughed and clapped her hands together.

"And I expect a picnic," Chase said. "It takes a lot of energy to steer a boat."

Paula gave him a dirty look. "I can manage a picnic, but I don't want a sunburn."

"With your fair skin? We'd have to hose you down with lotion. Maybe a pretty shade of pink?"

Aiden found that comment hilarious. *Boys!* Paula pulled up to the bar and dropped Chase off. His grin was unrepentant. But she found herself smiling on the drive home.

Chapter 21

Paula felt odd going to Chase's bar on Friday night, hoping to spend time with Jason. It was like she was a player. Her—Miss Faithful. She might not have held on to her chastity, like Jason's mother obviously expected girls to do, but she'd always been monogamous. A one-man-at-a-time woman.

Like before, the bar was crowded, and again, Buck Kreiger waved her to his table. She'd expected to see him here, and when he saw the white bakery box she carried, his face lit up with pure joy.

She grinned at him. "From Tessa. I told Ian I'd see you tonight."

"Is it . . . ?" He couldn't say the sacred word.

She nodded. "Blueberry."

He put a hand to his heart. The man loved his pies. "Be sure to tell Copperhead that I worship her. That woman's a keeper."

"Ian thinks so." When Louise came to take her order, she went with the burger and fries, and Louise set a beer on the table. "From Chase."

The man was too good for words.

Buck's expression went solemn. "How are you doing? How's your mom?"

"I'm doing better. Mom's not there yet."

He nodded. "It takes a while. Losing a partner's a horrible thing." Then he grimaced. "Sorry, you already know that."

"Life happens." Buck was a sweetheart. She vowed to find something the man liked and bring it to him. "How's the nursery business?" She needed a change of topic.

"I ran out of hydrangea bushes. Can you believe that? There was a run on them. Who knew?"

They talked gardens and landscapes until their food arrived, and then they ate in companionable silence. Jodi strolled in and went straight to watch Jason play pool. Yup, the girl was sinking her claws deep into her new prey. Paula drank another beer while Buck finished the cherry pie that he'd ordered. He grinned at the bakery box. "I'll save this for the weekend."

"The weekend? It's a whole pie."

His grin widened. "I know."

When Buck called it a night, Jason left his friends at the pool table to come and sit with her. He ordered them each a drink and leaned back to look at her. "You're not so easy to hang with."

"Tell me about it. I'm a chef with two kids and not much spare time."

"You're not just playing hard to get, are you?"

Paula blinked. Is that what he thought? "Not my style."

"So, are you thinking of settling in Mill Pond?"

"I love it here." They talked about the specialty farmers in the area and the wonderful selection of farm goods. Jason was as passionate about food as she was. They were yakking away when Jodi came up behind him and wrapped her arms around his shoulders.

"The guys are tired of my subbing for you. They've been sending you dirty looks, but you haven't noticed."

Jason grimaced, dropped money on the table, and looked at Paula. "I'd better get back. I told them I'd only be gone a minute."

She nodded and watched Jodi glue herself to him as they returned to the pool table. She'd picked up her beer and taken a long sip when Chase dropped into the chair Jason vacated.

"Give him two weeks," Chase said. "By then, he'll have bedded Jodi, and he'll be done with her."

"Done with her? Why?" But she suspected she already knew.

"Once he dips his wick, he's done."

She grimaced. "You make it sound pretty crude."

"As far as I'm concerned, it is. I don't like the way he treats women. If you want him, don't go to bed with him. Ever."

Before she could answer, the front door opened and Daphne entered the bar with her professor. Paula turned to study the man. Graying hair at his temples. Stooped shoulders. He wore glasses and a jacket with patches on the elbows. Really? Had he watched *The Absent-Minded Professor* one time too many? What did Daphne see in him? She nodded their way. "If you want her, I think you could have her."

Chase raised his eyebrows, curious. "What makes you think so?"

"She's lonely. She had to ask Tyne to help her move furniture in her sewing room. The prof doesn't do anything physical. If you hiked past her cabin, dropped by her shop a few times, she'd start thinking of you as a friend. You could take it from there."

He looked thoughtful. "That approach is pretty slow going."

"Are you in a hurry?"

"I'm patient, but I'm no tortoise. I like to see results after a while."

As they watched, Daphne leaned across the table to tell the prof something. He nodded, but didn't focus on what she was saying. It was clear he wasn't really listening. Paula pressed her fingernails into her palms. "The man's a dickwad."

Chase burst out laughing. "I like that, a perfect description."

Paula took another sip of beer. "I feel sorry for Daphne. When she finally sees the whole picture, it's going to hurt. You need to be there for her."

"Rebounds hardly ever work."

"They will for you. You're special."

"Really? How?"

Very aware that his entire concentration centered on her, she fidgeted, suddenly nervous. "You're a wonderful human being. One of the best."

"Is that so? And you think that will win her. What do you want in a man, Paula?"

"A best friend with benefits." The words rushed out before she could stop them. Wasn't that what her parents had had? Friendship? Devotion? Plus good times together? And what the hell—plenty of lust?

He grinned. "Smart girl, my mom and dad enjoy being together. They can share anything with each other."

She glanced across the room. "Do you think you can do that with Daphne?"

"No." His gaze bore into hers. "We don't have much in common. I want someone I can feel comfortable with, someone I can be myself with." He paused. "Do you think you'd have that with Jason?"

To her surprise, she answered, "No."

He nodded. "Neither do I. Maybe it's time to rethink your options."

Did she have options? And then she turned to look at him, to meet his gaze, and her breath caught in her throat. Maybe she did.

Chapter 22

On Sunday, Paula enjoyed working with Tyne for brunch. She hummed while she made the waffle batter. Tyne whistled while he folded the ricotta-filled crepes. Finally, Josh said, "Can you guys just quit? Your morning cheer is making me nuts."

They both laughed at him, but it made Paula realize she was feeling truly happy again. Tyne must be, too. He was turning into one of Snow White's seven dwarfs—whistling while he worked.

The dining room was full, every table taken. Some tables had a few empty chairs, but there must be about ninety people in the room. Was that possible? And then Paula realized she didn't recognize a few of the guests.

Tyne nodded toward the newcomers. "Harley let three RVs park at his winery this weekend, and Ian let them pay for brunch today."

"He knows we can only handle a dozen over the inn's guests, doesn't he?"

Tyne nodded. "We're not a restaurant. He knows that."

A good thing, because Paula made more omelets than she'd ever made before. By the time one o'clock rolled around, there were only a few slices of ham left, and most of the omelet fillings were gone. Tyne had been forced to make more waffle batter, and not one sausage patty remained.

Tyne surveyed the damage and shook his head. "I'd call that a success."

Cleanup still went fast with the two extra hands in the kitchen, and Paula found herself on the way to Chase's dock in half an hour.

The temperature had crept to seventy-eight. The kids wore T-shirts over their bathing suits. Paula wore her sturdy, one-piece suit that survived if kids tugged on it and pulled a pair of shorts over it. She might be a little chunky, but she still had a waistline.

Chase was waiting by his boat. "Come on. Let's spend as much time on the water as we can."

He lifted the kids aboard and held out a hand to help her. Her legs were short. Getting onboard was a challenge. He reached across the water and lifted her next to him. He made it look easy. How strong was he? Biceps bulged, and she decided he must work out. When he started the engine, she stumbled as the boat backed away from shore. He reached out to steady her. At his touch, shockwaves sizzled through her body—electric. She hurried to find a seat.

He headed toward the center of the lake as they settled in place. Paula moved to the front of the boat to see better, and he glanced at Aiden, raising his eyebrows.

Aiden grinned and nodded.

Chase turned sharply, speeding forward, and water doused her. Her hair dripped, her suit clung to her.

She sputtered, glaring at her bratty son. He and Chase burst out laughing. Even Bailey giggled. A fun prank. She shook her head. So much for taking more time than usual with her hair and makeup this morning. She undid the clasp in her hair and let it fly around her face to dry. The wind felt good. The boat's speed energized her. She closed her eyes and raised her face to the sun. When she opened them, Chase was staring at her.

She blinked. "Do I look like a raccoon? Did my makeup smear?"

"No, you're beautiful. You look like a Roman goddess."

A short Roman goddess. She snickered. "Yeah, I get that all the time."

But he didn't smile. He was serious. "I love how black your hair is."

Heat rushed to her cheeks, and she looked away.

He cleared his throat and said, "Who wants to go tubing?"

The water was warm. The kids wore their life jackets. Chase knew what he was doing, so Paula tried to stay calm.

Aiden went first. Paula sat in the back of the boat, keeping watch. When Chase purposely zoomed through another boat's wake, and the waves flipped Aiden into the air, he squealed with delight. Bailey was next, and Chase gave her a good ride, but a gentler one. When he finally hauled her in, he motioned toward two, large kites and said, "Give those a try. There should be enough wind to make them go high."

The kites reeled out from the back of the boat, and the speed made them climb skyward. They circled the lake, and then Chase started back to its center. "We'll eat out here, and then I'll get back to shore. We didn't have much time today. The next Sunday we go boating, you need to trade hours with Tyne so we have longer."

She'd made fried chicken to go with the potato and bean salads, along with buttermilk biscuits and corn on the cob. The kids broke their biscuits into crumbs and dropped them over the side of the boat to see if fish would come. She and Chase sat across from each other, their knees bumping, and Paula thought he could easily be one of the Fey with his sun streaked hair, turquoise eyes, and tanned skin.

He licked his lips, and her stomach clenched. "That tasted damn good." He smiled at her.

"You asked for picnic food."

"If I ask, will I receive?"

She blinked. She wasn't sure how to answer.

His grin widened. "I have a powerful love of cabbage rolls. My mom used to make them. I know it's the wrong season. They're a winter dish, but that wouldn't slow me down."

Her shoulders relaxed. Food. He was talking about food. "I make those every January. I can bend the rules for you."

His eyes glinted. "How much?"

"Don't push your luck."

He laughed. "In that case, let's head back to shore."

The day had been too short. She could spend an entire Sunday on this boat. On the ride back, he said, "By the way, my Sunday cookout is scheduled for two weeks from today. It will be at my place. Bring your A-game."

She sat up straighter. "Tyne's brother's coming?"

"Yup, get ready to rub elbows with the big guns."

"Shit."

He shook his head and bent to tweak her chin. "Take him down, Goth girl. You can do it."

"Tyne's competing, too."

"So am I." He gave her a look. "I flip burgers for a living. Watch out."

Paula wasn't really the competitive type, but for some reason, she wanted to beat them all. She started thinking about recipes and special grinds of meat. All of the suppliers were her friends, right? She should be able to come up with something. But then, they were friends with Chase and Tyne, too, damn it.

Chase broke into her reverie. "Your face shows everything you think. You're girding your loins for battle, aren't you? You want to take us down."

She flexed her arm to show her bicep. "I'm small, but mighty. You'd better come up with something good."

His expression puzzled her. She couldn't read it. "I wouldn't mind going down under you. But if you conquer me, you have to beat Tyne and Holden, too." Then he looked to the shoreline and concentrated on parking his boat.

She considered asking what the hell he was hinting at, but Tyne, Harley, and Kathy were waiting on the dock for their turn on the lake. She bit her bottom lip, and Tyne misunderstood her.

"Don't worry. I left the pork simmering on the back of the stove for carnitas."

"Perfect."

Harley and Tyne each grabbed a kid and hauled them onto the dock. Then Tyne grabbed her and dropped her next to them. What was she? A doll they could move from here to there? She groaned. It was probably that easy for them. Oh, well, let the men show their muscles. Soon, she'd be wiping her feet on them when she won the cook-off.

Tyne knew her too well. "Chase told you, didn't he?"

"I have two weeks to plan. Don't underestimate me."

"I never underestimate short people. They have so much to prove."

She punched him, and he laughed. Then she led the kids to the minivan, and they headed back to the resort.

Maya was waiting in the lobby when they got there. Paula had to hustle to be in the kitchen by four. Steph and Josh walked in a few minutes later. By six-thirty, everything was set up and loaded. Tyne's pork carnitas made her salivate, and her crab cakes would impress the guests. A nice balance. She couldn't have made them on her own, too time-consuming. But her two assistants were learning quickly. She was proud of them. They were both talking about going to culinary school in the fall.

When they finished up for the night, it was raining. Not a warm, friendly drizzle, but a pelting, stinging deluge of water.

"It's not safe to ride your bike home in this," she told Lane when he finished mopping the floor. "Load it in the back of my minivan and I'll drive you home." She pulled under the protective portico at the side of the resort, so that he wouldn't drown while he folded down her back seats and crammed his bike in the space.

She flipped her wipers on high and started down the road to his parents' farm.

"My Grandpa and I looked at an old gas station between town and the lake today," he told her. She knew where it was. West of Mill Pond, about five minutes away from the marina. "It's abandoned, overgrown with weeds, but it's perfect for my woodworking shop."

"Are you going to rent it?"

"Gramps is putting a down payment on it for me, so I can buy it. He said I can pay him back when my business is more established."

"You're that sure of yourself?" She tried to remember if she was ever that confident when she was young.

"Nick hired me to make a long kitchen table that would seat twelve," he told her.

"Sounds like you already have a good start." She turned into his driveway and pulled as close to the garage as she could. He jumped out, yanked his bike from the back of her van, and ran for shelter. He waved when he was under a roof.

She drove back to the inn, happy for Lane. She parked in the employee's lot and ran for the door. She was plenty wet by the time she reached it. She wondered if Chase and his friends had gotten caught in the storm. She hadn't noticed when it started.

Maya was already gone when she reached the apartment. The kids had gone to the kitchen to hang out with Cody until she got back. They stared at her when she stepped inside.

"You're all wet!"

She told them about taking Lane home, and Aiden nodded his head.

"Drivers couldn't see his bike when it rains this hard."

She ruffled his hair. "You're a smart kid. I might keep you."

After a hot shower and changing into her pajamas, she cuddled with them to watch a movie. The kids had had a big day, too, with plenty of fresh air and sunshine. When the movie finished, they were ready for bed.

Chapter 23

Paula made herself a cup of hot tea, turned out every light but one, and nestled on the end of the couch to unwind. The lamp glow lit the corner of the room, leaving everything else in shadows. The darkness comforted her, wrapped her in her own, private world. The tea warmed her, spreading a feeling of security through her body. The quiet embraced her.

This had been a good day. She saw more good days to come.

She let her mind wander aimlessly as she listened to the rain slow to a steady rhythm. Did ducks enjoy deluges? Did the ducklings huddle under their mother's wing? What was Jason doing now? Had it rained on his return drive from visiting his mother in Indy? What did he do for meals? Did he sit in his house on the edge of town and eat alone? She pictured him in front of a flat screen with a TV tray in front of him and wrinkled her nose. Who'd choose that at his age? Why hadn't he ever married? Had he been in a serious relationship that failed?

Her thoughts drifted to Chase. What was he doing right now? Was he alone? He didn't have to be if he didn't want to. Women would sprint to his place to leap into his bed. Was he with someone?

The cell phone jangled her thoughts. "Yes?"

"Everywhere I look, I expect to see your dad." Mom's voice sounded hoarse. Too many tears had roughened it. "It was too fast. I didn't have time to get ready. Can I stay with you and the kids for a while? I need to get away from here."

"Absolutely. We're here, Mom. We love you." She'd talk to Aiden and Bailey. They'd understand that Grandma would be sad and tired now. Grief does that. When Alex had died, she'd felt like her head was too heavy to lift.

"I'll call for tickets tomorrow," her mom said. "I need to get out of here."

"Come. Stay with us." Her mom would disrupt her rhythm, her routine. She'd be needy. That was all right. Everyone needed TLC once in a while.

"Thank you. I love your brothers, but . . ."

"I understand. I love them, too. I wouldn't want to live with them."

A harsh laugh. "I'll call you when I have times."

"We'll drive to Indy to get you."

"Thanks." The line went dead.

Paula's tea was cold. She got up and poured it out, turned off the last light, and went to bed. The darkness engulfed her. It didn't feel friendly now. She pulled her blankets closer and fell into a restless sleep.

Chapter 24

S he heard the kids rummaging around in the kitchen. Monday morning. She didn't have to work. She pushed one foot in front of the other to the kitchen. Her body felt tired, deflated. She'd set the coffee pot the night before and poured herself a mug.

The loaf of bread was open and a butter knife was smeared with peanut butter. Grape jelly was drying on the counter top. The kids were back in their room, playing a game on their computer. Paula sighed and sipped her coffee. She walked to the window and looked at a freshly scrubbed world. The sun beamed, and cotton candy clouds hung in a blue sky.

Too damned much wonderfulness. She went to drop onto the sofa and sipped her coffee in peace. Her mother called. "I've booked a flight."

"Let me get a pen and paper." Paula wrote down the airline, flight number, and times.

"I'll get into Indy at six tomorrow night." Her mother's voice held hope. Maybe this would work. Maybe new surroundings would help her cope. When Alex had died, every place Paula looked in New York reminded her of him. Their favorite bar. Their favorite walking trail. The restaurant they went to for Italian. Moving to Mill Pond had made things easier. Maybe it would help her mother, too.

She threw on clothes to find Tyne before he had to work the lunch crowd.

He stared at her in surprise when she told him her news. "You've looked better. You didn't sleep much last night, but you're determined to do this, aren't you?"

"Mom needs me."

"It sucks to be you." She told him the flight and times, and he nodded. "I'll cover for you if you work for me when Holden comes."

"You've already covered for me when I went to Dad's funeral. I'm okay tomorrow. If I leave here after the lunch shift, I have plenty of time to get to Indy, but my mom's a handful. She won't mind bugging you if she sees you. You've been warned." She turned to leave.

"If you need a break from your mom, let me know. I'll take her on a bike ride."

Paula snorted. "You're all heart."

"Really, though, if it gets to be too much, I'll take her somewhere, get her out of your hair."

She nodded. "Thanks."

"I'm starting to see the bright side of having parents who don't want me. My mom would rather have a root canal than visit me."

She turned to study him. "Even now? After you've grown? After you've turned out so wonderful?"

He grinned and blew her a kiss. "You're great for my ego, you know that? Mom likes to see me for quick visits. She misses Holden and me if she doesn't see us for a year or two." At her quick gasp, he shook his head. "We're not close. We send Christmas cards, and that about does it. My brother's another story. He's curious about the inn and the region."

"Your brother, the celebrity chef." Paula tried not to let that intimidate her, but Tyne's brother was written about in food magazines. He won awards. He ran a five-star restaurant. Okay, she'd be nervous if he stood behind her and looked over her shoulder. She wondered what he'd think about their menus.

Tyne grinned. "He makes me nervous, too, and he tries not to. He thinks I'm top-notch and just haven't found my audience yet."

"I can see that. He's right."

Tyne threw an arm around her shoulders and gave her a hug. "Yes, Mother. You're the best!"

The man was a sexy hunk, and his hug made her happy, but not in a girl/guy way. Were her hormones screwed up? What if Chase hugged her this close? Her pulse quickened. "Mothers get no respect. We're underrated, but I know my stuff. You *are* top-notch. And someday, the world will know it."

"We'll become famous together."

She stared up at him. "Are you thinking of staying here?"

"For a while. You?"

"As long as I can."

"Holden might like being head chef, owning his own restaurant, but I kind of like having you as a partner. Ian takes care of all the boring stuff—paying for the building and wages. I get to experiment and cook without worrying about all the other stuff."

Paula nodded. "I'd rather work in a restaurant than own one. At least, for now."

He gestured toward the door. "Get out of here. Enjoy your kids until you have to work the supper shift. I'm already marinating my tandoori chicken."

She wrinkled her nose at him. "Aren't you special?"

He grinned as she scooted out the door. Her mother would be here tomorrow. She took a deep breath. They'd make this work.

For now, she needed to get cash to pay Steph for babysitting her brats tonight. Next Monday, she needed to make better arrangements, but this would work for the moment.

Chapter 25

Paula's mind was on her mother through the breakfast and lunch shifts. She almost nicked her finger, chopping onions, celery, and green peppers for the Manhattan clam chowder. She made extra turkey wild rice soup—one of her mother's favorites—and stored some away. A good thing, because the guests finished both tureens and their refills. That surprised her, since she'd made turkey club sandwiches, which were pretty filling, besides PBJs and pulled-pork sliders.

One of the guests motioned her to his table and pointed to his empty soup bowl and plate. "I haven't enjoyed a meal this much for a long time. I own a restaurant in Indy. I could make you a good offer if you wanted to change jobs."

What a great compliment, but she shook her head. "You've made my day, but I'm happy here. I have two kids, and this job lets me spend time with them."

"If you ever change your mind, here's my card." He pressed it into her hand.

Paula tucked it into her pants pocket, but had no intention of following through on it. She wondered if he'd make the same offer to Tyne this evening and decided he probably would. Would it tempt him? She knew what he'd said, but Tyne was more ambitious than he realized. When the last guest left, and the dining room and kitchen were clean, she butterflied and pan-fried sixty quail for her supper offering. She placed them on beds of cornbread stuffing for Tyne to finish in the oven at the right time.

When Tyne saw her dish, he whistled. "I wish Holden was here to see those. They must have come from David Danza's poultry farm."

She nodded. "Darinda called me yesterday to tell me he had enough of them to send us." She took the card out of her pocket and handed it to him. "I got a job offer at lunch. You might get one tonight."

He read the name of the restaurant and looked surprised. "Top-notch, and you turned him down?"

"I'm happy here."

He rubbed a finger over the fancy engraving and shook his head. "So am I. No one will give me the freedom Ian does." He went to the refrigerator and pulled out a huge pan of trout. "I got a good deal on these. Pan-fried trout with lemon and caper sauce. How many restaurants can serve that?"

She shook her head. "We have to go with something more afford-able tomorrow. We're breaking the bank tonight." She and Tyne kept close track of the price of each item they served to stay on budget.

He nodded. "I'm doing grilled sausage and fennel pizzas, with a few pepperonis for kids."

"I'm making pork loin with Granny Smith apples. That'll even things out." She glanced at the clock. "Gotta go. I have a few things to do before we leave. And remember, if my mom bugs you too much, tell me and I'll make the kids keep an eye on her."

He laughed. "Your poor mom. Guess it works both ways, doesn't it?"

"That it does." She went to check on the kids. They all pitched in and cleaned the apartment to have it ready for her mom, then she loaded them in the minivan for the drive to Indy.

The scenery from the highway was flat and unremarkable. The kids got bored in less than ten minutes. She opened the glove com-partment and handed them their Nintendos, then turned on music. The rest of the drive passed quickly. They parked in the parking garage and crossed over to the airport.

The kids threw themselves on her mom when they saw her. She looked terrible, haggard and disheveled. Her blouse was buttoned cock-eyed. Her slacks had stains on them. Did she have more gray hairs than the last time Paula had seen her? Had she washed her hair in the last week? She'd brought enough luggage for a long visit. Paula stared at the five suitcases. Five? How long was her mom plan-ning to stay? That thought made her cringe. What kind of daughter was she? So she squelched it. They got a cart and toted her mom's bags to the minivan.

Once everything was loaded, Paula tried to make her mom feel welcome. "How was your trip?"

"Horrible. I'm starving." She patted her purse. "Let me take you out to eat."

Her mom looked one notch above a homeless person. The kids were squirming. Paula spotted a Five Guys a few miles down the road and stopped there. Aiden and Bailey gorged themselves on burgers and fries. Paula couldn't finish hers, and Mom picked at her food. When they were finished, they set off for home. Her mom looked so tired, Paula didn't try to force a conversation. She turned on music again, and the kids traded games to play on the way back. By the time they reached the apartment, they were all ready to relax.

Her mom looked around. "I only see two bedrooms."

"When you and Dad came last fall, the inn wasn't full. Ian gave you a guest room to stay in so you didn't spend much time in my apartment. The place isn't big, but the couch is comfortable, and I put clean sheets on my bed so you'll have some privacy. It'll work for now."

Her mom dragged a suitcase into the bedroom. "If you don't mind, I'm crawling into that nice bed. I hope I can sleep tonight."

"Here. This will help." Paula got a Benadryl from the kitchen cupboard and a glass of water. When Paula's allergies acted up, the pharmacist had recommended Benadryl, but Paula fell asleep every time she took one so she'd stopped. It wasn't nice to drug your mom, but the poor woman needed sleep.

Her mom frowned, gave her *the mother* look, but took it. In a while, Paula heard snoring coming from her bedroom.

Paula and the kids settled in front of the TV to watch a DVD they'd bought. She made popcorn and hot chocolate, and by the time the movie was finished, the kids were ready for bed, too.

Paula covered the couch with a sheet, plumped her pillow, and tried to get comfortable. She'd lied. The couch was great for sitting, not that great for sleeping. She woke to her alarm, stiff and sore. She had to stretch to get limber before going to work. When she had a good start on breakfast, she came back to check on the kids.

When Maya came, Paula told her to let her mom sleep as long as she wanted to. "I left the key for my minivan on the kitchen table, in case she wants to go somewhere. Chase serves barbecue at the bar on Wednesdays if she wants to eat lunch there."

Maya glanced at the clock, unhappy the kids were sleeping so late.

"They had a big day yesterday," Paula told her. "They can stay in their beds till ten. Then you can rouse them, if you want to."

Maya didn't approve, she could tell, but one of Paula's great joys as a kid had been sleeping in. The clock reminded her that she'd better get back to the kitchen, so she went to finish things up.

When Jason burst through the kitchen doors, he'd already heard the news about her mom coming to stay with her. Part of living in a small town. Everyone knew everything. "This is a win-win for both of you," he said. "Your mom can see the kids and enjoy them, and you have a built-in babysitter."

Paula stopped checking his list and stared. "I wouldn't do that to Mom."

He looked uneasy. "It might make her feel better, like she's still useful."

"Useful?" Her fingers tightened on the clipboard.

"Hey, I just meant that it helps to keep busy sometimes."

All right, that was true. When she was upset, she cooked. Her mom mostly ate out these days. The kitchen wouldn't comfort her, but the kids would keep her occupied.

He smiled when she handed back his clipboard. "Anyway, if you have more free time, you know where to find me."

She nodded. "Maybe I'll drag Mom along with me." She almost laughed when he looked horrified. He hadn't thought of that. She watched him hurry to his box truck, and Jodi walked out to meet him. If Paula knew body language at all, they were arguing. Finally, he pushed away from her and drove off.

Betty bustled into the kitchen with a smirk on her face. "Is your mom still attractive? Maybe he'll hit on her, too."

"Betty!" The woman looked too damned cocky.

When lunch was prepped and ready to go, Paula hurried back to her apartment for a few minutes to check on her mom.

"She's gone." Maya looked up from a book. "Took your minivan to town. Said she felt cooped-up and needed to get some air."

The kids were nowhere to be seen. "Did she take Aiden and Bailey with her?"

Maya motioned out the window to the back yard. Tyne, in swim trunks and a muscle shirt, was working with them on their karate moves. Bailey's black hair clung to her head. Sweat beaded on Aiden's forehead. Finally, Tyne took mercy on them, and as they headed to the beach, he yanked his shirt over his head. *Holy mother of hotness!* Paula finally understood how a body could be a temple. Women guests stopped and stared. Hell, Ian would never have an empty room if Tyne took a dip every day.

Her mind flew to Chase's biceps and flat abs. What did he look like shirtless? Would she be able to keep her hands off him if she knew?

Maya sighed. "He's been at it with them for an hour. I had a project planned for today. We're going to be lucky to get it done."

Paula patted the girl's shoulder. "Life throws you curves. Some of them are fun."

Maya grimaced. "I like schedules."

The girl had a lot to learn. Paula watched Tyne pick up Bailey and toss her in the water. He grabbed Aiden next. The kids squealed and laughed. Women smiled and enjoyed. The man had no idea how sexy he was. No, that wasn't true. He knew, but took it for granted.

"I have to get back to the dining room. Tell Mom I stopped to say hi."

Maya reached for a post-it note and scribbled a message, then she buried her nose back in her book.

Paula shook her head and hurried to the kitchen. Steph had already filled a tureen with today's goulash, and Josh had the corn chowder on the table. The sandwiches were arranged prettily on the plate tiers. They refilled the food often, and when lunch ended, they did a quick cleanup.

Paula's pork and apple dish was ready to go by three, but Tyne didn't blow into the kitchen as he usually did. She decided to start the pizza dough for him. Finally, he straggled in, only a few minutes before Austin was supposed to show up for work. He saw the mounds of dough she'd made for him and looked relieved.

"Sorry, but when I took your kids back to your apartment, your mom caught me." He grinned. "She's a neat old broad. You're lucky."

Who but Tyne could say it so aptly? "Yeah, she's the best, and I know it. I saw you with Aiden and Bailey. Thanks for practicing with them."

"Aiden's got the right moves." Tyne's brown eyes lit with excitement. "He could be good at karate. He's starting young enough."

"Ian taught him a few moves when a bully was picking on him," Paula said. "And Ian's brother, Brody, taught him how to punch."

"Ian knows karate, too? We've got one hell of a boss." Tyne's skin was bronzing from so much time outdoors. His hair was lightening from the sun. When Austin walked into the kitchen, Tyne looked pointedly at the clock. "Three minutes late."

Austin sneered. The kid *did* have an attitude.

"Drop and give me thirty push-ups."

Paula stared, but Austin dropped to the floor and Tyne started counting. When he reached thirty, he hitched his thumb toward the stainless steel table. "Wash your hands and get started."

Austin studied the menu and began slicing fennel.

Tyne looked pleased. "That kid's going to culinary school this fall if I have anything to say about it."

Paula pressed her lips together. "That kid doesn't have a penny to his name. He comes from a single mom—a good one, but a poor one."

"Doesn't matter. My mom makes a big deal about the charity work she does. She's going to sponsor him, or I'm going to fly out to visit her more often."

Paula stared. "You'd threaten your own mom?"

He paused, then grinned. "Guess I would."

She started laughing. She couldn't help it. She had to admire Tyne's chutzpah. "That kid's lucky he found you."

"I know, now get going. Your mom's in the mood to see you."

And she was. Paula didn't even get changed before her mom started telling her about her day. "I explored Mill Pond, visited your grocery store. Nice people. And ended up at Chase's bar for lunch. You're right. The pulled pork was delicious." Her mom wiggled her eyebrows. "The man's pretty delicious, too."

Aiden smiled. "He takes us fishing and boating."

"That's what he said. He's a real cutie. I'd go for him if I was forty years younger."

Bailey leaned into her grandmother. "We like him, but Mom likes Jason. He doesn't like kids."

"We don't know that." Paula's defenses came up; she didn't really want to talk about it.

Her mom gave her a curious look, but let it drop. "What's your schedule like? Chefs are always busy, aren't they?"

Aiden told her about Maya and Paula's hours.

"The babysitter could probably take some days off if she wanted to," Mom told them. "I can watch you two while your mom works."

Bailey's face fell. "We like Maya."

"And that's not why you're here," Paula added. "If you want to take off and go someplace, I want you to be able to. Maya can be here as backup. Besides, she could use a little attention herself."

"You like her."

"Her life isn't easy. She's a hundred years old in a fifteen-year-old body."

Her mom looked thoughtful. "You leave that girl to me. But I don't want to stay home and sit around tonight. I've done enough of that lately. I say we go into town for pizza."

The kids cheered and Paula gave in gracefully. Really, what were her options? So she drove her mom around the lake, showed her Harley's winery, and then stopped for pizza in town. By the time they got back to the apartment, her mom was dragging.

"My energy's gone. If I do much at all, I hit a wall."

"That's part of it," Paula said. But her mom looked a lot better today than she had yesterday. She got her another Benadryl and a glass of water and said, "Go to bed."

Her mom smiled. "Yes, ma'am!"

Chapter 26

Paula hurried through breakfast and lunch, then she took Betty to the apartment and introduced her to her mom. The two women hit it off. They were still yakking when Paula went back to the kitchen to start her supper dish for Tyne.

When Tyne got there, he had her mom in tow. "She said she'd like a tour of the kitchen."

Paula stared. "Really? I thought you'd sworn off those."

Her mom glanced around at the stainless steel and commercial appliances. "Yup, I've seen enough. I just came to spend time with your cute assistant."

"My partner," Paula corrected, and Tyne grinned.

He turned to her mom. "Wait till you meet my brother. He's coming the Saturday after next. He's famous."

"Is he as cute as you?" Mom's taste in food was a lot like the kids'. She couldn't care less about gourmet.

Tyne finished tying his apron around his waist. "Not even close."

"Then who cares?" Mom shrugged.

Paula cared. She turned to *Mr. Modest*. "Do you need some days off? What have you got planned while Holden's here?"

He looked sheepish. That made her nervous. It took a lot to make Tyne uncertain. "He gets in Saturday night, so you'll have to cover for me then. And he wants to work with us on Sunday brunch."

"In the kitchen?" Paula tried not to show the panic that welled up inside her. What did Holden's restaurant serve for brunch? Would he remember this was a resort, not a five-star dining room?

"That was the idea. After brunch, there's Chase's cook-off."

The cook-off was good. "He'll meet a lot of people there. That'll be nice."

"I work day shift on Monday, so after three I can show him the area and introduce him to our vendors." He hurried on, looking a little flustered. She braced for what came next. "On Tuesday, he'd love to take over the kitchen and cook with me the entire day."

"My kitchen?" She corrected herself. "Our kitchen?"

Tyne nodded. "If you're willing to give up breakfast and lunch, that is."

How did she feel about that? Would the brothers come up with something so wonderful, guests would think of her dishes as second-rate? She fought down her insecurities. "Is that your brother's idea of fun?"

Tyne laughed, relieved she hadn't gotten angry, she could tell. "We're both chefs. What can I say? We like hanging out in the kitchen together."

Paula shrugged. "Oh hell, why not?"

"I appreciate it. I know it's asking a lot of a chef."

"No biggie."

He hesitated again, and she tensed. "Chase invited him to compete in the cook-off, too."

"What?"

"Chase says you're going to wipe the floor with us, but he's wrong. I'm going to bury you all and dance on your wannabe chef graves." He wore a cocky grin.

Her mom laughed. "You don't know my daughter."

Paula stared at her, surprised. "You've never been to my restaurants."

"Doesn't matter. They're picking on the wrong girl."

"Is that so?" Tyne reached out to shake Paula's hand. "May the best chef win."

Paula rolled her eyes. When she and Mom walked back to the apartment, her mother threw her a look. "What about *that* nice boy? I didn't see a ring on his finger. And he's a looker."

"We're just friends."

Her mother sighed, ready to argue, but Paula distracted her. "On Thursdays, I take the kids into town for karate, then I eat supper at Chase's. As you know, he's a looker, too. So is my boss, Ian, and their friend who runs the winery, Harley."

"Four of them?" Her mother raised her eyebrows, impressed.

"Yeah, they could make a calendar and get rich. Are you up for going with us tonight?"

Her mom gave a quick nod, started to say something, then blinked and glanced away.

"Are you getting tired, Mom? Would you rather stay home?"

"No, I'm having a great time. Just once in a while, at odd times, I think of your dad. He'd have loved to see you here."

"He did."

"You weren't settled yet. You've found balance here, happiness."

Paula looped her arm through her mom's. "You'll get there, too. It gets better after a while, but it takes time."

Mom glanced away, sniffed, and then put on a brave smile. "Let's grab those kids and get out of here."

Paula bought Happy Meals on the way to town. She dropped Aiden and Bailey off, then took Mom to Chase's. He gave a wave, finished wiping down the bar, and came to sit with them. "It's going to be a slow night. Harley's introducing a new wine at his place. He hired a band to christen it right, and Grams's church is sponsoring a chili contest there. It's going to be fun."

"But you didn't go? You could have asked your new helper to cover for you." Paula looked around at the few, regular patrons scattered at different tables.

"And miss seeing you when you drop the kids off?" Chase reached out and put his hand over hers. He turned to her mother. "Your daughter's done a great job raising those two."

Paula's body woke at his touch. Every cell came to attention.

Mom gave a slow smile. "They've turned out pretty wonderful, haven't they?"

Chase nodded for Louise to take their orders. "What's your pleasure?" he asked Paula.

She decided to live dangerously. "A margarita." It was all she could do not to say, *You, sprawled on the bar, so I can lick salt off of every inch of you.* She swallowed hard. What the hell was wrong with her? When did her libido wake up and get funky?

He turned to her mom. "You?"

"Beer." Her mom's favorite—a brew.

"To eat?"

They all went with the special—chicken nachos. Paula was saving her burger for tomorrow night.

When Louise left, Chase settled his gaze on her mother once more. "So, how do you like Mill Pond?"

"What's not to like? Great people. Great food. It's a good place to raise kids."

He turned on his dazzling smile, but never released Paula's hand. "Paula should bring you and the kids boating with me this Sunday. I can show you the lake view of our town."

Her mom's face lit with excitement. "Betty invited me for supper at her cottage. You could drop me off at her dock."

"Perfect. We'll call it a date."

Paula tossed him a teasing glance. "You'd better be careful. If you spend two Sundays in a row with my kids, they're going to start expecting it."

His grip tightened. "I might like that."

She stared, not sure how to respond. Louise came with their food, and thankfully, the moment passed. Then customers started meandering in, and soon, Chase had to leave them. He pointed a finger at her, though. "Sunday, on my boat. And this time, trade hours with Tyne. I want you all day."

What had gotten into him? Then she looked at her mom and caught her smirk. When she started to protest, her mom shook her head. "I'm just enjoying my nachos and beer. After this, I want to find a bingo parlor I can visit sometime."

Paula decided to leave it at that. It was probably safer.

Chapter 27

Maya came to babysit on Friday morning, but had to leave at three. Mom volunteered to stay with the kids when Paula went to the bar, but Paula shook her head.

"Sorry, but you're coming with me. I was going to ask Grams to find me a babysitter for Mondays and Fridays, but Steph asked if she can keep doing it. She's trying to make extra money. The kids like Steph."

"Your nice little assistant?" Mom had been paying more attention to how the kitchen ran than Paula realized.

"Yup, she's trying to save as much as she can this summer. So get ready. We leave at five thirty."

Mom headed to the bedroom to change. Then it was Paula's turn. June had brought hot, humid weather, so Paula chose lightweight slacks and a T-shirt with KISS THE COOK sprawled across the front.

Mom grinned. "What if someone takes you up on that?"

"Everyone knows me here. They know better."

They spent time with Aiden and Bailey until Steph came, then they drove to town. This time, Paula pointed out the farms they passed. Vibrant green fields sprawled to a bright red barn at the Albertson's. "That's where Lane, the boy who rides his bike to work, lives." Livestock grazed in fenced pastures. She pointed to the next place. "The Kruses grow corn, soybeans, and wheat." When they passed a house with a pool in the back yard, Paula said, "That's David and Darinda's poultry farm."

Mom smiled and pointed at Garth's service station. "I met the owner at Ralph's diner. He told me that Grams's church has bingo every Tuesday afternoon."

"Be warned. Tessa's Grams knows everyone in town and volunteers in half of what goes on here. If she can sign you up for something, she will."

Mom looked thoughtful. "I could meet people that way. I could plug in for a while. I need to keep busy. When I slow down, the loneliness almost crushes me."

Paula's heart wrenched. Her mom was trying so hard. She'd done the same thing when Alex died.

They drove down Main Street, past the diner and Grams's little, white church. Paula motioned toward customers sitting at white, wrought-iron tables outside of Sadie's frozen custard shop. "Mill Pond is getting more and more tourists since Ian opened the resort." People browsed in the specialty shops around the courthouse square.

"You picked a pretty, little town," her mom said. "The awnings and flower boxes give it a quaint feel."

Paula nodded, proud of how charming it was. Cars filled Chase's parking lot, and Paula led Mom to Buck Kreiger's table when they walked inside the bar.

Buck gave a formal nod. "Nice to meet you, ma'am."

Her mom could talk to anyone, and before long, they were yakking about the changes in Mill Pond in the last few years. Louise came for their orders, but Buck didn't lose his focus.

"First, the farmers decided to specialize," Buck told them. "We raise things here that are hard to find other places. And then the shops started to go more upscale, so that people on their way to the national park would stop to browse through them. Then Art and his kids redid the exterior of the grocery store to make it look like an old-time, general store and added barrels of candies like taffy and stuff from the fifties."

"The fifties?" Mom asked.

Buck shrugged. "You know, candy necklaces, candy cigarettes, red vine licorice, root beer barrels, atomic fireballs . . ."

Her mom nodded.

"Anyway, tourists loved it, so the town went for broke with awnings and flower boxes, and more people came every day." He looked around the bar. "Mostly, this is still a local hangout, but tourists are starting to trickle in. Chase has been talking about adding an outdoor dining area to seat more people in the warm months."

"He'll have to," Mom said, "or he won't have enough room for everyone."

Louise brought their burgers and fries and another round of beers. "From Chase," she told them. When Buck's pie came, Mom ordered a piece, too. "I love lemon meringue."

Paula was happy to watch her mom finish her meal. She usually shuffled it around her plate, but the bustle and noise here made her eat without thinking. When Buck got up to leave, Mom looked sorry to see him go. Paula glanced at Jason, and he met her gaze, but stayed at the pool table with his friends.

That's the way it was going to be, huh? If she brought her mom, he was going to ignore her? Well, screw him.

Chase sent her and her mom another round, but was too busy to sit with them. Her mom shook her head when another woman touched his arm when he came for her drink order. "Women would stand in line for him. What are you waiting for?"

"It's too soon. I don't know what I want."

Her mom frowned when a woman rested her hand on his thigh. "Wait too long and he'll be taken."

Paula stared, distracted, when Jodi walked into the bar, alone. She went straight to the pool table and stood beside Jason. Without a word, Jason handed his cue stick to a friend, standing nearby, watching the game. The man stepped up to take Jason's place, then Jason came to sit with Paula and her mom.

Paula blinked. Jason had made plans with his friend ahead of time. She'd never seen a colder snub. She frowned at him. "You left your friend high and dry. She doesn't look too happy."

Jason raised his hand to order a beer. "She's not the kind of girl I want to spend time with."

A warning bell went off. Jodi must have slept with him. Paula glanced at the bar, and Chase was drilling her with his gaze. His expression didn't say *I told you so.* It was a warning. *Don't be the next girl Jason ditches.*

Jason's beer came, and Paula tried again. "I thought you and Jodi were pretty close."

A shrug. "I thought she was a quality date. I was wrong. She's too slutty for my taste."

The words popped out before she filtered them. "Most quality girls don't tell a man she can make them wet their pants when she dances with them. You knew that going in."

Her mom's jaw dropped.

Jason glowered. "She's trashy. That's all there is to it."

Paula was pissed, and she didn't care if it showed. She put her hands on the table and leaned forward, but Chase came up behind her and draped an arm over her shoulder.

"Hey, are we still on for Sunday?"

"What?"

"You and me? Boating with your kids and mom?"

Paula glared. "Yup, we'll be there at two."

"No need for a picnic. I thought I'd cook for you this time."

What the hell? Before she could respond, he grinned. "You still owe me a dance."

"The band's not playing."

"That's why I have a jukebox." He tossed his apron on the table and pulled her to her feet. He whirled her to the jukebox and dropped his quarters in. When the music started, he twirled her around the dance floor.

Between clenched teeth, she growled, "What do you think you're doing?"

"Giving you time to cool off. You looked like you were going to punch him. Not that he doesn't deserve it, but gossip will start. People will say *you've* been sleeping with him."

"He dumped Jodi."

Chase nodded. "He dumps all of them. None of them can measure up to his mom."

"That's sort of sick."

"That's why I warned you off."

She relaxed in his arms. "I'm okay now."

The song ended, and she tried to tug away, but he held her close. When the new song started, he twirled her some more.

"You can quit worrying about me. I've calmed down."

"I know. Now I'm dancing with you because I want to."

"What about Daphne?"

"What about her?" Before she could answer, a guy at the bar raised his voice, a little tipsy. Chase shook his head. "Sorry, gotta check on Earl. I have to cut him off before he gets himself in trouble." He gave her a light kiss on the cheek and hurried to the bar.

Paula felt people watching her as she made her way to their table. Jason was playing pool with his buddies again. Jodi was gone. She leaned forward so her mom could hear her. "I need to use the restroom before we leave. I'll be right back."

The bathrooms were at the end of a long hall. When she finished and was returning to her mom, a storage room door opened, and Jason yanked her inside, closing it behind them. He shoved her against the shelves and ground his lips on hers.

Paula gave him a hard shove. "What do you think you're doing?"

"You want it, you know you do. You're just trying to make me jealous by flirting with Chase."

"I don't want it, and I'll hurt you if you touch me again." She could, too. She was stronger than she looked. Alex had taught her some self-defense moves.

"If I'm gentle?"

Before she could answer, the door opened, and Chase grabbed Jason by the scruff of his collar. He looked at Paula. "Do you want him, or should I toss him out?"

Paula hitched her thumb toward the kitchen door.

"You heard the lady. Take a hike. Don't come back until you learn some manners." Chase was none too gentle as he marched Jason down the hallway and shoved him outside. When he returned, he looked worried. "I didn't overstep, did I?"

"It was less embarrassing for Jason to have you throw him out than to have me break his nose."

Chase laughed. "I'll try never to make you mad."

The adrenaline left her, and she was jittery. "Thanks for showing up."

"No problem. Any time. For you, always."

She locked gazes with him. To have Chase . . . for always. It wouldn't get any better than that. Then she laughed at herself. What in the hell was she thinking?

She pressed her lips together, not sure what to do next. Finally, she said, "I left Mom at the table. She'll be wondering what happened to me."

Chase grinned and offered her his elbow. "Let me lead the way."

She felt ridiculous, clinging to his arm as he escorted her to her table. He bowed to her mother, then kissed Paula's hand and twirled his dishrag in the air. "I'll be gone now, fair maiden."

Everyone stared. Paula could feel a blush climb to her hair roots. What was Chase thinking? People would gossip about this for days.

Her mom looked at her and laughed. "If you're trying to take my mind off things, you're sure giving me one entertaining night and plenty to think about."

All Paula wanted to do was get out of there. She paid their bill and they started for home. She couldn't concentrate. She still felt Chase's arms around her. She still pictured him marching Jason down the hallway and throwing him out the back door.

Chapter 28

Saturday was going to be a long day. Paula had traded shifts with Tyne so that she could spend Sunday with Chase. That meant working breakfast, lunch, and dinner. She looked out the kitchen window at a cloudless sky. The kitchen was already busy, but she loved the early morning stillness outdoors. Sunlight slanted across the water as a lone fisherman pushed a rowboat from shore. He paddled out far enough to turn on a small, trolling motor, then headed to a favorite spot close to where the channel emptied into the lake.

She'd put the Dutch babies in the oven and heated up the homemade oatmeal before Ian, his dark hair still damp from the shower, came to check on her. He grinned. "It smells good in here."

"We made breakfast burritos. Steph thought kids would like them. She did the bacon and Josh made the scrambled eggs."

"I'd eat those, too." He looked at how well the kitchen was running and nodded. "You guys have everything under control. I'd better get to the front desk."

She shook her head at him. Ian could hardly make himself stay out of the kitchen.

Paula and her team had the buffet ready to go with time to spare. They were cleaning heavy pots ahead of time when Josh gave her a shy look.

"What is it?"

"I've started watching cooking shows, and Geoffrey Zakarian made this baked egg dish on *The Kitchen* last week. I thought we could tweak it and try it some time."

"What's in it?"

"Tomatoes, olives, salami, and fresh mozzarella. He served it on garlic bread."

All stuff they had. "Sounds good. You'll be in charge of that for Sunday brunch."

Josh stared at her, in shock. "Me?"

"You can do it," Steph said. "I bet you can pull it together, and if you can't, I'll help you."

Her kitchen helpers were getting creative. She couldn't be any happier with them. "There you go, then. It's settled."

They finished the pots and went to check the dining room. Guests drifted in slower than usual on Saturdays. Most had stayed out late the night before and didn't get as early a start. The burritos were a big hit. Adults took the Dutch babies and oatmeal, but kids reached for the scrambled eggs and bacon wrapped in a tortilla.

Breakfast and lunch were both finished when Jason finally pushed through the kitchen door, later than usual. He glared at her. "I had to deliver to Ralph first today. He had a special order."

Was that true, or had Jason switched his route, hoping to avoid Jodi? She'd usually finished cleaning rooms and left the inn by now. He'd probably avoid Paula, too, if he could. She braced herself. She motioned for Steph and Josh to help Betty in the dining room. When they were alone, Jason shoved his clipboard to her. "You could have told me you were seeing Chase."

Paula went to inspect the boxes. She thought Jason was too professional to bring her inferior products out of spite, but she wanted to make sure. "We've only seen each other a few times, usually with the kids. We're just in start-up mode, and it might not go any further."

"A little hard to believe. He seemed pretty damned possessive at the bar."

"Yeah, that surprised me. I didn't think he was the jealous type." She signed the sheet and returned it to him.

"Are you exclusive?"

"I don't know what we are. Last week, I would have said no. Now I'm not sure. He hasn't asked, but I think he made his point last night."

Jason shook his head. "I should have made my move sooner. I took too long, didn't I?"

"I've been into you for a long time. Thought you knew it and weren't interested until Tyne started working here. Then I watched you with Jodi and finally gave up."

His ego somewhat mollified, he looked her up and down. "If you and Chase don't work out, you know where to find me."

She nodded. "At the bar playing pool or at the bowling alley."

"I won't dither around if you show up this time." He tipped his dolly and headed to his truck. Paula glanced out the window to watch him. To her surprise, Jodi walked out to meet him. This time, tears fell. Jason yelled. It got ugly. Paula was glad she couldn't hear their exchange. When she turned back to the kitchen, Steph and Josh were watching her.

"Are you okay? Are you into that guy?" Steph's cheeks reddened. "I'm sorry. It's none of my business."

Paula shrugged. "Hey, you caught me watching him. And yeah, I used to have a thing for him. Not anymore."

Betty flew into the kitchen. "Did I hear you right? Tell me you're not tempted by him."

"Nope, not anymore. I learned my lesson."

Ian slipped into the kitchen, too, ostensibly to help with clean up. Did a woman have no privacy at this inn? "I heard that you and Chase are doing the come-hither dance. Is it true?"

Paula thought about dodging the question, but this was Mill Pond. If she sneezed in the bathroom, people would know. "We danced to two songs last night. Chase was trying to keep me from embarrassing myself with Jason."

Ian looked disappointed. "Too bad, you two would be good together."

"Says who?" Betty raised an eyebrow at him. "The matchmaker expert? I told her about Chase first."

Ian protested. "Told her, yes. Encouraged her? Not enough. I helped my brother, Brody, win over Harmony. I could help Paula, too."

"What girl wouldn't fall for Brody? He's like adding gasoline to a roaring fire." They harassed each other until Paula heard a motorcycle pull to the front door.

She glanced at the clock. "What's Tyne doing here? I'm working his hours today so he'll work mine tomorrow."

Ian's smile was downright ornery. It looked good on him. His chocolate-brown eyes sparkled. His white teeth gleamed. He had a natural charm that was hard to resist. "Tyne's not here to cook. He promised your mom a ride around town. They're going to stop at Harley's winery for a tasting, too."

Her mom? And wine? Paula shook her head. Not likely, but she should have known. Mom was always one step ahead of her. "Tyne had better be careful. Mom will enjoy hanging on to him a little too much."

Ian laughed and went back to work the front desk. Betty finished up and left for the day. Paula put ribs in the oven to finish on the grill later. Steph started the homemade barbecue sauce for them. Then Paula took a huge batch of chicken wings—not a common item on the buffet—from the refrigerator. She'd cook them in her homemade sauce until they were sticky. Grownups and kids alike would be happy tonight.

She had a lot more hours to work, but the time was flying by. And tomorrow should be even better.

Chapter 29

Ian and Tessa came for Sunday brunch. A rarity.

"I woke up starving today," Tessa told them. "But I didn't want to cook. And the resort's so close. . . ."

Paula smiled at Tessa's rounded belly. "How far are you now?"

"Six months." Tessa unconsciously rubbed her stomach and murmured an endearment.

Could this baby be any more wanted?

Tessa winced. "He's getting really good at kicking."

Paula remembered those days. Aiden had been an active baby, too, but nothing like Bailey. That girl did somersaults in her belly.

Ian tilted his head, inhaling deeply. "Do I smell tomatoes? And salami?"

Paula raised her eyebrows at him. "You're getting really good. Josh made a baked eggs dish today with both."

"Sounds good." Tessa licked her lips, but Ian shook his head.

"Nope, too much acid. Remember what happened the last time you ate tomatoes?"

Tessa's expression fell. "There's plenty of other things to eat, right?"

Tyne finished fussing with the dining room and came to give Tessa a warm hug. "You've come to the right place. How you doing, Copper?"

"If someone doesn't feed me soon, I'm going to get dangerous."

Tyne laughed and tugged on her coppery curls. "Sorry, you're too nice to instill fear."

Tessa scowled, but Paula handed her a plate with one of Tyne's crepes with lemony cheese filling, and she gave a satisfied smile. "Thank you. You're a saint."

"Hardly, but I remember the days of intense cravings." With

Aiden, Paula couldn't eat enough deviled eggs. Go figure. And with Bailey, Alex swore he wouldn't buy her one more gallon of ice cream.

With her appetite somewhat assuaged, Tessa tugged on Ian's arm. "Let's go find a table."

He shook his head at his wife, but followed her.

Then things got busy. Josh carved the ham, Tyne refilled food trays, and Paula worked the omelet station. Steph filled in wherever she was needed. By one, the dining room cleared out, but they felt like they'd survived a blitz.

"We always offer so much food, and it always disappears," Tyne said, shaking his head.

Paula pointed to the large, steel tray that had been filled with Josh's baked eggs. "They were a hit, Josh. Maybe we should offer a specialty egg dish every Sunday. I thought the omelets would be enough, but some people want something unusual."

"Huevos rancheros?" Steph asked.

Tyne shrugged. "Why not?"

They all pitched in for cleanup, and by two, the kitchen and dining room sparkled. Tyne grinned at her. "You're finished for the day. Time for sun and water. Enjoy yourself."

She was ready. She hurried to the apartment, grabbed her mom and the kids and drove to Chase's dock. He'd told her not to worry about a picnic, but he'd be doing enough work entertaining them, so she packed ham sandwiches, pasta salad, and lemon bars.

When Chase saw them, his entire face lit up. "I brought a golf club for each kid and buckets and balls. They can hit them off the back of the boat."

Paula was amazed at how much thought he put into entertaining her kids. They boated around the perimeter of the lake to show her mom the cottages and scenery. Then Chase anchored the boat in his favorite spot and fished with Aiden and Bailey. Bailey didn't want to bait her own hook, and Chase looked at Paula to help her.

Paula shook her head. "Not gonna happen. I hate bugs."

Her mom took charge. Crickets and worms got no mercy.

"That was one of your dad's rules," Mom told her. "If you went fishing with him, you baited your own hook."

"I can't remember ever going fishing with Dad."

Mom set down the bait can. "He was probably sick of it by the time we had you. Your brothers begged to go all the time."

That was fine with Paula. Her hook would have stayed empty if she had to take care of it herself.

"You should put that in Grandpa's memory box," Aiden said.

Her mom frowned. "What's that?"

Aiden and Bailey explained. When they finished, her mom said, "You'll have to show it to me sometime. I'd like to see it."

"Chase thought of it." Bailey sent him an adoring gaze. Her bobber dipped, and her mom nodded toward it.

"It seems to me that Chase comes up with lots of good ideas." She helped Bailey reel in a blue gill, too small to keep. They threw it back.

The sun shone down on them, and Paula could feel her skin tighten. She started to rub on more sunscreen and Chase came to help her. His hands on her body took her breath away. How long had it been since she'd enjoyed a man's touch?

"Maybe we should find some shade, or we're all going to have sunburns." He steered them to a shady part of the shore, where tall trees reached their branches over the water. They ate their picnic, anchored in shallow water.

After lunch, Chase took them to deeper water, and they all jumped in to cool off. Their life jackets kept them afloat, so that they could paddle and splash with no worries. Then later, he took the kids tubing. After that, it was time to get Mom to Betty's cottage.

Mom exhaled a long breath. "I can't remember the last time I felt this relaxed."

"Sun and water do it every time," Chase told her.

"That, and good company. I've had a wonderful day. Thank you." Mom's suit was dry enough to slide her slacks over it. Betty and her husband were waiting for her when Chase pulled up to their dock.

"When should we come to get her?" Chase asked.

"About eight? We won't eat until six-thirty," Betty said.

"See you then." Chase waved as he pulled away. This time, he returned to his own dock and let the kids play on the equipment by the marina while he grilled hot dogs. Paula didn't think she'd be hungry, but swimming and boating worked up an appetite. When they sat down to eat, the food disappeared.

The kids ran back to play, and she and Chase stayed at the picnic table to keep an eye on them. She was shading her eyes to watch Aiden climb to the top of the playset when Chase placed his hand on her bare thigh.

Sparks exploded inside Paula, zinging up her nerves, and making her want his hand to move higher. The heat of his touch burned her bare skin. She licked her lips. She could almost feel his hands rove her body, stopping to explore. He turned to her, and their gazes locked. He lowered his head and this time his kiss was passionate and possessive.

She leaned into it, her hands on his shoulders. Need welled up inside of her until she thought she'd climb on top of him. Then Bailey screamed. Paula jerked away and searched for Aiden. She saw him, lying on the ground.

She was running to him before she realized she'd leapt to her feet. Chase was right behind her. When they reached Aiden, he pushed himself onto his elbows and shook his head, his eyes unfocused. "That wasn't a good idea."

Paula gulped for air.

Chase held him in place. "Don't move yet. Let us check you over." He ran his hands up and down his bones. "It doesn't feel like anything's broken."

Aiden squirmed, then rolled onto his feet and smiled at her. "I can almost skip bars when I cross the jungle gym."

She might hurt him. The urge was there. What the hell had he been thinking? But she fought to slow her hammering heart instead. Had panic made it do double time? Or Chase?

"From now on, be more careful." Her voice sounded strained. He'd scared her, and she couldn't hide it.

Aiden hugged her, then winced and hugged himself. "My hands were slippery, or I wouldn't have fallen."

Her expression gave her away, but before she lost her temper, Chase reached out to ruffle Aiden's hair. "You're not a monkey, kid. Don't act like one."

Aiden grinned. "Got it."

Their romantic interlude was shot. Hormones had given way to adrenaline. Chase loaded the kids back on the boat and took them to a sandbar where they could play until it was time to collect her mom.

Slowly, Paula relaxed again, too. And by the time Chase helped them load up the minivan for the trip home, her carefree mood was almost restored.

He leaned down to kiss her cheek before he shut her car door. "I'd be happy spending every day with you."

She stared at him. "I'm grumpy."

"One of my favorite characters in *Snow White*. Let's do this again soon." And he waved them off.

Paula drove in a daze. What did Chase expect from her? If he got her into his bed, what then? And did she care? A frolic with Chase might last her a long time.

Chapter 30

Monday was the only morning Paula didn't work. She didn't wake until the kids wandered out to the living room and pestered her on the couch. When her mom heard them, she came rushing out of her bedroom, her eyes swollen and crusted. She'd cried before falling to sleep. It was the quiet hours that got you.

"Oh lord, it's already eight." She tugged Paula to her feet. "You'd better get ready."

Paula yawned, glancing toward the coffee pot. She hadn't set it the night before since she could sleep in. "Ready for what?"

"Chase is going to be here at nine to take you out on his bike."

"Today?" Paula went to the kitchen to flip on the coffee.

"It's the only day he can. It's the only day you're free." Her mom folded Paula's blankets and sagged onto the couch. "Go take a shower. I'm claiming the kids today. They're mine."

"Until Steph comes tonight."

"That's long enough. Now hurry. He's taking you to Columbus to poke around shops and have lunch."

Paula frowned. "When did you two set this up?"

Her mom gave a casual shrug. "When you were busy with other things."

"He never asked me."

"I know. When he called, I told him I'd make sure you were ready."

Paula went to hug her mom. "Thanks, it's been a long time since I've been on a motorcycle."

"Too long. Get out of here. And don't come home until you have to."

Paula hurried to get ready. By the time Chase came, she had on her best jeans and one of her new tops. She shook her head when she looked at herself in the mirror. If she was going to keep going out and being social, she needed to buy more clothes. But Chase didn't seem to notice. He grinned when she walked out of the resort and climbed on the back of his bike.

"You ready?" When she nodded, he handed her a helmet and they zoomed away. She clung to his back, pressing herself against him. She probably didn't need to, but it felt good. His hard back and muscled belly made her fingers itch to touch. It was a hot day, but the wind made the ride comfortable. If she'd worn shorts, she might get a suntan, but on this long of a ride, she worried about a sunburn instead. Chase wore jeans, too. They rode low on his hips, and she could dip her hand under the waistband, but she didn't dare. He was already too tempting.

They didn't talk until they reached the outskirts of Columbus—a beautiful town full of architectural interest. Chase pulled to the curb in the shopping district and reached for her hand. They walked up and down its sidewalks, window shopping, until it was lunchtime.

"Do you have a favorite place?" he asked.

She shook her head. "I've only been here one other time."

"Good, there's an outdoor café I like." He led her to it.

She ordered a Cobb salad, and he got a Philly cheesesteak sandwich. They sipped their beers and ate a leisurely lunch. It was easy spending time with Chase. She didn't strain to think of something to talk about. They enjoyed each other's company. When they finished, he said, "I thought if we got back to Mill Pond a little early, I could show you my apartment. There's plenty of room for kids, but it's over a bar. Some women wouldn't like that. But if there's something you'd like to see before we leave . . ."

"It can wait." She wanted to see where he lived, see how he furnished it. "My kids have grown up around restaurants. A bar's not that much different. Hanging out there won't corrupt them."

He grinned. Her heart skipped a beat. How much time would they have when they got back? Enough? Her palms grew sweaty, and she wiped them on her jeans.

He drove faster on the way home. She clung on tighter. When they reached his place, he parked in back, where no one could see his motorcycle. "No reason to let the world know I'm home." He unlocked the back door and led her up the stairs to his apartment.

It spanned the same dimensions as the bar. She hadn't realized it would be so roomy. A large open space held a living room, with two leather sofas and matching chairs, a dining area, and then a kitchen. Paula liked the open concept, but the kitchen had seen better days. She doubted Chase used it often. The speckled counter tops were dated, and the harvest gold appliances must have been there since the sixties.

Chase followed her gaze and groaned. "I know. Everything needs to be updated."

"It's a lot bigger than I expected."

"Four bedrooms and two full baths," he said. "Come on. I'll show you."

The wooden floors needed work. The walls could use fresh coats of paint, but every room was good-sized. The smallest bedroom had been made into an office with an old wooden desk and a laptop. Metal files sat in a corner. The second bedroom held two twin-sized beds. "For when buddies need some place to crash," he told her. The third bedroom was a jumble of storage boxes, but the master bedroom held a king-sized bed. A dark comforter, with geometric shapes splattered across it, had a hole—with stuffing peeking out of it—near the center. "I took in a stray cat. It clawed there."

Chase and a cat. She could see it. "No cat now?"

"It lasted twelve years, and it was older when it came." He scraped his hand through his hair. "Nothing to brag about, is it?"

"It has potential."

He laughed. "A diplomatic answer, if ever I heard one." Then he leaned down and kissed her nose. "Do you like it? I want you to know that if I have my way, no other woman will come up here. It's too soon to be sure, but I think we'd make a great team. We can redecorate together."

She felt hot. He was so close. His bed was only a few steps away. He glanced in that direction, too, and she pulled him toward it.

He stared at her, his expression serious. "Are you sure? I'm not pressuring you. We can go in the kitchen and have a beer."

"Afterward." She pulled her T-shirt over her head and let it drop to the floor. Then she unzipped her jeans and stepped out of them.

His turquoise eyes blazed with passion. His shirt and jeans followed hers. Then he pulled her to him. His hard body tensed, and his lips locked on hers. He pulled away. "Wait. Let me get . . ."

She shook her head. "I'm on the pill."

His hands roamed everywhere, teasing, touching. Her breathing quickened to sharp gasps. When he unhooked her bra and pushed it off her shoulders, she squirmed with pleasure. His hands grabbed her ass, pressing her closer. When his mouth claimed her breast and his tongue licked her nipple, she groaned with need. His fingers teased her other nipple while his lips grazed lower and lower. Then he slid his hand under her panties and slipped them off. His fingers moved against her slickness, and she thought she'd explode. Then he lowered her on the bed, stripped himself naked, and was on top of her. His erection teased her until she was so wet, she raised her hips to receive him. She met his lunges with her own until they erupted in unison.

Paula went limp, spent and satisfied. Chase grinned and nipped her ear lobe. Even that made her nerves frizz. When he finally withdrew, she sighed. Having him inside her was so good she felt empty when he rolled over to gaze at her. He reached to brush a strand of hair off her cheek.

"You're so beautiful." He meant it.

She started to shake her head, to disagree, but at the moment, she *felt* beautiful. She decided to enjoy it.

He propped himself on an elbow to stare at her. "I want you to be mine, Paula. I know you're not ready for that yet, but promise me you'll think about it."

How could she not? She nodded. "You'll be taking on two kids. That's a lot to ask of a man."

He shook his head. "Aiden and Bailey are a bonus. You three make a perfect package."

Happiness bubbled inside her. Then she glanced at the clock on his nightstand and closed her eyes, pretending she hadn't seen the time.

He smiled. "I know. If I don't get you back soon, Ian will never forgive me. Neither will Tyne. You can have the first shower."

She rinsed off in record time, and he was even faster. On the ride back to the inn, she leaned against the length of his back. She held on tightly and never wanted to let go. But before they pulled into the drive, she scooted back a respectable distance, and Chase let her off at the front door.

"Next Monday?" he asked.

Lord, she hoped so. Would this happiness last? A knot clenched in her stomach. Probably not. Men always left her, one way or another. Nothing was permanent. But she'd enjoy this as long as possible.

Chapter 31

Paula was glad she worked Monday night and Tuesday morning. She needed distractions, or all she'd do is think about Chase. Since when had she turned into a mooning, lovesick female? That wasn't her style.

Maya had come to watch Aiden and Bailey, and Mom took off to play bingo at Grams's church. Mom had warned her that when Paula was done cooking for the day, she intended on grabbing all of them and heading to Indy to shop.

"It's about time you owned more than jeans and chef pants. I'm buying you some new clothes."

"I have my own money . . ." Paula started, but Mom cut her off.

"I'm your mother. If I want to spend money on you, I can."

Paula knew better than to argue, so when Tyne came to take over the kitchen after three, she had everything ready for him.

He glanced around the room. "Where are Steph and Josh?"

"I sent them home. We got done ahead of time."

He cocked an eyebrow at her shrimp and white bean salad over watercress. "That looks delicious. It'll go perfect with my pan-fried sirloin steaks with country gravy."

She nodded. "Kids like steaks, so I could make something more chef-y."

"I saw your mom. She says she's dragging you to Indy to go shopping."

Paula sighed. "I might get a makeover whether I want it or not."

Tyne laughed and gave her a knowing look. "Don't need one. Chase thinks you're almost perfect, as is."

Her cheeks grew hot. "He's not too bad himself."

"I knew it! I just knew you two would be good together."

She grimaced. "Apparently everyone did but us."

"Can't see the forest for the trees." He tied his apron around his waist. "Chase thinks you'd look pretty in pink. Just saying."

She let out an exasperated sigh. "Really? Pink?"

"All I hear about is your black hair and sapphire blue eyes. If I didn't like you so much, I'd get sick of how Chase goes on and on about you."

She tilted her head at him. "What about you? Have you ever fallen hard for a girl?"

He shook his head. "Not on my agenda."

"Ever? Or just for a few years?"

"First I have to check everything off my list."

"How long is your list?"

"Finish culinary school. Done. Travel the world to try different cooking methods. Done. Decide what kind of restaurant I want to start. I'm working on that one. That's why I'm here; to experiment with different styles and ingredients, get a feel for things. Own my own restaurant. In my near future. Be rich and successful. That might take a while."

"Sounds like I won't get an invitation to your wedding for a long time."

"Don't hold your breath." He pulled the steaks out of the refrigerator to let them reach room temperature, then nodded to the door. "When I see you tomorrow, I expect an upgrade."

"What? You want me to wear a pink chef's outfit to work? Won't happen."

"Hmm, I'll settle for new lipstick and a snazzier hairstyle."

"In your dreams. Everything melts in the heat of the kitchen."

He wiped his brow. "You have a point. I'll just have to put up with you as is."

Laughing, she left him. Her mom hardly gave her time to shower and change before herding her to the minivan.

"Let's go. This is serious. We're on a mission."

Paula sighed. She'd seen her mom do Christmas shopping. She didn't stop until she had everything she needed. "I'm not the best shopper. You remember that, don't you?"

Mom had a determined look on her face. How much did she think Paula needed? A new pair of Dockers? A couple of tops? But from the glint in Mom's eyes, Paula began to worry.

They headed to the closest mall on the edge of the city to avoid five o'clock traffic. Mom scanned the stores and gave a satisfied nod. "We can find everything here."

"What's everything? I was thinking a few tops, a . . ."

Mom took a sheet of paper from her purse. "We'll start with summer slacks, three pairs of capris, shorts, and two skirts."

Paula cringed. "I never wear skirts."

"It's time you did." Mom set off and Bailey reached for Paula's hand.

"It's okay, Mom. We're all going to help you."

Oh Lord. "Somebody just shoot me."

Aiden laughed.

They found two pairs of slacks at the first store and three plain T-shirts with V-necks.

"For everyday casual," Mom said.

Paula frowned as the clerk rang them up. "You're not buying it all. It's too much."

"You can pay at the next store."

That made Paula feel better. Bailey chose a flowered skirt for her to wear and Aiden found fancy clips for her hair.

"My teacher wore these sometimes. She looked pretty in them." Aiden had loved everything about his teacher.

Her mom brought her three more tops to try on. "These are dressier, perfect for when you go out."

"They're all different shades of pink."

"Chase likes pink," Bailey said.

Paula frowned at her mother's tan slacks and white knit shirt. Her mom shrugged. "At my age, if I'm presentable, I'm happy."

"It's not like you're ancient, Mom. You were two years younger than Dad." Paula bit her bottom lip. She hadn't meant for *Dad* to slip out.

"That's what Dela—Tessa's Grams—told me. She lost her husband, too. She said that life goes on." Mom grinned. "And then she signed me up to help with the bazaar next month. We're collecting things now and labeling them."

"I warned you." Paula toted the clothes to the cash register to pay for them. She was glad she was buying this lot. She didn't want her mom paying for any more.

"I like Dela. She's a survivor. She won't let me sit around and feel sorry for myself."

Paula snorted. "Like you'd do that anyway."

"I was tempted." Her mom blinked quickly, then looked at her sheet of paper. "You still need shorts and makeup."

Paula sighed. "I'm going to go into retail overload. Don't we have enough?"

Her mother's eyebrow rose. She had the expression she used when they were little and she scolded them. "I haven't crossed off shorts or makeup. The sooner we finish, the sooner we can get supper."

"Come on, Mom." Bailey tugged Paula to the next store. "I'm hungry. Buy something."

Aiden pointed at a display of shorts. "Hey, Grandma, how many does she have to buy?"

"Three pairs."

He gave Paula a small, friendly push. "Those look good, don't they?"

An unsubtle hint. Shut up and buy something. So she tried them on, they looked good, and she paid for them. Bailey and her mom hovered at the makeup counter, and when she and Aiden got there, they'd already picked out three eye shadows, pink lipstick, and a rosy blush.

"Do you like them?" Bailey's eyes sparkled with excitement. Her daughter loved girly things. Maybe she'd be a hairdresser or a makeup artist when she grew up.

"They're perfect." Paula started to open her purse, but her mom handed the cashier money first.

"This one's on me."

They loaded all of the bags in the back of the minivan, locked up, and headed back inside the mall to find a restaurant. Mom picked. "I like this chain." She ordered the appetizer platter for them. "We can each try a little bit of everything. You kids already eat enough hamburgers. It's time you try something new."

They didn't protest. Obviously Grandma could get away with things she couldn't. And when the food arrived, they surprised her with all the things they liked. Aiden loved fried ravioli, and Bailey asked if she could have Paula's mozzarella stick.

They yakked all the way home, and by the time they walked into the apartment, they were ready to plop on the couch to watch the movie *Stardust* together. Her mom had never seen it. Bailey fell asleep before the end, and Paula carried her to bed. Aiden wasn't far behind. When THE END rolled on the screen, her mom stretched and yawned. "My turn. See you in the morning, kid."

Paula glanced at the bags that leaned against the far wall. They could wait until tomorrow. She spread the sheet on the couch and slept until her alarm woke her.

Chapter 32

After the rush of getting breakfast ready for the dining room, Paula looked outside the kitchen window. Maya had the kids setting off along the shoreline on a nature scavenger hunt. Paula had seen the items Maya put on this one: a duck's feather, a dandelion, a twig with leaves on it, a cattail, a smooth stone, and more. It would take a while for the kids to mark everything off the list.

A movement near the tennis courts caught her eye, and she looked over to see her mom sitting on the bench under the tree. Her mom's head was bowed, and her shoulders shook. Paula looked away, giving her mother privacy to express her grief. She'd done that when Alex died. Cried at random moments. Eventually, it had passed.

Josh came in the kitchen, and Paula's attention returned to work. With her two helpers and the new dishwasher Ian had hired, breakfast went so smoothly, Paula felt spoiled. They were cleaning up and starting the soups and sandwiches for lunch when Jason hurried through the door.

The thrill of seeing him was gone, but they still talked about the supplies he brought and any town gossip he might have heard. When he left, Betty popped into the kitchen and shook her head. "Rumor is he's interested in the new waitress Ralph hired at the diner."

"Has anyone warned her?" Steph asked.

"Ralph will. Everyone knows Jason's routine."

Paula had finished the gazpacho and carried it to the buffet table when Tessa nudged the kitchen door open and brought her the desserts for tonight's meal.

"Kayla usually brings these," Paula said, surprised. "That way, she can see Luther."

Luther had worked for Tessa before Ian offered him a full time job. The boy was a little rough around the edges, but a good worker. The lawn was always mowed, the landscape trimmed, and every-thing outdoors in good order.

"Emilia's cutting teeth, and her babysitter got sick and couldn't come today. She brings the baby with her while we bake together, but Emilia can crawl now, and she gets fussy when she's in the playpen too long. It's getting trickier. I've thought about that. Ours is due in September."

Paula nodded. "I remember those days. It's hard to juggle things before your kids start school."

Tessa pursed her lips, thinking. "We'll have to come up with something. But in the meantime, get ready for a call from my Grams. She's organizing a big church dinner to raise money for missions."

Paula frowned. "I thought she was doing a bazaar."

"Oh, she is. She'll probably call you about that, too. She signed me up for cakes and pies."

"That's a lot of work."

Tessa laughed. "Have you tried to say no to your own grandma?"

"I don't see mine that often." Maybe that was a good thing. But she loved Tessa's Grams. She knew she couldn't say *no* to her. She hoped whatever she had in mind wasn't major.

"Remember. Once Grams gets you in her clutches, she never lets you go. She'll call for more things."

Oh, great. Paula waved Tessa off, then filled tureens with her sec-ond soup—chicken and rice. Josh and Steph helped her plate the fin-ger sandwiches for the day, and they switched into dining room mode. Josh had a knack for talking with guests. Steph was shier. But between the three of them, guests left happy.

They were cleaning up when Lane poked his head through the back door. He saw Paula and came to talk with her.

"What are you doing here?" she asked. "You work the supper shift during the week."

He hung his head. "That's why I came. I have to quit pretty soon. Gramps put money on the garage we've been looking at, and we're going to start working on it. It won't take long to make it into a work-shop and display floor."

The boy looked worried. Paula offered a broad smile. "I'm so happy for you."

Lane's shoulders relaxed. "I thought you might be aggravated that I'm not staying for the summer. That's your busy time."

"Why would you do that? You graduated from high school and you're starting your own business. Congratulations!"

He grinned. "If you ever need anything built, I'll give you a special price."

"Thanks, I'll remind you of that."

"I'd better go then, but I wanted you to know." He started for the door. "I have chores to do before my shift tonight."

Such a good boy. Paula watched him pedal away. She wished him all the luck in the world. She'd have to tell Ian he needed a new employee. He could call Grams and talk to her. Paula was afraid to. Grams already had plans for her.

It wasn't until later that evening, after Mom and the kids were in bed, that Grams's call came. "I know you're a busy girl, but Chase volunteered to supply half of the beef for our church supper if you'd help him grill the kebabs."

"When is it?"

"On a Friday night, a month from now. Chase said you have that night off."

"I do. He doesn't."

Grams laughed. "He's going to have someone cover it for him. He doesn't expect to be busy. A lot of people come to this supper."

Paula thought about working side by side with Chase. She didn't see any downside to it. "Sure, put me down."

Grams hesitated. "I'm just curious, but why did he ask for you?" Grams liked to be on top of the town scoops, if she could.

"Because I'm a chef?"

"So is Tyne, and those two hang out a lot."

Paula might as well confess. Grams would hear about it anyway. "We're seeing each other."

Another pause. "Chase is *dating* someone?"

"Sort of. I guess. Nothing formal."

Grams's voice grew a little sharper. "Not just any girl will do for that boy. He needs someone who'll love him, who won't try to change him."

Did everyone in this town love Chase? Dumb question. Why wouldn't they? "What needs changed?"

Grams laughed. "Oh, honey, that's the right answer. Good luck to you."

Would she need luck? Did Chase make a habit of getting cold feet when things got too hot and heavy?

"You know, neither of you are spring chickens anymore," Grams told her. "More people would come to the supper if you two got hitched before then. They'd want to catch up on all the news."

"In a month?" *Was she for real?*

"Oh, well, just a thought." Grams said her goodbyes and left Paula staring at the phone in her hand.

Chapter 33

On Thursday, Bailey woke before Paula left the apartment. "Did something startle you?" Paula smoothed the snarls back from her daughter's forehead.

Bailey held up her arms for a hug. "I heard you getting ready in the bathroom. You were humming." Bailey smiled. "You used to hum when Daddy was alive."

A knot formed in Paula's throat. She felt half guilty for feeling so happy when her mother was struggling with grief. She wasn't sure what to say. She settled on, "I like it here. Do you?"

Bailey wrapped her arms around Paula's neck. "I love Mill Pond."

"Can you go back to sleep if I tuck you in bed?"

Bailey glanced outside. "The birds are singing."

If Paula left her alone in the apartment, she'd wake her mom and Aiden. "Why don't you come in the kitchen with me until Maya gets here? Would you like that?"

Bailey ran to her room to get dressed. She sat on a high stool in the kitchen, stirring whatever Paula, Steph, or Josh put in front of her, chattering away with them. At eight-thirty, Paula led her back to the apartment to meet Maya.

Maya frowned when she saw her. "What are you doing up so early?"

Paula blinked, taken aback. "I woke her up getting ready this morning. She couldn't go back to sleep."

Maya snapped, "Why don't you watch TV for a while until Aiden wakes up? Then we'll think of something to do."

"Are you all right?" Paula stared at a bruise on the girl's arm.

Maya pulled her sleeve lower. "I'm sorry. I'm just tired. I hate my other job. I wish I could quit."

Mom came out of her bedroom, still in her robe, and headed to the kitchen for coffee. "If you want to take a nap, I'll watch some cartoons with Bailey for a while."

Maya looked horrified. "Not while you're paying me."

"You have dark circles under your eyes. I can manage for an hour or two," Mom assured her.

But Maya wouldn't hear of it.

Paula felt sorry for the girl. She was having a tough summer. "We have to serve the food pretty soon. I need to go."

Mom waved her off, but Paula hesitated, reluctant to leave. She'd never heard Maya snap at one of her kids before.

"Go!" Mom motioned to the door.

Paula went. She was leaving Maya in good hands. Mom would find a way to talk to her, to maybe give her some ideas to make things better.

Had her stepdad hit her? Paula's hands balled into fists. But if that were the case, Mom would find out, and Mom or Grams would know what to do.

The guests swarmed into the dining room en masse instead of trickling in, as usual. Everything got busy and stayed busy for an hour. People loitered, getting second and third cups of coffee, grabbing pieces of fruit to snack on. Kids ran around the dining room tables. By the time the last few tables emptied, Paula needed two aspirin for her headache. Steph blew out a loud breath, and Josh stared at them, stunned.

"What do you think happened?" he asked. "They've never done that before."

"My horoscope said the planets formed an angry conjunction today," Steph said.

Josh wiped his sweaty hands on his apron. "What have *they* got to be pissed about?"

Steph shrugged. "Who knows? Maybe they had a wonky orbit."

"Doesn't matter," Paula told them. "The sooner we clean up this mess, the sooner we can prep for lunch. Let's get moving."

Betty shook her head when she saw the dining room. "Looks like a war zone."

"It was." Josh filled a bus pan with dirty dishes and carted them to the dishwasher.

They all got busy. A half hour later, Brian—the new guy—had everything rinsed and ready to wash. Betty was sweeping the dining room and scrubbing the tables, and Paula, Steph, and Josh got started on the soups and sandwiches. Paula was serving three smaller portions of soups today, because not everyone liked oyster bisque. Most kids would eat beef and vegetable, but some people liked chilled cucumber soup in the summer.

The food made a hit. On a happy high, they rushed into making their dish for Tyne that night. They'd started the tarragon halibut in parchment when he walked into the kitchen early.

Paula glanced at the clock. "It's only one forty-five."

"I know, but I wanted to look at our menus again for the next few days."

"For when your brother's here?" Paula couldn't blame him for being nervous. She was nervous, too, and she wasn't related to Holden. Tyne's father and mother would weigh Tyne against his brother, and he'd come up short. He always did, but she understood why he wanted to impress Holden.

Tyne scrubbed his hand, back and forth, in his short, dirty blonde hair. The more he mussed it, the sexier he looked. "This is my first serious gig since I got home. Holden's owned his own restaurant for three years."

Tension oozed off him. Paula went to wrap him in a hug. "You're going to be okay. We're good together. We make top quality food."

"Can we up our meals for a few days until he leaves?"

"For you, anything."

Tyne rested his chin on the top of her head. "You're the best. You know that, right?"

They were standing like that when Jason walked through the door. He looked at Paula with disgust. "I should have known. You're just like the rest of them. First, you probably did Chase. Now your assistant. Was I further down the line?"

Tyne's body went rigid. He pushed away from her and started toward Jason. Paula hurried to step between them.

"It doesn't matter what he thinks. He hates women. Just let this go."

"He shouldn't talk to you like that."

"He won't anymore, or I'll tell the vendors and he'll be out of a job. But I'm fine. He didn't hurt my feelings."

Tyne took a few breaths, then leaned forward, pushing his face close to Jason's. Between clenched teeth, he said, "Get out of here before I lose control. And if you ever look cross-eyed at Paula again, you'd better have a damned good reason why."

Jason shoved the clipboard toward him. "You haven't signed."

Tyne's brown eyes glittered. "Do you really want me to take that clipboard?"

Jason pulled it close and tucked it under his arm. "Never mind." He hurried out the door.

Tyne slammed his fist on the steel table and made Steph jump. "That bastard! You should have let me hit him."

Paula patted his arm. "I'm over him. I don't care what he thinks."

Tyne tilted his head back and closed his eyes. "I need some fresh air. I need to walk off my temper. When I come back, we can look at the menus."

Paula nodded. When he left, she looked at Josh and Steph. "Let's get the fish ready to go. When it's done, you guys can take off."

They set to work, and by the time he returned, Steph and Josh could easily finish on their own. Paula handed Tyne a beer, then sat at the worktable with him. They sipped while they decided what to serve. They ended up with some high-ticket items.

"We can switch Friday and Saturday menus." Tyne scribbled down notes. "I'll have Holden back in time for supper Saturday night. Instead of prime rib, you can make Beef Wellington, and I'll fix Thai curry seafood over rice instead of the usual salmon."

"Save me some of the curry. I love it."

He nodded. "Then we can serve salmon mousse for Sunday brunch, and since I work the early shift on Monday, I'll do a chicken terrine with crackers for lunch."

He was going all out. Why not?

When they finished, Josh and Steph had gone. He sighed. "Thanks for doing this for me."

She realized how much she cared for him. She wanted to mother him like she did Aiden and Bailey. After listening to him talk about his family and its lack of love, he could use it. Instead, she finished her beer and slapped his shoulder. "You don't need to impress Holden, but he'll appreciate it that you went all out for him."

He grinned. "Yeah, that'll be nice."

He was whistling again just before she left him, and when Austin walked in five minutes late, he didn't even turn around. "Drop and give me fifty."

He missed the slight smile on Austin's lips. The kid was starting to like him. He counted out loud as he began his push-ups.

Paula changed into comfy clothes to take her mom and kids to town. She dropped the kids off for karate, then headed to Chase's bar. On the way, she asked her mom, "Did you get any feel for what's bothering Maya?"

"That girl would make a clam look gabby."

Paula had been afraid of that. The bar was busier than usual, but Chase stopped at their table every chance he got. Each time, he threw his arm around her shoulders. Making a statement. Letting people know they were an item.

And Paula liked it.

On the drive home, her mom said, "Tonight would be a good night to show me your memory box."

Paula turned to glance at her. "Are you sure?"

Her mom nodded. "I want to remember the good times, not how fast he went."

So that's what they did. The kids brought the box out of Paula's closet, and they took out one item at a time, explaining why they'd chosen each one. When they finished, tears flowed down her mother's cheeks. Her shoulders shook, but she was smiling.

"These are good tears. I'm not thinking about everything I lost, but everything I got to do and share with him."

"If you're sure . . ."

Her mother touched her cheek. "Thank you. I think I'll be able to sleep all night tonight. It feels like something heavy has lifted."

Paula nodded. It was a start. That's all it was, but one step forward was a good thing.

Chapter 34

On Friday night, when Paula and her mom walked into Chase's bar, Jason wouldn't look her way. The tiny, little evil part of her was amused. If he slept with too many more women, he wouldn't be able to make eye contact with most of the customers who came here.

Buck Kreiger was happy to see them when they settled at his table. "I've heard gossip about you," he told Paula.

Her mom grinned. "It's all true. Grams signed her up to pole dance at the charity supper."

Buck threw back his head and laughed. "I'd pay to see that."

"To see what?" Chase came to take their orders and gave each of them a beer.

"I bet Paula would make one hell of a pole dancer," Buck said.

"So do I. When's she performing?"

"At Grams's charity supper."

Chase looked smug. "She won't have time. I'm keeping her busy at the grill."

The joke had gone on long enough. Paula said, "I'll take my usual—the burger and fries."

Buck and Mom ordered the same, but Buck added his usual piece of pie.

When Chase left, Buck said, "I heard some fancy-schmancy chef was coming to visit Mill Pond for the next few days."

"Tyne's brother, Holden. Tyne's pretty excited."

Buck leaned forward and lowered his voice. "I've met Tyne. I like him, but Chase has invited me to his big grill-off. Hell, he's invited most of the town, and we want to see you win. So don't let us down."

Paula blinked. "That's a lot of pressure. Holden's a five-star chef."

Buck shrugged. "We won't throw our votes. We'll cast them fair and square, but you know what we like around here. Keep that in mind."

She winked. "I've pulled out my trump card. I talked to Carl Gruber." When Mom frowned, she said, "He raises grass-fed beef and his kids run the butcher shop on his property. They're grinding me a special order of burger—part brisket, part chuck, and part sirloin."

Buck leaned back in his chair, satisfied. "No one has better beef than Carl."

"I know, and then I'm adding minced garlic and onions to it." Paula could hardly keep the gloat out of her voice.

"If you don't win, no one can say you didn't try." Buck took a sip of his beer. "I heard you were going to keep plenty busy while the chef was here, too."

Paula let out a breath. "Tyne covered for me when I had to leave town, so I'm happy to cover for him Saturday night when he picks up Holden from the airport."

"And then you cook at the restaurant *and* the cook-off on Sunday?" Buck asked.

"No one ever gets bored with a restaurant job," Paula told him.

Louise came with their food, and they got busy eating. They hadn't finished yet when Jodi walked into the restaurant and headed straight to Jason. He lowered his cue stick to the floor and leaned on it, his eyes narrowed.

The entire restaurant hushed when she squared off in front of him. Loud enough for everyone to hear, she said, "I'm pregnant."

"You told me you were on the pill."

"I was. I'm still pregnant."

Jason shrugged. "So? That doesn't mean it's mine."

"You're the only one I was sleeping with."

Paula wondered at that. It must not have been a one-shot deal with Jodi. Jason must have enjoyed her more than usual. What had made him walk away?

Jason didn't change his stance. "You can't be that far along. Get rid of it. I'll pay half."

"Ain't gonna happen."

"Don't expect money from me to raise it. I don't want it."

She put her hands on her hips. "You haven't met my brothers, have you?"

Buck Kreiger straightened in his seat.

Jason frowned. "What about them?"

"They're meaner than spit and super protective of me."

Jason looked at his buddies. One of them said, "We grew up with them. They'd bust your head as soon as smash pumpkins."

Jason laid his cue stick on the pool table. "What do you want?"

"I want to get married. I want a dad for my kid. You're going to make this right."

Jason picked up the stick and pointed it toward the door. "If you're going to act like a whore, you should protect yourself like one. Not my problem. If you want me to help with the abortion, let me know."

Jodi stared, then turned on her heel and left.

People sat stunned for a moment, then the bar buzzed with gossip.

Chase came to sit at their table. He reached for Paula's hand. "Do you want more kids?"

"What?" Her mind was still on Jason and Jodi.

"Whatever you want is fine by me. We already have Aiden and Bailey."

We. She could hardly speak past the lump in her throat. Chase was *so* a keeper. "You're rushing it, aren't you? You might not like kids underfoot twenty-four/seven. They're a lot of responsibility."

He kissed her cheek. "Anything worthwhile takes work, but I can't wait."

Right at that moment, she wanted Chase so badly, she could hardly stand it.

Chapter 35

Saturday flew by like a whirlwind. A good thing, Paula didn't have time to get nervous before Tyne led his brother into the dining room. Not as tall as Tyne, only about six feet, with sandy-colored hair and a lean build, he was attractive, but not a showstopper like his brother. Tyne had made his dish before he left for the airport. Beef Wellington wasn't hard to make, but she didn't make it that often, so she worried. Would it meet with Holden's approval? Steph and Josh had made a butter lettuce salad with orange segments and sliced red onion before they left for the day. She'd added a watermelon salsa and roasted potatoes.

She watched Tyne's chest puff with pride when he looked at the buffet. Holden looked like he'd burst with happiness when one table after another called Tyne over to compliment him on the seafood curry. Tyne introduced each guest to his brother, then the men filled their plates and came into the kitchen to eat at the stainless steel work table.

"People, come meet my brother!" Tyne called. He started introductions. "This is Howard, our extra help, and Lane—he's leaving us soon. Austin's my assistant"—Austin looked surprised and pleased—"and Cody's our dishwasher. You have to watch him. He's trouble."

Cody wiggled his eyebrows and laughed.

Holden was warm and friendly with everyone. Paula didn't see any trace of a big ego anywhere. Then Tyne turned to her. "And this is my kitchen partner and best friend, Paula."

She pressed her lips tight. She loved her Tyne. Holden smiled and shook her hand.

"I've heard a lot about you. Tyne says he's going to bury you in his dust tomorrow at the cook-off, but you're one hell of a chef."

She smiled. "Let's just hope your brother's not a sore loser."

Tyne laughed. So did Holden. "I didn't travel all this way to let him beat me."

She shook her head. "Sorry, fellas, but you know the saying: boys drool, girls rule."

Lane snickered and turned away, embarrassed. He hated calling attention to himself.

Paula headed back into the dining room to check on guests, and the brothers finished their meals and left. Tyne had plans to take Holden to Harley's for wine and jazz before it got too late.

When the kitchen closed and Paula turned off the overhead lights, she heaved a sigh of relief. Their first night with Holden had gone well.

Maya was still at the apartment when Paula got there. Mom and the kids were playing a game of Clue at the kitchen table, but Maya was sitting on the couch, reading. Paula blinked at the book's title—*The Girl with the Dragon Tattoo*. "That's sort of gritty for you, isn't it?"

Maya gave her a steely look. "I've already read most of the books for kids my age. I like adult literature."

"I get it. You're a super brain, but that movie was almost too much for me. You're only fifteen."

"Being a kid isn't all fun and games." Maya put a bookmark between the pages to mark her place. "My mom should be here pretty soon."

The girl had never been smiles and giggles, but she'd never been this distant before. Paula studied her. "Is everything okay? If you're in trouble . . ."

Headlights swept past the window. Maya stood. "Mom's here. Gotta go."

Paula stared after her. Mom waited for the girl to leave, then said, "I can't get a word out of her. She's polite and all, but something's eating at her, and she's holding it close."

Paula decided to try harder the next time she saw Maya. No, that would be tomorrow, when she came to cover for Sunday breakfast. Paula wouldn't have time. She'd have to hurry to get to the cook-off at Chase's. But she'd see her Sunday night. She'd try then.

They all called it an early night since tomorrow was going to be a big day. Mom and the kids were excited about the cook-off. Paula was nervous. She was worried she wouldn't be able to sleep, but the minute her body hit the couch, she was out.

When she hurried to the kitchen Sunday morning, Holden was there with Tyne, dressed in a chef's coat, ready to work. No, correction. When she opened the refrigerator to start the waffle batter, a salmon mousse already gleamed on a plate.

"When did you two get started this morning?" she asked.

Tyne shrugged. "We got here a little early. Holden couldn't stand it, wanted to try out our kitchen. Can he pitch in?"

"Are you kidding? He can be in charge of the omelet station."

Holden laughed. "Every chef's worst nightmare. It must belong to you most Sundays."

She grinned. There was no down time when you cooked on demand. "I won't miss it for a week."

They happily fell into their routine, but when Steph and Josh started the *huevos rancheros*, Holden went to see what they were doing. She heard him yakking about different recipes with them and offering advice without seeming to. Yup, Tyne's brother was pretty cool.

After brunch, Tyne came to give her a hug before they left. "Friends forever, even when I make you eat my dust."

Holden shook his head. "I love my little brother, but I'm going to have to school him and show him how things are done on the West Coast."

Josh and Steph gave her a conspiratorial look. "They wish. Don't worry about the dishes tonight. We'll get them started, then we'll see you at Chase's."

She wasn't worried about Sunday's supper. She always kept it simple, and she didn't doubt Steph and Josh. They'd learned a lot in a short time. When Paula went to get her mom and kids to drive them to the bar, they were more nervous about the cook-off than she was. Bailey hugged Paula's legs. "We like Chase, but we want you to win."

"Winning isn't everything . . ." Paula started, but her mom interrupted her.

"Show no mercy. Take no prisoners. Crush them."

Paula shook her head. This rivalry had gotten a little out of hand.

Chase's parking lot was full. She had to park on the grass at the back of his property. When she reached the grills, she saw that Chase had brought in extras. Each cook had his own, already preheated.

Picnic tables stretched across the back and sides of the lot, and Ralph had carried in huge pots of baked beans and cole slaw from his diner. Women came with pies and cakes. People milled everywhere.

Buck Kreiger made his way to her grill. "Remember, kid. Knock 'em dead."

"I'll try." She'd already mixed the beef with the seasonings and formed patties. She'd sliced mountains of onions and sautéed them. Maxwell was supplying all the buns.

Chase finished carrying baskets of plastic silverware and paper plates to the end table, then came to see her. "You ready for this?"

"Do I have a choice?"

He laughed. "Not a one. Let's feed the hungry masses."

Chase, Tyne, Holden, and Paula lined up at their grills. "May the best hamburger win!" Chase called, and they started throwing patties on the hot grates.

They drank beer and talked smack while they cooked, and Paula found herself having a great time. When Holden's burgers hit the grill, she smelled lamb. He opened containers of feta cheese and tzatziki to serve with them. She had an advantage. The natives around here, except for a few, liked their beef. Tyne offered Asian burgers with baby sprouts and hoisin barbecue sauce. Chase did old-fashioned bacon cheeseburgers, and she did her special blend burgers with an avocado spread, sliced tomatoes, and grilled onions. People lined up, and by the end of the meal, most of the food, including the burgers, was gone.

Ian had volunteered to count the votes that had been dropped in a cardboard box. When he finished, he grinned. "Paula's the winner!"

People cheered. Buck jumped to his feet, excited. Chase and Tyne lifted her onto their shoulders and paraded her up and down in front of the grills. When the fanfare was finished, Ian and Tessa chanted, "Speech! Speech!"

Paula kept it short. "Thank you, everyone. Thanks for coming, and thanks for voting. My win is thanks to Carl Gruber and his special blend of beef. Thank you, Carl."

Tyne pointed to Carl, sitting at a nearby picnic table with his family. "No fair! I thought we were friends."

Carl raised his hands, trying to look innocent. "When my Ellie was sick, Paula brought us a pot of soup once a week. I'll grind her any kind of beef she wants."

Tyne turned on Ian. "Did you know about this?"

"Sure did"—Ian wrapped an arm around his Tessa—"but Paula made Tess soup, too, when she had morning sickness."

Tyne shook his head, a savvy smile on his face. "I see that the barter system thrives in Mill Pond. Next year, I'll be ready."

"You can't beat karma," Holden told him. "Paula's good deeds came back to her."

The contest over, Tyne and Holden went to talk to Carl. Paula and Chase settled at the table with her mom and kids. Paula finally got to relax and glanced around at all of the people who'd come. "I didn't see Jason or Jodi."

"I invited them, but I'm glad they didn't show up. There'd be drama." Chase raised an eyebrow at Aiden and Bailey. "Your mom has to leave for work soon. No rest for the wicked, but if you guys want to hang out a while, I'll drive you home later."

"Can we?" Aiden turned to her.

"Maya's coming to babysit." When Aiden sighed, Paula shrugged. "Stay here, and I'll pay her anyway. She's looked so tired lately, she can take a nap until her mom comes to get her."

"Really?" Bailey bounced up and down. She glanced to another table where her friend, Maddie, sat with her family. "Can I go play with Maddie?"

"Go for it!" Chase motioned the kids off.

Paula smiled as they raced to see their schoolmates. She turned to her mom. "You ready to go?"

Her mom stood to leave them. "Sorry, kid, but I'm going to hang out with Dela and Betty. Have a good night at work."

When Paula started to her minivan, Chase walked with her. He pulled her to him for a quick hug. "Hang in there, champ. This is going to be a long day."

But when she got to the restaurant, Steph and Josh were already there. In no time, pans of lasagna were ready to join the corned beef and cabbage in the oven. It was a good thing she kept Sunday suppers simple. After the big Sunday brunches, the guests preferred that. By eight-thirty, though, when they finally closed the kitchen, Paula was feeling the effects of being on her feet all day.

All she wanted to do, when she got in the apartment, was change into her pajamas and collapse, but first, she planned on cornering

Maya for a long talk. It hadn't taken much to convince the girl to curl on the sofa and sleep and still get paid.

"It's my fault, I changed the schedule at the last minute," Paula told her. "You came when you were supposed to, so let me pay you, like I'm supposed to."

That's all it had taken. Maya looked tense and haunted. Paula didn't see any new bruises, but something was wrong. When she opened the door, though, determined to have a serious talk, Maya was already gone. Chase and her mom were working on a jigsaw puzzle with the kids at the kitchen table.

Paula blinked. "Where's Maya?"

"I drove her home." Mom glanced at Chase. "Chase offered to give her a ride, but she freaked out, so I took the minivan."

Thankfully, Paula had already paid her for the week. She didn't have to worry about that. "Her stepdad wouldn't let her bum rides with Tyne either. She probably thought she'd get in trouble if he saw Chase drop her off."

Chase scooted his chair back and pulled her onto his lap. She glanced at the puzzle. Three edges were finished and part of a corner was done. They'd been at it a while. "You've had a long day," he told her. "I'll get out of here and let you unwind."

Both kids circled her to hug him goodbye.

He grinned at Paula. "I've won them over. Even your mom likes me. Someday, you'll have to keep me."

Aiden's eyes grew wide. "Do you like my mom?"

"Sure do."

Aiden turned to her. "Do you like Chase?"

She hesitated, then gave herself a mental shake. Why the hell was she stalling? He wouldn't announce they were a couple in front of her kids unless he was serious. "Sure do, but we've only started seeing each other. Keep that in mind."

Aiden hugged her next. "Does this mean Chase will keep taking us boating and fishing?"

Chase gave a wide grin. Not his smile to charm, but a look of pure happiness. "Sure will."

Aiden and Bailey jumped up and down.

Paula lifted an eyebrow at Chase. "That wasn't really fair, you know."

"I never said I played fair, but I have your best interests at heart."

Her mom waved her toward the bedroom. "Change out of your work clothes and get out of here. I'll put the kids to bed and get up with them in the morning. You don't work until the supper shift, and you're a little old for a curfew."

"Are you sure?" Paula couldn't remember the last time she'd spent a night away from the kids.

Her mom smiled. "You've got to be tired. You're not going to last long. You'd better hurry."

"Thanks." Chase lifted her with him as he rose. He snagged her robe off the back of a nearby chair and carried her to his pickup.

Paula wiggled to get down. "I need my pajamas, a toothbrush, some clothes for tomorrow."

He opened the truck's door and set her inside. "No, you don't. All you need is a sheet."

Her jaw dropped, and then she laughed. Maybe he was right.

Chapter 36

Chase sat her on the bar to grab a bottle of wine before he carried her up the stairs.

"I can walk," she protested, but he just laughed. He didn't even get winded, acting as though she didn't weigh more than a bag of groceries. He was so strong, so solid. He finally set her down in front of the sofa.

"Wait here." He disappeared into his bedroom and then she heard water running. He stopped in the kitchen to uncork the wine. In a few minutes, he came to lift her again and carry her into the master bath. Steam covered the window and mirror. The claw-footed tub was filled with hot water. The bottle of wine and two glasses sat on the long sink top. A clean, fluffy towel draped on a hook.

"Your legs must ache. A long soak will ease your muscles." He stood behind her and lowered his lips to her neck. She stepped out of her clogs and used her toes to push off her socks. His hands went to her chef jacket and began unbuttoning it. He slid it off her shoulders and then tugged on her black pants. They fell to the floor and she kicked them away. Her bra went next and then her panties. Still behind her, he circled her body with his arms, and his hands began moving from her neck to her breasts, stroking and teasing. When her breaths came in quick bursts, he lifted her and lowered her into the tub.

The hot water caressed her. It soothed her muscles and aches. He handed her a glass of wine, and they clinked glasses. "To pure lust," he said. Then he soaped up a washcloth and began scrubbing her back. Long strokes woke up her senses. He dropped the cloth and soaped her neck and shoulders with his hands. Skin against skin. He cupped her breasts and his fingers circled her nipples. He squeezed and kneaded. He lifted one leg and massaged it gently. He kissed the bottom of her foot. He rubbed the other leg, loosening the muscles in her calves. Then his hands moved higher up her thighs. They dipped below the bubbles and his fingers squirmed inside her. Her body stiffened, and he leaned her against the curved back of the tub. He could explore more freely and his fingers found her pleasure spot, stroking and probing. A coil tightened inside her. She couldn't breathe. When she arched her back and groaned, he lifted her in the towel and carried her to his bed.

"No rush this time." He removed his clothes, and she stared at the beauty of him. Over six feet of hard muscles, a square jaw, and blue-green eyes. He smiled, and his dimples showed.

She reached for him, and he lowered himself on top of her. But they were in no hurry. Yes, her body wanted him, but her hands wanted to touch, to caress, to claim. Their kisses lingered. Their tongues probed. They clung together, then pulled apart to whisper kisses across hot skin. She straddled him and stroked him until he lifted her and settled her on his hardness. She rode him, and he pressed deeper and deeper until she clenched herself around him and they burst in unison. She fell forward on his chest. He stroked her back, kissed her forehead. When they parted, she spooned herself against him and he kissed the top of her head. He held her close, and she drifted to sleep.

When she woke in the morning, he was gone. She stared at the ceiling, unsure of herself. She hadn't slept with anyone since Alex. The bedroom door opened, and Chase carried in a tray of coffee and toast.

"You okay?"

She blinked. "You're the first since . . ."

He nodded. "I thought I might be. Alex would want you to be happy." He grimaced at the toast. "I don't have much in my refrigerator. Most of the supplies are downstairs in the bar. How do you like your coffee?"

"Just black."

He looked relieved. "Good. My milk went sour."

She laughed. As usual, he'd lifted her mood, eliminated the awkwardness. She tried to pull the sheet higher as she sat up, and he handed her her robe. She tugged it on and was about to close it when he pushed it wider.

"I like the view."

She blushed. Silly, since he'd seen everything before, but he'd been naked, too. At the moment, he had a large towel wrapped low on his body. His sun-streaked hair was still damp from his shower. He smelled of soap and aftershave.

She sipped her coffee—strong, just the way she liked it. Then she nibbled on her toast. But her entire attention kept returning to the towel around Chase's hips. When she drained her mug, he asked, "Do you want more?"

In answer, she scooted forward and tugged at the towel's knot. The towel fell free. He looked surprised and then grinned. With a satisfied sigh, he said, "Me, too." He pushed the tray out of the way and returned to bed with her.

By noon, her muscles felt like Jell-O, and she was famished. They took quick showers and got dressed. Then Chase took her down to the bar's kitchen and made bacon sandwiches for lunch. No bacon sandwich had ever tasted as good as his.

He laughed. "Now I know how to win food contests. First, I screw everyone to starvation, and then I cook for them."

"Sorry, but *I'm* the only one who gets to vote on your bacon skills."

He kissed her nose. "Then I'll be content being the man behind the champion." He pushed a bottle of beer toward her. "I'm glad we did this now."

She gave him a look. "Why?"

"My parents are coming next weekend. I won't have any privacy. But at least you can meet them."

Her stomach clenched. Alex's parents had liked her, but they'd never been close. She didn't see them that often. Alex had three older siblings, all with kids, all close to home, so his parents didn't mind only seeing Aiden and Bailey a couple of times a year.

Chase noticed her hesitate. He shook his head. "They're going to love you. Hell, they'll just be happy I finally found someone."

She felt awkward when Chase loaded her in his pickup and drove her home. When she entered the resort and headed to the apartment, it wasn't really the walk of shame, but then Tyne stuck his head out of the restaurant. "Well, you finally made it home." Holden came to stand beside him, smiling.

"Don't!" Paula warned.

"You picked the right one." Tyne looked too damned full of himself.

Paula scowled. "Don't break your arm patting yourself on the back."

Holden laughed at him. "He's always been good at that."

"Easy to believe." She mustered what dignity she had and went to her apartment.

Her mom grinned when she walked inside. "Did you have a good night?"

Paula choked on a gasp. "Mom!"

Her mother chuckled. "Chase is a keeper. I hope this works out for you, hon."

Paula looked around the apartment. "Where are the kids?"

Mom pointed outside to where Steph was playing in the lake with Aiden and Bailey. "Steph came early, was pretty excited to see the kids."

How lucky could a girl get? Maya was a great babysitter. Her mom was nuts about her kids. And Steph was awesome.

While Paula showered and got ready for work, she thought about Chase. Mom was right. He *was* a keeper, but nothing in her life had been permanent. She loved her dad, but he was gone a lot. She loved Alex, but he was gone a lot, too. And then they both left her. Maybe it wasn't safe for her to love too much. She always got hurt.

When she went to work the evening shift, Tyne and Holden had made a gorgeous crown rib roast with stuffing in the center.

"We had to impress you after you beat us yesterday," Holden said.

She shook her head. "You both impressed me at the cook-off. You just didn't know the crowd you were playing to."

Tyne nodded. "You had the hometown advantage."

"Yeah, and I'll work that angle again next year."

Tyne laughed. "So will I."

The brothers left so that Tyne could introduce Holden to the local vendors and show him around. The night sped by, and she was happy to return to her apartment to see her kids at the end of her shift. She'd been glad to get away from them for a night, but that was long enough. She needed to satisfy her motherly urges again.

Chapter 37

Paula didn't work on Tuesday. She had the whole day off. Tyne and Holden were taking over the kitchen. When she woke at eight, she wondered what they'd serve for the breakfast buffet. When they put their heads together, what had they come up with? But she resisted the urge to wander into the kitchen to find out. She'd ask Steph and Josh about it later.

She was flipping pancakes for Aiden and Bailey when Chase called. "I don't have to work tonight. My college guy is manning the bar. I was wondering if you and the kids could come over and help me get this place ready for my parents' visit."

She loaded the pancakes on plates, and the kids carried them to the table. "What time do you want us?"

"As soon as you can get here. Wear old clothes. I'm thinking of cleaning out the spare bedroom."

She was pouring herself a cup of coffee and paused. "What do you usually do when they come?"

"Give them my room and sleep in one of the twin beds. Not very comfortable. My feet hang over the bottom edge."

She laughed. "Mom's spending the morning with Grams, making plans for the charity benefit. I'll drop her off and swing by your place, but I have to be back to eat Tyne's supper at six. Cooking with his brother is too big of a deal for him. They even put up a sign, announcing that Tyne would be cooking with a guest chef today."

"Hell, I'll come with you, if that's all right," Chase said.

"After all the cookouts you've done for us? You're invited." A spurt of happiness shot through her. It would be nice to have Chase come to something of hers. So far, she'd gone to his events, and they'd all been good. She was flattered he wanted to attend something because it was important to her. And this was important. She wanted Tyne and Holden to come up with a dinner that would be talked about for months. For now, though, they'd better hustle if Chase needed much done. "Okay, then, I'll see you as soon as I can."

"Thanks. Really. I'm going to get started, so I might not hear if you knock. I'll leave the door unlocked, so just come up."

"Will do." When she told the kids, they loved the idea. So did her mom.

"This isn't play time," she warned them. "Chase is going to put you to work."

"That's what Dad used to do." Aiden squared his shoulders. "We helped him."

Paula glanced at her mom. Mom nodded. "Kids are part of a family. Everyone pitches in."

A family, yes, but she and Chase weren't together yet. What if they split? What if they didn't work out? She didn't want the kids to be disappointed. She wanted stability for them.

Her mom watched her expressions and shook her head. "Relax. Aiden and Bailey are smart. They know you and Chase aren't married. You're friends. And maybe that's all you'll ever be, but that's all right."

Her mom was voicing her concerns, bless her, making the kids aware of them. Paula glanced at them, and Aiden nodded. "We know the difference between dates and getting married, Mom. Besides, Chase will still be our friend even if you break up."

He was right. Chase wasn't the type who'd dump her kids just because the romance fizzled. But even as the thought crossed her mind, she hoped the romance didn't fizzle. She wanted Chase. For herself and for the kids.

Mom finished her pancakes and carried her plate to the kitchen. "I, for one, have places to go and things to do. Let's move it."

A half hour later, they were on their way into town. A haze of heat hung over Mill Pond—late June in the Midwest. Paula had put on a sleeveless top and short-shorts. Sure, she'd get dirty, but she wouldn't melt from the heat and humidity. Even if Chase cranked his air conditioning to high, in this kind of weather, when you worked, you perspired.

On the drive, Mom asked, "What does Mill Pond do for the Fourth of July? It must be prime tourist season. Do you go all out?"

"Last summer, the town had a big picnic at the lake, and then we watched fireworks over the water!" Bailey had talked about it for weeks. She thought it was the best celebration she'd ever seen. Ian had told guests at the inn that the dining room closed on the Fourth of July and everyone ate outside unless it rained. Paula had made huge pots of shrimp boil. She'd smoked and grilled barbecued chicken. Everyone ate off paper plates with plastic silverware, and a table was loaded with slices of watermelon and cantaloupe. Gallons of ice cream were cradled on ice, along with toppings for sundaes.

Her mom smiled. "Chase's parents will be here for the Fourth. They probably help at the bar. I bet it's busy."

"Everything's busy, but it's great." Paula pulled into the driveway for Grams's snug ranch-style house in town. These days, Miguel's pickup was always in the garage.

Mom got out, and Grams opened the door before she got there. "I thought we'd spend the day together," Grams called. "I'll drive her home when we're ready." She waved at Paula as she backed out and headed to Chase's.

She parked in back of the bar and noticed that smoke was already drifting from Chase's smoker. He was getting the ribs and pork ready for lunch tomorrow. The kids flew up the stairs to Chase's apartment. Paula heard laughter and greetings as she climbed the steps to join them.

"My work crew showed up!" Chase led them into the spare room.

Aiden grabbed Bailey's hand, and they ran to peek into the other rooms off the hallway. He stopped at the room with the two twin beds. "We could spend the night some time."

Chase nodded. "That would be perfect for early morning fishing trips. We need to fix the room up if you're going to spend time in there, though."

Bailey clapped her hands. "I want a yellow room!"

Paula raised her eyebrows at Aiden.

Aiden shrugged. "Anything but pink."

Chase led them back into the storage room. "That can be our next project, but for now, we have to clean all the boxes out of my extra bedroom." He'd opened the window and taken out the screen. "A dumpster's under that window. Let's start sorting."

They made a line. He'd take items out of a box and if he wanted them, they went in one pile. If he didn't, they passed them down the line and Aiden tossed them out the window. When a box was empty, the box flew to join the rest of the trash. Most of the things he'd saved had belonged to his parents, but they no longer wanted them. Once in a while, he found something with sentimental value or a tool or possession he'd misplaced, and they'd go in the save pile.

Paula was surprised how fast they sorted through everything. He opened a closet door and it was clear he'd already dusted and cleaned inside it.

"For now, we'll put all of these in here, and later, I'll decide where they should go." They filled the top shelf and a far corner, but there was still plenty of space to hang clothes. The room stood empty. The floor needed to be swept and mopped. Chase frowned at the walls. "These are in good shape. They're clean, but they could use a coat of paint." He looked at Aiden. "What color?"

Paula knew what he'd choose before he said it. They'd stayed in a hotel on their drive from New York to Mill Pond that had walls the color of grocery bags, and Aiden fell in love with it. When he told Chase, Chase frowned. "Could you pick it out if you saw it on a paint chip?"

Aiden nodded.

"Good, then you two come with me to the hardware store. Bailey can find the yellow she wants, and you can find your brown. We'll buy brushes and rollers, too. I have some, but they've seen better days." He looked at Paula. "Do you mind hanging out here until we get back? I'll stop and buy lunch while we're in town."

"If you show me where you keep your cleaning supplies, I'll sweep and mop while you're gone."

"You don't have to do that."

She motioned to the floors. "Yes, I do. Don't worry about it. That way, you can start painting right away. You'd better buy a drop cloth or two, though."

He led them downstairs to a closet off the kitchen that held every cleaning supply anyone would need. Then he took off with the kids.

Paula had the floors cleaned and dry when they got back. They brought a bag of coney dogs with them, and after they ate, Chase showed the kids how to paint.

"If you get tired, you can quit, but if I see you get sloppy, I'm firing you. First, though, you have to let me get the painter's tape on the woodwork, so we don't ruin it."

They took his warning seriously. Once he and Paula taped the oak woodwork and laid the drop cloth, they carefully started work on their end wall. Chase taped everything else, because Paula couldn't reach the top of the long, narrow windows without a ladder. She painted while he worked. He'd bought high-quality paint, so they'd only need one coat, and by midafternoon, the walls were done.

Chase crossed his arms to inspect their work. He was as dirty and sweaty as they were, and he still looked good. "Well, what do you think?" he asked Aiden.

Aiden looked like he'd hug a wall if he could. "It's perfect."

"Good, then let's start on Bailey's room."

That room was smaller, but it was five before they finished it.

"Your vote?" he asked Bailey.

"I love it!" She twirled in a circle by the window.

Chase looked pleased with himself. The rooms did look nice. "This way, if you want to spend the night to go fishing with my dad some morning, you can. Your room's ready."

"Will your mom and dad like my brown room?" Aiden asked.

"Why wouldn't they? It's beautiful. And when they leave, that's where you'll stay when you visit."

"My own room?" Aiden stared.

Bailey squealed, she was so excited. "Can I put a dollhouse in the yellow room then? Please?"

Paula discouraged that idea with a scowl. Bailey had wanted a dollhouse for over a year now, but they didn't have enough room for one.

Chase shrugged. "I don't see why not."

"If they have their own rooms, you'll never get rid of them."

"Maybe that's the point."

She didn't know how to answer in front of Aiden and Bailey. Instead, she glanced at her watch, now splattered with paint. "I don't want to be a spoil sport, but we need to get back to the apartment to clean up before supper. We have to look good for Tyne."

The kids loved Tyne, too, so they didn't argue. They scrambled down the stairs to leave. Chase brushed Paula's lips with his before she followed them.

"I'll be there at six. And thanks for all the help."

"I enjoyed myself." And she had. She was hot and sweaty. Dirt smeared her face and legs, paint speckled her arms and part of her hair, but she'd loved helping him work on his place.

He smiled at her. "You're cute when you're a mess."

Yeah, right. "So are you." Oh hell, he was always yummy. She didn't know if it was possible to make Chase look bad. She had to force herself to turn and head down the stairs. Spending time with him was addictive.

Mom, already dressed in her casual finest, laughed at them when they tumbled into the apartment. "I knew you'd be dirty, but you've outdone yourselves. You'd better hurry. You have lots of scrubbing to do."

Paula didn't have time to wash her hair, but she worked the paint out of most of it and was squeaky clean when the four of them made their way to the inn's kitchen.

"Good, you have time to see the buffet before the guests come." Tyne herded them into the dining room.

Her mother sucked in a surprised breath. Aiden and Bailey blinked, trying to take it all in, and Paula stared. An ice statue of a horse, rearing up on its hind legs, sat in the center of the beverage table, and tonight, bottles of wine nestled around the statue in silver ice buckets. The antique pink glass plates normally on display in the lobby held paté and crackers. A mixed green salad with artichoke hearts, hearts of palm, grape tomatoes, and feta cheese filled a huge, cut-glass bowl. That was followed by small dishes of mixed olives and pickles, and a cheese tray. The two entrees were stunning—Lobster Thermidor and steak Oscar: beef filets topped with asparagus, béarnaise sauce, and sautéed shrimp.

Chase came to stand behind Paula, and he whistled. "Holy crap, I feel like I'm in some topnotch, exclusive restaurant."

Holden locked gazes with Tyne. The two men looked pretty proud of what they'd accomplished. Rightfully so. "That's what we went for. We talked to Ian and we might do this once a year."

Chase blew out a breath. "If he advertises it, he won't have a spare room in the whole resort."

"He doesn't now," Tyne said. "He thought we might do it sometime in the off-season to bring people in, and charge more than usual. Maybe for Valentine's Day."

Paula shook her head. "You can't count on the weather. A blizzard could shut us down."

"Easter?" Tyne asked.

"Yup, that would work." Paula heard footsteps approaching.

Guests were on their way. "We'll wait in the kitchen so that the guests can get the whole effect before you open up the dining room."

Holden nodded. "We'll bring you plates when we come in for some quick bites."

Once in the kitchen, Paula noticed that Steph and Josh had stayed to help with tonight's special. "Well?" she asked them. "Do you think it's fancy enough?"

"The steak Oscar was Tyne's idea." Austin's voice swelled with pride. "He taught me how to make béarnaise sauce."

"Ian and Tessa are coming to eat here tonight," Steph said.

Josh added, "Ian's talking about offering special holiday meals and rates. He wants to do a medieval dinner for Christmas with a roast goose and venison. He went to one of those once."

So had Paula. The weather was safer in December than in February. That might work. She shrugged. "We'd better learn to make plum pudding."

As usual, in a kitchen, the talk turned to food and menus. They were discussing what they'd serve at Thanksgiving when Tyne and Holden carried in plates with a little bit of everything for people to try out. Every item on Tyne's menu was a success. Before Paula got ready to leave, Tyne said, "Do you remember you're covering all three shifts again tomorrow so I can drive Holden to the airport?"

"I've got it. No worries." She held out her arms to hug Holden. "It was great having you here. Have a good trip home."

The others would say their goodbyes at the end of the shift. Holden gave her a cuddly hug and said in her ear, "My brother's happy here. Mill Pond is a great place to cook. Thanks for seeing his potential."

Paula laughed and dipped back. "What's not to see? He's always trying to show me up."

"Good luck with that. Tyne's right. You're good. This resort, the entire area's great. I'm glad I came. I'll brag about him to Mom and Dad, but they won't listen."

"Their loss." Paula glanced at Tyne. "I hope we keep him for a long time."

Holden gave a knowing look. "I think you might. There's more to life than just cooking. He's found friends and . . ." He shrugged. "There's a lot on offer here."

Paula frowned at him, but didn't push it. His words made her curious, though. Aiden tugged her arm, and she smiled. "Gotta go. Come again any time."

And it sounded like he just might. He and Tyne might take over the kitchen again next year at Easter time.

Chapter 38

On Wednesday, Paula listened to all the gossip in the kitchen and thoroughly enjoyed it. Steph informed her that the brothers had debated lots of different recipes for breakfast, but after they studied their budget, had decided to stay with what they always made on Tuesdays—plain and fancy pancakes, frittatas, and the usual morning fare.

"What kind of pancakes did they do for the adults?" Paula asked.

Steph looked smug. "They made your recipe for pecan pancakes with Bananas Foster syrup."

Josh nodded. "That's hard to beat. The guests love it."

"What about lunch?"

Josh chuckled. "Holden made a hot and sour soup, and we brought half of it back."

"Not his fault," Paula said. "I tried that once, and it just doesn't go over here."

"Tyne made chicken and dumplings, and we ran out of that," Josh said.

"Traditional is a safer bet." Paula helped load today's breakfast on the buffet. Even kids were starting to try her baked eggs in ramekins.

"They went cheaper on the sandwiches," Steph told her. "They had to, the dinner menu was so expensive."

"Tuna salad and turkey wraps." Josh grinned. "They were really good, though."

They headed back to the kitchen to let the guests help themselves, and Steph shook her head. "You should have seen those two brothers together. They got downright silly sometimes, snapped each other with towels, threw radishes at each other."

That would have been fun to see, but if Paula had stuck her nose in the kitchen, they'd have put her to work. She knew better.

Once breakfast was finished, Betty came to work in the dining room, and Paula got busy on the day's lunch menu. Steph and Josh chopped and diced beside her. She'd learned from experience that after guests ate a feast, like they did last night, they wanted a lighter lunch. She opted for egg salad sandwiches, cucumber sandwiches, and sloppy joe sliders. Even the soups were simple: white cheddar cheese and alphabet vegetable.

Steph and Josh were loading the food into tureens and onto the tiered, glass plates when Jason came with supplies. His foul mood preceded him, permeating every nook and cranny. Steph and Josh glanced at her, then without a word, left the kitchen. Even Brian, the dishwasher, followed them.

"Are you okay?" Paula asked.

"Someone slashed my car tires last night, all four of them. It had to be Jodi's brothers, but I can't prove anything."

Paula blinked. "Why would they slash your tires?"

"They want me to marry their whore of a sister."

Paula didn't know what to say. "Even if you don't like her?"

"They don't care about that. They'll do a DNA test to prove paternity and charge me for everything they can and *still* torment me until I make her legal."

"How does Jodi feel about marrying you?"

"She's all for it." He slammed his clipboard on the steel table. "Damnit, even my mother told me I should." He glanced out the kitchen window, taking a moment to rein in his emotions. "She told me I let the snake out of my pants. Eve was tempted by the snake in the Garden, and it still tempts women to this day. When they succumb, childbirth is their punishment."

Paula stared. "That's how your mother views sex?"

"The pill lets us enjoy the snake without consequences, but once a baby's made, a man has to face his responsibilities. She said she and Dad are still paying for their sins. Now I have to pay for mine."

Paula couldn't be any more shocked. "Your mom got pregnant, and that's why your dad married her?"

"He never lets her forget that she trapped him, that he wouldn't have chosen her if he didn't have to."

"Your poor mother." She thought a minute. "Poor Jodi. You don't want what your mom and dad have, do you?"

"What choice do I have?"

"You don't have to be like your dad. Why did your mom stay with him?"

"She had four kids. She kept thinking he'd see that she was a good mother, a good wife. But it never happened."

"Your dad's an asshole."

"I already know that."

"That doesn't mean you should be one."

He glared at her. "I'm stuck.

"You and Jodi had fun together. You could try to make this work."

"Yeah, right. Lucky me. I get to marry a whore." He dumped the boxes off his dolly and stalked away.

Betty, Steph, and Josh came into the kitchen. Paula looked at them and shook her head. "You listened to everything, didn't you?"

"What a jerk!" Steph picked up the first box and started unloading it. Paula hoped there were no eggs on top. Steph wasn't being gentle.

Betty shook a finger at poor Josh. "That boy judges every woman he sleeps with, but still thinks *he's* pure as snow. If you ever treat a girl the way he does . . ."

Josh threw up his hands in self-defense. "I love my girlfriend. I'd never do anything to hurt her."

Something clanged in the dining room, and they hurried to check on their guests. A kid had accidentally banged a metal spoon on the side of the coffee urn, nothing to worry about. The rest of lunch went fast, and Paula started on the dishes for supper before Betty left for the day.

Betty shook her head on the way out the kitchen door. She opened her mouth to say something, then decided against it. Steph said it for her. "He's a lost cause. Not worth thinking about."

As usual, when Paula was upset, she concentrated on food. After last night's buffet, anything ordinary would look sad. She'd decided on balsamic-glazed stuffed chicken breasts and red snapper.

The food was more labor-intensive than usual, and Steph and Josh stayed an extra hour to help her before Austin arrived. Austin got excited about the red snapper, so she let him do the majority of the prep. If Tyne could really talk his mom into funding culinary school for the boy, Austin would turn into a good chef. So would Steph and Josh, but Steph had been making noises lately that she might marry her boyfriend instead of leaving Mill Pond. They'd been together since ninth grade.

"Could I work part-time during the slow months?" she asked Paula. "And would you hire me again full-time during the peak season?"

"I'll ask Ian, but we could use another sous chef around here, even in the winter."

By the end of the night, when the kitchen was cleaned and Paula headed back to her apartment, she thought about Jason. Nope, Steph was right. Not worth the bother. That made her think about Steph. She was a little disappointed in her. She had so much potential, but each person had to follow her own path. Not everyone was cut out to be a chef. The hours were terrible.

When she stepped through the apartment door, the kids hummed with excitement. They pointed at the kitchen table. A bouquet of two dozen red and white roses lay there. She went to read the note and tears misted her eyes. I MISSED YOU TODAY. HOPE YOU MISSED ME. CHASE.

All other thoughts flew out of her mind. She bit her bottom lip. He'd worked lunch and dinner today, too, and he'd still found time to send her flowers. She fussed with the green wrapping paper. Her mom came to wrap an arm around her waist.

"He really does love you, you know. I know you're waiting for him to get called away somewhere, but it's not going to happen. The man's in this for the long haul. He isn't your dad. He isn't Alex. He wants to be here for you."

She had to fight back tears. How had she gotten so lucky? Most of her fear was disappearing. Chase was what he said he was. He loved her kids. He loved her. She just needed to accept that.

Chapter 39

On Thursday, she worked breakfast and lunch, so she didn't see Chase until she dropped the kids off for karate and went to his bar.

When he came to sit with her, she greeted him with a bigger smile than usual. "Thanks for the roses. They're beautiful."

"You liked them?"

She leaned across the table to kiss him, lips on lips.

He looked surprised. "A PDA from you? That doesn't happen. I'll have to send flowers more often."

She laughed. "Then flowers will get old. This time, they were a nice surprise."

"Where's your mom?"

Paula sipped the beer he'd brought her. "She said she needed a quiet night, that she was going to enjoy having the apartment to herself."

"I understand that." He reached across to lay his hand on hers. He was the touchy-feely type. At first, that had bothered her. Now she liked it.

She pursed her lips, thinking. "I'm worried that once everything slows down, and the quiet settles around Mom, the tears will fall." But tears *had* to fall, didn't they? It was part of losing someone you'd shared most of your life with.

He squeezed her hand. "Tears can be good. They wash away the heartache."

She'd never thought of it like that, but he was right. She glanced around at the customers scattered at different tables—a good crowd. "Do you have everything ready for your parents?"

"Yup. The queen-sized bed for the brown room came today. So did the chest of drawers. Mom's pretty stoked about staying in her own guest suite." There was a Jack-and-Jill bathroom that connected their room and the yellow one. Admittedly, it needed some updating, but it was there.

"Do you have to pick them up on Saturday?"

He shook his head. "They're renting a car and driving from the airport. They're pretty independent. They want their own wheels."

She arched an eyebrow, gave him a naughty look. "You'd let them borrow your motorcycle, wouldn't you?"

"Mom would hurt me." He snorted, then gave her a sideways glance. "They're excited about seeing you and the kids."

"You've told them about us?"

"My parents and I talk about everything. Part of being an only child."

He *was* an only child, wasn't he? He didn't fit the mold. "Was that hard for you?"

"Nah, I ran around the bar a lot, always had people around me, and I had lots of friends. I spent a lot of time at the lake in the summers." He fidgeted, nervous. "I hope you like my parents. They mean a lot to me."

She hoped she liked them, too. "Alex's parents and I never really warmed up to each other."

He looked surprised. "Did they get to know you very well?"

"We didn't see much of each other."

"Well, there you go."

She frowned. "They didn't want to."

"My parents will."

That made her nervous.

He smiled and shook his head. "They're going to love you as much as I do."

He'd said it. The words. Everything stilled inside her. The truth flooded her. He *did* love her, and she loved him. "I love you, too."

His blue-green eyes blazed with emotion. "Thank you for saying it. I needed to hear it."

She frowned. "Who could *not* love you?"

"It's a matter of loving *enough.*"

There was something in his voice, the shadow that crossed over his handsome face. She stared. "You were hurt in the past, weren't you?" She couldn't imagine it. Someone had walked away from him.

He sighed. "The very first woman I loved was ten years older than me. She was twenty-nine. I was nineteen. She was lonely. I was enthralled. Then the summer ended, she kissed me, told me I'd meet someone wonderful someday, and said goodbye."

"Did she love you?"

"At the time, but she went home to marry the guy she was luke-warm about."

Paula could feel his pain, the hurt of betrayal that still lingered after all these years. She was leaning toward him, to comfort him, when Louise called, "Hey, boss, I could use some help!"

He jerked his attention to the bar. More customers had wandered in. "I guess I'd better get busy."

She thought about that young Chase while she finished her dinner. Maybe that's why he'd been attracted to Daphne. Maybe he chose women who were elusive because they reminded him of his first love. Well, she wasn't mysterious or out of reach, but he'd chosen her any-way. And they were going to be happy together, she could feel it.

Later, when she left to get the kids from practice, energy hummed inside her. Blue skies were ahead—for all of them. She was driving down Main Street when Aiden yelled, "Mom! Stop the car! Stop!"

Paula slammed on the brakes, looking for what she'd missed. Had a dog run in front of her and she'd missed it? Was there someone on the sidewalk, in trouble? Her heart thumping, she pulled to the curb. "What, Aiden? What's the matter?"

Aiden pointed out the window to a narrow opening between two buildings. Maya sat with her back pressed against the hardware's brick wall, her head down, her shoulders shaking.

Oh crap!

"Stay here." Paula went to see if she was all right. On a Thursday night, Maya should be babysitting.

Maya heard her coming and lifted her head. Eyes red and puffy, she rubbed tears off her cheeks. She turned her face away, embar-rassed.

"Hey, what's up?" Paula kept her voice calm and squatted down to lean against the wall with her.

"My mom . . . kicked me . . . out." Maya's words came in bursts, shakily. "I lost . . . my job . . ."

"With the couple who work nights?"

Maya nodded. "The husband . . . keeps touching . . . on accident."

She took a breath to steady herself. "His arm against my boob. His hand bumps inside my thigh. His wife noticed, but never said anything."

Paula's mind flew to *The Girl with the Dragon Tattoo*. She braced herself. "What happened tonight?"

"Before they left for work, he pushed me against the wall and kissed me."

Relief. Not as bad as it could have been. "Did the wife see?"

"She walked in and screamed at me. Told me I was a tease. Told me I was fired."

"Oh, good." When Maya stared at her, she sighed. "It's better this way, honey, it would only get worse. The husband would only get braver, do more."

Maya pulled her knees to her chest and lowered her head to them.

"It wasn't your fault. You know that, don't you?"

Voice muffled, face hidden, she said, "I walked home and told my mom. She said I ruined the job on purpose, that I was too lazy to make money for them."

That didn't surprise Paula, and that in itself was sad. "So you ran away?"

"No, she told me to get out. She told me I was trying to steal my stepdad, too. She told me I was too ugly for any man to want me except for bad things." She raised her head and scrubbed at tears that rushed down her cheeks.

Paula's fingers curled into fists. But her anger wouldn't help Maya. "What are you going to do now?"

She leaned back against the wall, exhausted. "I don't know."

"I do." Paula stood and reached out a hand to tug her to her feet. "You're coming home with us. The kids love you. So does my mom. So do I. We'll think of something."

Maya's entire body started to tremble, and Paula pulled her into a tight embrace. She rubbed her back. "It's going to be okay. Come on. You'll have to sleep in a sleeping bag on an air mattress, but we'll figure out something."

The kids didn't ask questions when Maya climbed into the passenger seat. They sat, quiet, on the drive home. But when they got inside the apartment, they plastered themselves against her, offering comfort.

Maya's breath evened out, and she started to calm down. "I'm sorry." Tears welled, but she blinked them away. "I feel like such a loser."

"Not you." Mom hadn't even heard the story yet, but she championed the girl. "You didn't do anything wrong. Tomorrow's Friday. You can help me watch the kids, and from what Dela told me, there are more people who could use good, reliable babysitters around here."

Paula frowned. Where was Mom going with this?

"Tessa and Kayla are having a horrible time watching Kayla's little girl while they bake. Soon, Tessa will have a baby, too. I think you and I could earn some decent money if we opened a daycare."

"A daycare?" Paula blinked. "Where?"

"Well, here, if Ian would let me move in and take your place. I've called to break my lease in Texas. I like it here."

Paula stared. Mom had given this some serious thought.

"If you and Chase get together, you'll move in above his bar. Maya and I could live here and babysit. If that doesn't work, I'll buy a place of my own in town. I have enough money from your dad's insurance. I like Mill Pond, and I like being close to you and Aiden and Bailey."

It wasn't a bad idea. Her mom loved kids. But it might not be that easy to save Maya. "Maya's mom could make her move back with them."

"She might try, but then Grams and I would have to pay her a visit. I think she'll let us keep Maya."

Paula rubbed her forehead, trying to massage her mind into keeping up. Mom had seen this coming. She sounded serious. She must know something Paula didn't. *Good.* Mom was easygoing and loving, but Lord help anyone who got her dander up.

Mom smiled. "I'll fill you in later, but for now, we have a plan. Let's sleep on it, and in the morning, I'll take Maya home to get her things."

"Without me?" Paula had to work the morning shift on Fridays.

"Oh, honey, it's probably better if you don't see me when I'm mad." Aiden and Bailey stared, and her mother shook her head. "You two can stay with your mom in the kitchen for a while. We won't be long. But remember, moms are like mother bears. Mess with a cub, and they turn deadly."

Aiden nodded. He understood that analogy. So did Bailey.

Mom fussed around, blowing up an air mattress for Maya and finding enough blankets for her. Then they settled in front of the TV, and Maya didn't complain as they watched a silly show. At bedtime, Paula curled on the couch, but had trouble falling asleep. She could hear Maya moving around on the air mattress on the other side of the room. The girl sniffled off and on. She thought about her mom and Grams. Were they planning on blackmailing Maya's mother? Did she care? And she realized she'd do whatever she could to protect Maya, too. That thought eased her mind, and she drifted into slumber.

Chapter 40

Paula found that she was anxious when Tyne came to take over the kitchen on Friday. Fridays were always simple—prime rib and salmon. She'd purposely made three side dishes, just to keep her mind off Maya.

Tyne raised an eyebrow when he saw them. "You can quit cooking now. Your minivan's in the parking lot, and your mom and Maya made it back with all of her clothes loaded on the back seat."

"You've heard?"

He rolled his eyes. "It's Mill Pond. Everyone knows, but Grams is spreading the word that Maya's mother wants what's best for her, so she's letting Maya go into business with your mom."

"What a crock!"

He looked serious for a moment, but then shrugged. "Your mom and Grams are letting Maya's mom save face. They have to tell everybody something."

It would be better that way. Paula knew it, even if she didn't like it. "Have they talked to Ian yet?"

"Are you kidding? He's so relieved he can offer daycare for his employees, he's already hired a contractor to build a small, fenced-in play area off your apartment's side door. He figures by the time Tessa has his second kid and Kayla's babies go to all-day kindergarten, your mom will be ready to retire."

Paula could feel her insides unwind. She hadn't realized she'd been so tense until her shoulders relaxed. But Ian was the type of boss who always looked ahead. With Mom and Maya here, Tessa and Kayla would have on-site babysitters. Jodi would be having a baby soon, too. And Ian could pop in to coo over his little boy between guests.

Tyne grinned. "If you and Chase break up, you're going to mess up everything."

"We'll just have to hang in there then. It will be a sacrifice to move in with a hot, awesome man, but I'll force myself to do it." He laughed, and she watched him tie on his apron, then remembered what Holden had told her. "What about you? If you're going to stay in Mill Pond awhile, you could move up your plans on finding someone."

"Not me. Not ready."

That's what he said, but had Holden heard or seen something that made him think otherwise? She grew serious. "How's Daphne doing? Is she still happy with her professor? Chase won't be there to cheer her up if things go sour."

He pinched his lips together. "The bastard's been seeing his wife. He says they have things to work out. And he's still seeing Daphne."

Paula hung her apron on its hook. "She's going to need a friend before this is done."

"I know that. She's a good person. I'll be there for her."

He would be, too. She had no doubt about that. He was always there for *her* when she needed him. She patted his arm on the way out the door. "You're a good person, too. So is your brother."

"Yeah, that's us, the dynamic duo. Get ready. Holden's already thinking of things to do and make on his next visit."

"No." Paula couldn't stop a groan. "It's too soon."

Tyne laughed at her. "He's going to keep us on our toes." He whistled on his way to the refrigerator, and Paula smiled. He loved a little friendly competition with his brother.

On the way to her apartment, she flew through a mental list of what might greet her. More tears from Maya. Her mother, ready to do battle. The kids in an uproar. She was surprised to see Steph there, watching Aiden and Bailey.

"I heard about Maya moving in with you guys," Steph said, "but your mom wanted to take her out tonight, said she needed a little fun in her life."

"I can't argue with that." Paula glanced at Aiden and Bailey. "What are you two up to?"

"Steph's going to help us build Mill Pond's Main Street with boxes." Bailey pointed to piles of shoeboxes in the corner.

"One box for each store in town. Some can go sideways and some will go up and down for the tall buildings," Aiden said. "It was Maya's idea, but Steph likes it."

It would keep them busy for a while, that's for sure. Paula looked at another pile of colored paper and a box of Sharpies. "That looks like a project Maya would think of."

Steph grinned. "We might not finish it tonight, but we'll get a good start."

"I'll leave you to it." Paula hurried to change and drive to the bar. She'd be walking in on a Friday to see Chase, not Jason. She dressed in a short flowered skirt and a pink silky top, and took extra care with her hair and makeup.

When Chase saw her, his whole face lit up. She smiled back at him and made her way to Buck Kreiger's table. Glancing at the pool players, she saw Jason with his friends. Jason wore what looked like a permanent scowl.

Buck grinned at her. "Gossip's been flying all week. Jason and Jodi. You and Chase. And his parents are coming to town tomorrow."

"We're trying to wear out the grapevine." She smiled at Louise when she put a beer in front of her. This was going to be one of those nights. Her cheeks would ache by the time she got home. Smiles for all.

"Same order as usual?" Louise asked.

"Burger and fries."

Louise winked. "I've never seen the boss happier. Way to go, girl!"

Chase came to sit with her when he could, but the bar was busier than usual. More tourists milled with the regulars. By the Fourth of July, the bar would be overflowing.

"A work crew's coming tomorrow to throw a roof over the back patio," he told her. "They can get it done in one day, and then we can serve outside. A dozen of the picnic tables we used for the cook-off are mine. They're stacked on the side of the building."

Buck frowned. "You have a lot of cement back there. You need to soften it up with some potted plants."

"What have you got in mind?"

Paula sat back and let them talk. She only half-listened, watching the people mingle and talk at the tables around them. Finally, Chase glanced at the bar and said, "Gotta go. Orders are piling up. Take care, babe."

He bent to give her a quick kiss, then went back to work. *Babe.*

That was new. She liked it. She visited with Buck until he finished his pie and then excused himself. The open chairs were an invitation for more people to stop by. Grams and Miguel came to talk to her.

"Don't worry. I'm not trying to twist your arm for any more charities," Grams teased. "But your mom and Maya want to start a daycare. Did Ian like the idea?"

"Loved it."

They talked about Tessa and Kayla, Jodi, and some other pregnant woman Paula didn't know. When Grams returned to her other friends, Jason stalked across the room to sit with her. Damn. Paula had no idea what to say to him.

He motioned for Louise to bring him a beer. *Bummer.* He wasn't in a good mood and didn't bother to hide it. "My friends' wives can't stand me. They even tried to warn women away from me, so they all came to the bar tonight to support Jodi." He sounded bitter as he pointed to a table of women, sitting with Jodi, near the pool area.

Paula recognized one of them—the woman who'd cornered her in the clothing shop to tell her to steer clear of Jason. "You must have good friends if they're still hanging in there when their wives give them grief about it."

"They keep telling me things are only going to get better with a good woman by my side." He snorted. "Like Jodi's a good woman."

"Give her a chance." Not that Paula thought Jodi was a saint, by any means, but maybe Jason and Jodi deserved each other.

"She's moving in with me this weekend. Maybe then people will shut up."

"Maybe." People didn't change overnight. It would take Jason and Jodi time to work things out, if they ever did.

One of the men at the pool table motioned for Jason, obviously not happy he was sitting with her.

Jason grunted. "Life's going to be shit for a while." He grabbed his beer and walked away. Chase came to sit with her for a second. "Everything all right?"

"Jason's not going to be a happy man for a while. If ever." Paula was surprised when Maya's mom walked through the bar doors with a tall, rough-looking man by her side. She'd never met Maya's stepdad, but she'd heard enough about him to know he'd never pay for a babysitter. "Don't they have young kids at home?"

Chase nodded. "Your mom and Maya picked them up to spend the night at your place. Those two don't like being stuck at home."

At her place? The apartment? Paula sighed, but then decided it was for the best. Maya's little sister was ten. Who knew when her mom would blame *her* for trying to steal her husband?

The music started up, and Paula was surprised when Jodi pulled Jason onto the dance floor. Chase snuck in one dance with her, but by then, she was fizzling and he had to get back to bartending.

"Catch you later?" he asked.

"Sorry, it's gonna be an early night for me. This has been a busy week, and I work the early shift tomorrow."

Chase pressed her to him for a moment. "Will you come meet my parents when you get off work tomorrow?"

"Won't you be tending bar?"

"Yeah, but it's slow on Saturday afternoons. We'll have to keep it short, but then you'll have more time to get know each other on Sunday."

She was letting Tyne sleep in on Sunday during brunch, in exchange for him covering her evening shift. Austin was going to man his duties. That way, she could stay longer to visit with Chase's mom and dad.

She left the bar earlier than usual and braced herself on the drive home. There'd be three more kids underfoot. But when she got there, Maya had them all busy, finishing shoeboxes to build Main Street. She'd forgotten that Maya watched over them more often than their parents. They were used to following her lead. They watched a movie after that, and then everyone found a spot on the floor and fell asleep.

Maya's brothers and sister had been so careful about everything they did or said that it broke her heart. They weren't just on their best behavior. They treaded softly, so no adult would scream at them. Lying on the couch, Paula had to fight back sadness. If Maya wanted to bring them here every Friday, it was all right with her.

Chapter 41

After work on Saturday, Paula dressed carefully in casual slacks and a pink top. She pulled her hair into three different styles and didn't like any of them. She put on eyeshadow, but thought she looked too drab. She added eyeliner and thought she looked like a strumpet. Finally, her mom said, "You look great. Quit stalling. Go meet them."

On the drive to Chase's, she thought of all the things they wouldn't like about her. She was too short. She was too plump. Her hair was too dark. Her nose was too long. But when she walked through the bar's doors, a woman rushed to greet her.

"You've made us so happy!" She wrapped her in a hug until Paula thought she might never let go. Then she pushed away from her, held her at arm's length, and beamed. "You're just perfect, everything Chase said you'd be."

A man came up beside her. "For God's sake, Poppy, let the girl breathe." He was as tall as Chase, but with long graying hair pulled back in a low ponytail. He wore jeans and a tie-dyed T-shirt.

"Don't start with me, Troy. I've waited a long time for this." The woman's turquoise eyes sparkled. Her white hair hung down to her waist. She wore a long, flowing skirt and a skinny white tee.

Chase came up behind them and wrapped them both in a gentle hug. He smiled at Paula. "Now you know. My parents are both old hippies."

She relaxed. These weren't people who'd judge her. They'd accept her. She smiled. "Chase told you about my kids?"

Poppy looked around. "You didn't bring them?"

"Not today. All of us—my mom, too—are coming tomorrow."

Ripsaws and hammers sounded at the back of the building. The work crew was adding the roof over the patio. Plastic hung over the doors and windows to keep the dust out.

Troy rubbed his hands together, ignoring the noise. "Chase says your kids like to fish."

"Love it." She might be signing Aiden up to fish more than he ever wanted to.

Troy turned to the customers, who were craning to catch everything they said and did. "We're going to be grandparents! It's about damned time. You know Aiden and Bailey. They're going to be ours."

People raised their beer mugs in toasts, and Poppy reached to hug her again. "We waited so long to settle down, and we were beginning to think Chase was never going to. This is wonderful!"

Chase led them to a table near the bar where he could jump up and fill drinks between visiting with them. No food was served until four, so people just came to drink and hang out in the afternoon. A few wandered over to congratulate them, but mostly everything was low-key.

She stayed an hour, until the bar started getting busier, then promised that she'd return tomorrow with her kids and mother in tow.

"How soon can you get here?" Poppy asked.

"I told you, Mom. She works the brunch shift."

Poppy waved Chase's comment away. "I need a time."

"We'll try to be here at three." And that would mean rushing.

"And then you can spend the day with us!" Poppy beamed, excited.

A few customers wandered in and shouted hellos to Poppy and Troy. "'Bout time you two showed up!"

Troy laughed and went to see them. More people followed, happy to see them, and Paula made her escape.

On the drive home, she had to pull to the side of the road. She pressed her face in her hands and fought to calm herself. She'd never been so totally accepted, except by Mom. She couldn't imagine a life with a husband who'd always stand beside her and in-laws who wanted her, who'd dote on her kids. She gazed at herself in the rearview mirror. "Enjoy this. Don't screw it up."

Squaring her shoulders, she made the rest of the trip home. Aiden and Bailey ran to her, and her mother gave her a knowing smile. A lump caught in her throat. So many blessings. She couldn't say enough thank-yous.

On Sunday, she worked brunch without Tyne. She went in earlier than usual to do his part of prep work. Austin came through on keeping everything refilled, and Steph and Josh flowed smoothly between slicing the hams and helping with the waffle station. She, as always, flipped omelet after omelet. When one-thirty came and they switched into clean-up mode, they plowed through it quickly. And then, Steph and Josh stayed to help her prep the Sunday dish for Tyne.

Josh wrinkled his nose. "Did you have to pick crab cakes? They're a little tricky."

"Not when we work together." Paula started mixing the aioli to bind the cakes together. "Steph and I will do these if you make the hoppin' john salad."

"Deal." He got busy boiling the black-eyed peas.

In under an hour, they had the crab cakes on large sheet pans for Tyne to slide into the oven and the salad was cooling in the refrigerator. Paula waved Steph and Josh out of the kitchen, then went to collect her mom and kids.

Bailey squirmed on the drive to the bar.

"There's nothing to be nervous about," Paula told her. "If they liked me, they're gonna love you."

But the kids remembered the lukewarm reception they'd gotten from Alex's parents. It wasn't until they walked in the bar, closed on Sundays, and Chase's parents scooped them up that they started to relax.

"Are you the fisher boy?" Troy asked Aiden. "Chase has never taken you out early enough to catch the big fish. They go deep when the sun heats the water."

"We have a surprise for you!" Poppy told Bailey. "Come on."

Chase grinned at Paula and her mom and motioned upstairs to his apartment. Her mom looked around the large, open space that combined living room, dining room, and kitchen. She pressed a hand to her throat.

"You're going to love this." She gave Paula a little squeeze.

Chase led them into the hallway at the back of the apartment, and they passed the master bedroom, the brown bedroom his parents were staying in, and entered Bailey's yellow room with the two twin beds. At the end wall, a low, wooden table held a huge dollhouse. Bailey and Poppy were already on their knees, examining every room and tiny piece of furniture. Troy was sitting on a bed next to Aiden, showing him the games loaded on a chocolate-brown laptop.

Mom wiped at her eyes. "These are the kind of grandparents Aiden and Bailey deserve."

Paula felt a little weepy, too, but leaned against her mom's shoulder. "They have you. That's nothing to sneeze at."

Chase squeezed between them and wrapped an arm around each of them. "I don't know who's the most excited, the kids or my parents. Come on. Let's let them get to know each other. I could use a drink."

They sat around his kitchen table, sipping beers. He asked her mom about her plans for a daycare, and she asked him about the covering he'd had built over his back patio.

"See for yourself." He led them back downstairs, and Paula was surprised how big the cement area was. A dozen picnic tables were spaced under the roof. The workers had added half walls to provide some privacy and protection from the elements, and Buck Kreiger had delivered a dozen huge, clay pots filled with geraniums and petunias. A lantern was centered on each table, and the effect was inviting and cozy.

"Well, what do you think?" he asked.

Paula shook her head. "I couldn't picture it, but it's great. You have plenty of space for tourists during busy season."

He'd added a commercial ice machine near the back door and a large counter with closed shelving underneath to make life easier for the servers. "They'll still have to run in and out for food, but they can grab napkins and silverware and fill water and soft drinks out here."

A smart idea. Kids could come here with their parents.

They settled at a picnic table, and he went to fetch them more beers. After a while, his parents came to sit with them. Poppy grinned. "We can't tear the kids away from their new toys."

The yak turned to the getting-to-know-you stuff that's the start-up for any friendship, and Chase's parents surprised Paula again. They'd traveled almost as much as Paula's family had.

Troy leaned forward on his elbows. "I was born with a wanderlust and not a whole lot of sense. I worked my way across the country, staying in small towns and cities until the next one looked greener. I saved up enough to hitchhike through Europe, and then I finally got a hankering to settle down."

"That's when we met," Poppy said. "I was a traveling nurse, worked in hospitals from Maine all the way to Hawaii. I met Troy in Oregon, but it rains a lot there. We'd both grown up in the Midwest and wanted to go back. Saw this place and bought it. We both love Mill Pond."

"Not enough to stay here," Chase teased.

Troy gave a wry grin. "The sunshine likes us, boy. Keeps us young."

The conversation went to some of their favorite places and before they realized it, the kids came down, looking for food. Troy and Chase threw steaks on the grill, along with corn on the cob, and Poppy tossed a green salad. After they ate, Troy motioned for the kids to walk the few blocks to the lake with him. "We like a short boat ride after supper."

Poppy and her mom joined them. Paula stayed behind to help Chase with cleanup. When they returned to the back patio, he walked to the counter and slid open one of its doors. He was carrying something when he returned to the picnic table. She frowned when he put a small, velvet box in front of her.

"Marry me, Paula?"

She blinked back tears when she stared at the simple, white-gold ring in the box. Perfect. She always preferred simple.

He tilted her chin so he could see her face. "Do you like it?"

"I love it."

"So?"

"Yes." She burrowed into his arms, as close to him as she could get.

He sighed with relief, and she wondered that he'd been nervous. How could he be? "I'm not rushing you?"

"I'm not a patient person."

"No? In that case, we could go to the Justice of the Peace, then have a reception here next Sunday while my parents are in town. Unless you want a big wedding with all the works. That takes a little more planning. We'd have to . . ."

She turned to press her lips over his. "Now is fine."

He blinked, his blue-green eyes glowing with pleasure. "Quick is good." Before she could stop him, he lifted her off her feet and swung her in circles.

When their families returned, Poppy took one look at their faces and started twirling. Bailey joined her.

Paula laughed. "What is it with circles? It can't be heredity. They're not related."

"Not yet." Troy tensed up, nervous. "Is it official?"

Chase held up her hand to show them the ring. "I called Wilbur, and he's marrying us in his office on Friday. We'll have the reception here on Sunday. I already called Tessa, and she and Kayla are making the cake."

Mom dropped onto a picnic bench, as though her knees gave out on her.

"Are you all right?" Paula asked.

"No, I'm too happy. I can't breathe."

Aiden laughed at her, and Bailey climbed on her lap.

Troy waved Chase to a halt. "That's all you get to plan. We'll take care of the rest. Is a barbecue okay? With all of the fixin's?" He looked at Paula.

"Works for me." Mill Pond would expect to celebrate with Chase.

Poppy ran inside and returned with two bottles of champagne. "I've been saving these for a special occasion."

Troy popped the corks, and they all toasted. Aiden and Bailey ran from one person to the next, looking for hugs.

It took a while for everyone to settle down. Then Paula said, "It's getting late. Maya's at home, alone. We'd better go." She needed a moment of calm. She felt like she'd spun too fast on a Ferris wheel and needed to stand on terra firma to regain her bearings.

Chase didn't argue. Instead, he picked her up and kissed her thoroughly. "I can't wait till Friday."

Mom shooed him away. "We have a lot to do before then. I'm taking Paula to Indy. She's going to buy a decent dress. And the kids need something, too. So do I. And we need to order flowers . . ."

Chase whispered, "Maybe we should have eloped."

Poppy overheard him and swatted his arm. "You two will survive if you don't see each other this week. I want to take the kids out for a day, and your dad wants to take them fishing."

Paula held Chase's inquiring look with a speaking gaze.

He laughed. "Tell Ian and Tyne to find extra help this weekend. After we get hitched on Friday, I'm renting a room somewhere, and you're mine."

She grinned. "Until Monday at supper. That's my shift, remember?"

He shrugged. "Mine, too. Isn't restaurant life fun?"

Chapter 42

Paula wore a knee-length, white dress to be married in. She'd worried about the stud in her cheek and her tiny eyebrow ring, but Chase shook his head.

"They're a part of who you are, what shaped you. They stay."

He wore a suit that made him more handsome than she'd ever seen him.

"Do you like the look?" he asked.

"Oh, yes, but your jeans are sexier." Riding low on his hips, they hinted at pleasures to come.

Aiden fussed with his tie, but was pleased with how he looked. Bailey wore a frilly, pink dress that matched her pink nail polish. Even their parents had dressed up. Chase's dad didn't own a suit, but he wore a short-sleeved shirt and dress pants. Poppy had tried to get him to wear a tie, but finally gave up. Poppy and her mom had both chosen light-blue dresses that went well together.

Wilbur kept the ceremony short, then Chase carried Paula to his motorcycle and they roared off together. Friday and Saturday were everything a short honeymoon should be, and when they returned on Sunday, she had been thoroughly loved and was ready to celebrate with friends.

Most of the town showed up. Poppy and Troy had smoked and grilled enough briskets and chickens to feed all of them, and Harley and Tyne manned the grills for hot dogs and hamburgers. Women carried in side dishes and desserts. The town celebrated in grand style.

Tyne came to hug her before he left. "Told you," he whispered in her ear.

Paula laughed. "Thanks for everything—grilling today and covering my shift." She frowned. "I didn't see Daphne. Is she okay?"

"The professor came to pick her up. She was planning on being here, and I was going to give her a ride, but she had to cancel on me."

She'd always thought Daphne was smart. Now, she wasn't so sure. A ride with Tyne? Or the professor? Tough choice. "But he lives in Mill Pond. Why didn't he come?"

Tyne raised his nose in the air. "He'd rather associate with his fellow academics. I've met a few of them. They're nice, not like him."

Paula shook her head. Daphne talked to Tyne almost every day since he lived above her stained glass shop. Maybe someday she'd wake up and see the hotness. It had taken her long enough to appreciate the wonder of Chase. "Thanks again, Tyne."

"I'm happy for you." He left to saunter over to join Harley and Kathy. They were riding their bikes back to Harley's winery.

When the last person left, Chase took her hand and led her inside the bar. He motioned for the kids to follow them. "Welcome home." He bent to kiss her.

She glanced toward the stairs. "Your mom and dad?"

"Are staying with friends tonight. They'll be back tomorrow. Aiden will have to stay in the yellow room for now, but when they leave, the brown room is his."

The kids raced up the steps, and Chase bent to lift her and carry her to the apartment. *Home.* She and her mom had moved all of her and the kids' clothes here. Chase and his parents had brought the rest of their belongings. Paula had left the furniture for her mom and Maya. This was her new home. *Their* new home. And she couldn't be happier.

Please turn the page for an exciting sneak peek of
Judi Lynn's next Mill Pond romance
SPICING THINGS UP
coming soon!

Chapter 1

The alarm buzzed. Tyne Newsome rolled over and hit snooze. Five minutes later, it buzzed again. He pulled the pillow over his head and then thought better of it. *Might as well get up.* He usually beat the alarm, but he'd stayed up later than usual last night. Silly, since he worked early shifts on Mondays, but he and Harley had gone for a long motorcycle ride after Tyne got off work yesterday. Tyne glanced out the window of his apartment. A blaze of leaves glowed in the streetlights.

He and Harley hadn't meant to stay out as long as they did, but Harley's wife, Kathy, had told them to do whatever felt good. She was going to catch up on the winery's bookkeeping all day. The crisp air and glory of autumn had pulled them deeper and deeper into the national park south of Mill Pond. They hadn't returned to the vineyard until close to sunset, and then Kathy had insisted Tyne stay for supper. By the time he got back to his apartment, upstairs from Daphne's stained glass shop, it was late, and then he'd stayed up reading another hour to relax.

Oh well, the lack of sleep had been worth it. He hustled into the bathroom, took a quick shower, and tugged on his chef's pants and coat. Ian's resort was too swanky for line cooks. Tyne had to look the part, though he usually wore his worn jeans into work for supper shifts and changed before any guests got to the dining room.

He zipped down the inside staircase and stopped to glance at Daphne's shop in the dim light. Most people didn't move at four-thirty in the morning, with good reason. When he returned later this afternoon, would the shop be decorated with dangling crepe paper and balloons? The professor she'd been seeing was supposed to be a free man today. All he had to do was sign his divorce papers. Patrick could finally ask Daphne to marry him. Nothing Tyne would celebrate. The man was as exciting as porridge, but Daphne thought she'd be happy with him.

On his way out the door to his Jeep, he inhaled the crisp, clean autumn air. It perked him up, cleared his head. Driving down Main Street with its brick buildings, striped awnings, and old-fashioned streetlamps, he saw Maxwell step out of his bakery to snag the morning paper by his door. Another early riser. When Maxwell saw Tyne's orange Jeep, he raised a middle finger and grinned. Tyne laughed and returned the gesture. As usual, Maxwell's Chihuahua, Chester, was close to his heels. Tyne had never met a man so attached to his dog.

Tyne passed Ralph's diner and saw lights on in the kitchen. Garth's gas station was still dark, with only a security light shining on its four pumps. Once outside town, Tyne passed the farms that lined both sides of the road until he came to the drive for Lakeview Stables, Ian's resort. He glanced past the tennis courts to the lake at the back of the property. The water lay still as a mirror.

He drove around to the back of the building—a three-story limestone center with a wing off each side—and entered the kitchen through the back door. Monday breakfasts weren't as rushed to prepare. He'd made the potato-sausage strata ahead of time and left them in the refrigerator to soak up the custard filling. All he had to do was put them in the oven. Steph, the morning sous chef, walked through the back door while he was sliding the sausages and bacon into the second oven. She started putting ramekins in a stainless steel pan for them to start the eggs en cocotte with smoked salmon.

"Have a good weekend?" Tyne asked as they lined each ramekin with salmon.

"We spent the weekend at Ben's parents' place on the lake. Had a great time, played lots of cards, and ate too much food."

Tyne grinned. "The scenery's gorgeous right now. Bet the lake was beautiful."

Steph started breaking an egg into each ramekin. "It's hard to beat Mill Pond when the leaves change."

"It's hard to beat Mill Pond in lots of things." He slid her a sideways glance. "You happy you stayed on as the early shift sous chef?"

Paula, his fellow chef, had trained Steph and expected her to go to culinary school, but Steph had decided to stay in Mill Pond, near her high school sweetheart. She slid the eggs into the oven and filled the steel pans with hot water to create a water bath. "What's not to like?"

Tyne couldn't think of anything. The area farmers had worked together to raise their standards so that specialty goods were easy to find. The area had become a foodie's delight, one of the reasons the inn was so popular. That and all the things Ian had to offer—a golf course, tennis courts, horseback riding, and lake activities. Things always slowed down once kids had to return to school, but the inn still did all right. Couples used it as a romantic getaway. This week, enough couples had doubled up to rent the cabins by the lake that sixty people came for meals each day. Ian had decided to add special weekend packages for holidays. Every room was booked for Halloween in a couple of weeks.

Steph began slicing oranges for a fresh fruit salad. "Have you and Paula decided what to serve for the long Halloween weekend yet?"

"We just talked about it. Ian wants us to go for fun instead of fancy. We're leaning toward a barbecue of some kind with gory desserts."

"Gory?" Steph raised an eyebrow.

"Dirt cakes with jelly worms and gravestones, eyeball popcorn balls . . ."

"Good idea." She glanced out the windows at the long shoreline. "It's not like kids can trick or treat here, though. How's Ian going to keep them busy?"

The owner himself walked through the kitchen door before she finished the question. "I'm doing a movie night—fun stuff early in the evenings for kids, like *Hocus Pocus*, and horror movies later for the adults. I have hay rides and scavenger hunts planned, pumpkin carving, and bobbing for apples. The Kruses are building a corn maze." Their boss held his five-week-old baby boy, Drew. The baby had lots of black hair like his dad and hazel eyes like his mom. Steph loved babies and would have hurried to grab him, but everyone knew you practically had to use a crowbar to pry the baby away from Ian.

"Hey, Big Daddy!" Tyne called, teasing him. "You gonna wear a pouch and teach the kid how to work the dishwasher later this morning?" Ian would stall as long as he could before he handed Drew over to Paula's mother, who lived in an apartment in the inn's east wing and babysat for the employees.

"Tessa would hurt me. My wife has the temperament that goes with her wild, coppery hair."

Tyne glanced at the clock—close to nine—and he and Steph carried food out to the long buffet tables, then watched over things for the next hour until the last guest left. Betty flew in at ten to help with cleanup.

She looked Tyne up and down. "Lookin' good, hot stuff. Heard you had a full weekend."

Ian, who'd settled into work mode, turned to hear his answer.

"Harley and I spent Sunday riding through the national park, enjoying the fall colors."

Ian nodded. "Another reason we have so many guests now. The park's good for business."

They had the kitchen and dining room clean in no time, and Tyne and Steph got busy on lunch. Tyne settled on two international soups—classic posole from Mexico and lemon chicken soup from Greece. He didn't want to push his luck, though, so went for traditional sandwiches—BLTs and chicken salad. Lunch went smoothly and before long he and Steph finished his contribution for the supper menu. He provided the international dish each night, and Paula did the traditional.

Their jobs done, Steph took off her apron. "I'm out of here. See you tomorrow."

"Not for long." Tyne worked dinner shifts for the rest of the week. Paula did the early hours. On Mondays, she dropped her kids Aiden and Bailey at her mom's apartment before she zipped into the kitchen.

Paula rushed in, glanced at the menu, then frowned at his scruffy chin. She tsk-tsked. "What? You didn't have time to trim your whiskers this morning?"

She always gave him grief about his chin strap. He returned the favor. "What? You didn't have time to do your hair?" Her thick, black tresses were pulled up in their usual clip, spiking at the back of her head.

She laughed. "What have you got for me tonight?"

"Thai curry with pork and eggplant over rice." Tyne had lived and cooked in Thailand for a year before he returned to the United States. He loved its food and flavors. Thai and Vietnamese cuisine were two of his favorites.

Since he loved it spicy, she asked, "You toned it down a little, right?"

He grinned. "For you, Miss Wimpy? Of course. I wouldn't want to send you home too hot for Chase to handle."

She smirked. "Like that could happen."

She had him there. Chase could handle most anything. He'd been tamed by his little goth mama, though, and Tyne had never seen him happier.

Paula came over to taste a spoonful of his dish. "Oh, this is good."

Tyne untied his apron and hung it on the peg by the door. "You should talk Aiden and Bailey into trying it."

Paula snorted. "It has too many vegetables. They might accidentally get healthy."

Kids. They resisted what was good for them. Come to think of it, though, so had he. Tyne gave her a quick wave and headed to his Jeep. He was going to take it easy tonight, make himself something simple for supper, and chill out.

He drove past Daphne's shop to turn at the corner and pulled into the alley that ran behind the buildings. He glanced at the stained glass pieces displayed in her front window. Was the shop dark? He frowned at the CLOSED sign hanging in the door. What was up? Tourists crowded the sidewalks. They'd come to see the leaves and stopped in Mill Pond to shop and eat. Had she closed up early to run off with Patrick?

Nope, Daphne's SUV was parked in the back lot next to his spot. No matter. They probably took Patrick's car, but when he stepped through the back door to head upstairs, Daphne sat behind the cash register, her head in her hands, her shoulders shaking. *Oh, no.* He'd never trusted the professor. Tyne went to her. "Hey, you okay?" Dumb question. Who sits and sobs when life is good?

She turned away from him. He bent to wrap his arms around her. "He dumped you?" Did the asshole have another girl on the line in some other town?

No one but Daphne's parents had been impressed with Patrick. The professor was so self-absorbed, Tyne wondered how he could relate to his students. He probably didn't. Chase had been interested in Daphne before he met Paula. Chase didn't think much of Patrick either. He'd made Tyne promise to be there for Daphne if the misery came. Not a hard promise to keep. Tyne liked her. He'd never make a move on her—she was a for-keeps type girl—but Tyne didn't just rent his apartment from her, they were friends. Or at least friendly to each other, good neighbors.

She turned and pressed her face against his chest. Tears and snot soaked his T-shirt. Gross, but what were friends for? He patted her head. Love sucked. Sometimes, it worked—like it did for Ian and Tessa, Chase and Paula. But usually? It wasn't worth the bother, the pain. That's why Tyne had promised himself he'd never fall for someone until he reached forty. Maybe not even then, but he might be ready for the crush of romance once he was older and his friends were more tied down. Maybe then he'd be bored enough that a relationship would look good.

Chapter 2

Daphne clutched Tyne's T-shirt and buried her face against his hard chest. So different from Patrick's that it made her cry more. Not that Patrick would appreciate it if she sobbed into one of his expensive tailored shirts. He took pride in his looks, how thin he stayed for his early forties. He cultivated his professorial look with baggy trousers and button-down shirts and cashmere sweaters. He took pride in wearing wire-rimmed glasses. He loved the status of academia.

"I should have seen this coming." *Had* seen it coming, but she hadn't wanted to believe Patrick would leave her to return to his wife. The wife he swore was cold and bitter, the wife he couldn't please no matter what he did. The wife that was too much like him. He swore she drained him of any creative energy, that he'd only stayed with her to raise their two kids. "I'd have never, ever dated a married man except that he and his wife had separated, and his wife lived in their house in Bloomington, and he moved to an apartment in Mill Pond. They'd been separated for five months and the papers had been filed." She swallowed hard. The divorce took an ugly turn, and Patrick's wife would receive much more money than Patrick had anticipated. His income would be severely limited. She choked on a sob. "Patrick likes money. So does his wife. Neither of them enjoys penny pinching, so they reunited. I got cast aside as a budget cut."

Tyne shrugged. "Doesn't surprise me. The man's priorities didn't add up."

"I met his wife once. I could see why Patrick had been attracted to her. She carries herself regally, gives off the essence of money." Patrick, deep down, believed he should be treated like aristocracy, believed he should have more attention and privilege than he did as a professor. He wrote poetry and he'd been published in journals and poetry websites, but once his kids left the nest he'd decided it was time for him to write a book, his ode to a man who'd bedded many women before he turned to more cerebral pursuits.

Daphne knotted her hands into fists. "Patrick was full of himself." Shame on her. She'd fallen for his drivel because she'd turned thirty-six and decided it was now or never. "We had a lot of common interests—books, music, plays. I hoped that would be enough."

She was a damn coward, and she knew it. Patrick wouldn't demand too much from her except constant support and occasional worship. And even that hadn't been enough.

Buggers! The stinking idiot dumped her. Her tears were as much for her own stupidity as for losing him.

Tyne patted her on the back. He pulled away to bring her a Kleenex. She grimaced at his T-shirt, probably ruined with smudged makeup. The man was a luscious length of temptation who didn't seem to think about his looks. Maybe when you were that sexy, you took it for granted. He handed her one tissue and dabbed at her eyes with another. "Hey, people break up all the time and live through it. It's going to hurt for a while, but you'll move on and find someone else."

She snorted. Unladylike. "Bullshit. I've heard that all my life."

He stared, but his brown eyes sparkled. "I've never heard you cuss."

"Neither have my parents. It's my own private pleasure, but the words hardly ever leave my lips."

His handsome face lit up, curious. "What other naughty things do you think about?"

"Like I'd tell you!" She rubbed at her eyes, smearing her mascara, she was sure. She probably looked like a puffy-eyed raccoon. But what did it matter? Even when she'd decided to settle for less, the professor had kicked her to the curb.

Tyne tried again. "You have a right to be angry. Anger's good, but you can do better. Just wait and see. You'll meet someone . . ."

She didn't let him finish. "That's a load of crap. I'm not buying it. I bought Patrick's stupid lies for months, and I'm sick of it. Don't you lie to me, too."

His lips curled at the edges. "So why did you buy into his massive ego? The man was nothing but a spoiled snob."

She winced. Tyne never minced words. She'd forgotten that. He wasn't the best person to spar with verbally. He'd have eaten Patrick alive. She frowned. "You make me sound stupid. No one's talked to me like that. Ever."

"Then it's time they did. Own up. What the hell were you thinking?"

"I'm tired of dating. I'm tired of looking for Mr. Right, and I'm not getting any younger."

"So what? I'd rather be by myself and enjoy my own company than be stuck with a jerk."

She sighed. No one else would say that to her either. But Tyne wasn't like anyone else. He was his own person. Yes, the man was gorgeous with his dirty blond hair and scruffy beard, his body that rippled with muscles and pheromones that permeated a room, but that's not what she liked about him. She liked his keen wit, his quick mind, and his outspokenness. At least, she *usually* liked his outspokenness.

Her shoulders sagged, the fight seeping out of her. Defending herself took too much energy. Tyne would be too demanding day in and day out. He'd make her tired. "Look, you're the type who goes for it. You've traveled all over the world. You wanted to be a chef, so you became one. I never dreamed that big. I'm happy here in Mill Pond, I love working with stained glass. I just wanted a *little* more. That's all."

He circled the counter to get a better look at her. "Maybe you didn't dream big enough."

"Not all of us can get everything we want." She went for another Kleenex and turned her back to blow her nose. She took another to wipe under her eyes. The sheet came away covered in black.

Tyne leaned his hip against the counter. "I'm glad you won't be smothered by Mr. Brain Drain."

That was a new one. "Brain drain?"

"He loved to hear himself talk, but never said anything of importance."

Hmm, she'd never thought about Patrick's rambling lectures that way. "We enjoyed a lot of the same things. I like concerts, books, poetry—Patrick wrote good poetry—and art exhibits."

Tyne crossed his arms over his chest. "Boring."

She blinked, surprised. "You don't like any of those things?"

"Sure I do, but what else did he have to offer?"

"There's more?"

Tyne gave her a look, and she could feel her hackles rise. How could this man annoy her more than anyone else ever had? And still, if she needed something done—furniture moved in her sewing room at home or new shelves put up in the shop—he could make it fun. He knew how to make her laugh. And suddenly, she realized that if she spent too much time with him, he could ruin her equilibrium. So she took a deep breath and smiled. "I'm fine now. The worst is over. I knew I was expecting too much. I'll go back to my work and my sewing. I'll get through this."

His face scrunched. He obviously didn't like her answer. "Oh, for Pete's sake. Get your sweater. Let's get out of here. The leaves are gorgeous. The air smells like energy. Let's go for a hike."

She shook her head. "I can't." She withdrew into herself. She felt it happening. He was going to mock her now.

He looked her up and down. "What? When your heart broke, did your legs break, too? Do your feet still work?"

"I never hike."

He stared. "Why not? You live on the edge of a national park, and you never hike it?"

"I look at it. I enjoy its beauty."

He let out a long breath. "I'm gonna love this, I know, but why just look when you can experience it?"

She pressed her lips together, gathering her thoughts. "My parents weren't happy I moved there. They said it wasn't safe for a woman to hike alone on the trails. I was too far from town. There could be snakes. People have fallen on some of the steep trails and broken their ankles."

He threw back his head and laughed, and she cringed, but he didn't stop there. He grabbed her elbow and pulled her to her feet. "You won't be alone. If we see a snake, I'll lift you on my shoulders so it can't reach you. And if you start to fall, I'll grab you. Enough already. Let's go."

He tugged her along with him, and she wasn't sure she had a choice. "I look horrible. My makeup's a mess. I'm ugly when I cry."

He put a finger on her lips. "You could never be ugly. You don't need makeup. You're one of loveliest women I've ever met. So hush up and move it."

Lovely. He'd called her lovely. But then he yanked again, and she had no choice but to follow. She stalled when he opened the door to his orange Jeep—a deathtrap on wheels. But he gave her a small push, and she slid onto the passenger seat. He slammed the door and went to climb behind the steering wheel.

"Have you ever been in a Jeep before?"

"No." And she was sure that was a good thing.

He grinned. "Then you're in for a treat."

Treats weren't healthy for you, were they? The Jeep jerked forward, and she braced her feet. If she could survive being cast aside, she could survive this.

Author's Note

If you like the sound of some of the food served in this book, I used my *Wolfgang Puck Makes It Easy* and *Nigella Express* cookbooks for inspiration.

Judi Lynn received a Master's Degree from Indiana University in elementary education after attending the IPFW campus. She taught for six years before having her two daughters. She loves gardening, cooking, and trying new recipes. Readers can visit her website at www.judithpostswritingmusings.com and her blog www.writingmusings.com.